Born in the Kingdom of Fife in 1960, Ian Rankin graduated from the University of Edinburgh in 1982, and then spent three years writing novels when he was supposed to be working towards a PhD in Scottish Literature. His first Rebus novel, *Knots and Crosses*, was published in 1987, and the Rebus books are now translated into over thirty languages and are bestsellers worldwide.

Ian Rankin has been elected a Hawthornden Fellow, and is also a past winner of the Chandler-Fulbright Award. He is the recipient of four Crime Writers' Association Dagger Awards including the prestigious Diamond Dagger in 2005 and in 2009 was inducted into the CWA Hall of Fame. In 2004, Ian won America's celebrated Edgar Award for *Resurrection Men*. He has also been shortlisted for the Anthony Awards in the USA, and won Denmark's *Palle Rosenkrantz* Prize, the French *Grand Prix du Roman Noir* and the *Deutscher Krimipreis*. Ian Rankin is also the recipient of honorary degrees from the universities of Abertay, St Andrews, Edinburgh, Hull and the Open University.

A contributor to BBC2's *Newsnight Review*, he also presented his own TV series, *Ian Rankin's Evil Thoughts*. He has received the OBE for services to literature, opting to receive the prize in his home city of Edinburgh. He has also recently been appointed to the rank of Deputy Lieutenant of Edinburgh, where he lives with his partner and two sons. Visit his website at www.ianrankin.net

BY IAN RANKIN

The Inspector Rebus series

Knots and Crosses
Hide and Seek
Tooth and Nail
Strip Jack
The Black Book
Mortal Causes
Let It Bleed
Black and Blue
The Hanging Garden
Death Is Not the End (*novella*)
Dead Souls
Set in Darkness
The Falls
Resurrection Men
A Question of Blood
Fleshmarket Close
The Naming of the Dead
Exit Music

Other novels

The Flood
Watchman
Westwind
Doors Open
The Complaints

Writing as Jack Harvey

Witch Hunt
Bleeding Hearts
Blood Hunt

Short stories

A Good Hanging and Other
    Stories
Beggars Banquet

Non-fiction

Rebus's Scotland

Omnibus editions

Rebus: The Early Years
(Knots and Crosses,
Hide and Seek, Tooth and Nail)

Rebus: The St Leonard's Years
(Strip Jack, The Black Book,
Mortal Causes)

Rebus: The Lost Years
(Let It Bleed, Black and Blue,
The Hanging Garden)

Rebus: Capital Crimes
(Dead Souls, Set in Darkness,
The Falls)

All Ian Rankin's titles are available on audio.

Also available: *Jackie Leven Said*
by Ian Rankin and Jackie Leven.

IAN RANKIN

HIDE AND SEEK

An Orion paperback

First published in Great Britain in 1990
by Orion
This paperback edition published in 1998
by Orion Books Ltd,
Orion House, 5 Upper St Martin's Lane,
London WC2H 9EA

An Hachette UK company

Reissued 2011

A CIP catalogue record for this book
is available from the British Library.

Printed and bound in Great Britain by
Clays Ltd, St Ives plc

The Orion Publishing Group's policy is to use papers
that are natural, renewable and recyclable products and
made from wood grown in sustainable forests. The logging
and manufacturing processes are expected to conform to
the environmental regulations of the country of origin.

www.orionbooks.co.uk

To Michael Shaw,
not before time

'My devil had long been caged, he came out roaring.'
— *The Strange Case of Dr Jekyll and Mr Hyde*

INTRODUCTION

A year or two after *Hide & Seek* was published, there was a break-in at Edinburgh's police headquarters. Among the items rumoured to have been stolen was a list of names of men prominent in Edinburgh society. Allegations had been made that these men had been using rent boys, leaving themselves open to blackmail, and a police inquiry had been instituted. There were enough similarities between the real-life case and aspects of my novel that people would stop me in the street to ask how I'd known so much so soon. I would explain that my sources had to be protected.

There were no sources, of course: I'd made the story up.

I saw *Hide & Seek* very much as a companion piece to *Knots & Crosses*. Reviewers had failed to pick up on the earlier book's use of Robert Louis Stevenson's *Dr Jekyll and Mr Hyde* as a template. I was determined to try once more to drag Stevenson's story back to its natural home of Edinburgh, and to update the theme for a modern-day audience. In fact, the book's eventual working title was *Hyde & Seek*, but only after I'd ditched *Dead Beat* (at the behest of my agent, to whom the book was eventually dedicated). The final version of *Hide & Seek* opens with a quote from *Dr Jekyll and Mr Hyde* and goes on to use quotes from Stevenson's book at the start of each section. Moreover, I lifted many of the character names directly from Stevenson's masterpiece – Enfield, Poole, Carew, Lanyon – while *Dr Jekyll and Mr Hyde* provides Detective

Inspector Rebus with his night-time reading, when he's not busy mulling over his latest case.

Not that I was keen for readers to get the connection or anything . . .

Between *Knots & Crosses* and the events of *Hide & Seek*, Rebus has been promoted from detective sergeant – his one and only promotion in the series so far. Other changes have taken place. Rebus has a new sidekick called Brian Holmes (a none-too-subtle nod to another Edinburgh writer, Sir Arthur Conan Doyle). And Edinburgh is changing, too, as new money moves in. The book was written in 1988 and 1989. By then, I was living in London, at the height of Thatcherism. Red braces and Moët were all the rage. In some wine bars, rising property values seemed to be the only currency of conversation. I'd been in London for a couple of years and was not making much of a go of it. My wife and I lived in a maisonette in Tottenham, and having failed to find full-time writing a lucrative enough proposition, I was working as a magazine journalist in Crystal Palace, entailing a three-hour commute each weekday. I seemed to be surrounded by people more successful than me, people with fat salaries or five-figure publishing deals. My situation at the time seems to me now to explain the bitter edge to much of the writing in *Hide & Seek*, and is reflected in Brian Holmes's memories of his few student months in London ('a season spent in hell', as he himself remembers it).

The novel did not come hard on the heels of *Knots & Crosses*: there had been two other novels in between. One was a spy adventure, *Watchman*; the other, *Westwind*, my attempt at a techno-thriller. The latter, however, was struggling to find a publisher of any kind, while the former had sold a scant 500 copies in hardcover. *Hide &*

Seek was actually begun in the summer of 1988, but failed to make much headway. My job got in the way, as did attempts to turn my first novel, *The Flood*, into a useable screenplay, and various frustrating efforts to get work as a script-writer on *The Bill*. I was also reviewing books most weeks for a new broadsheet called *Scotland on Sunday*.

One other reason why I may have held back on a second Rebus novel: plans had been afoot to film the first one, with Leslie Grantham (Dirty Den in *EastEnders*) as Rebus. This plan eventually fell through in January 1989. My guess had been that Grantham would want the action of *Knots & Crosses* relocated to London. Now that he would not be taking Rebus to the screen, I felt free to write a second Edinburgh-based adventure for my character. The final draft of the book was completed in May.

It's a less overwrought work than its predecessor, the prose leaner, though the Rebus we meet is still not the fully formed character of later books. For one thing, he's still too well-read, quoting from Walt Whitman – someone I'd studied at university but of whom Rebus couldn't really be expected to have had knowledge. He also quotes from the Romantic poets, and listens to Radio Three in his car. On his hi-fi at home, there's jazz, but also the Beatles' *White Album* (I'd soon have him preferring the Stones). My own time as a hi-fi journalist is reflected in the expensive Linn turntable owned by one character, while a scene inside the library at the University of Edinburgh takes Holmes to the fifth floor, which I'd haunted during my three years as a postgraduate student.

There are other literary references in the book: to James Hogg's *Confessions of a Justified Sinner*, and to the poet George MacBeth, who had shared a writers' retreat with me a couple of years before. A character from *The Flood* pops up in the first few pages, and Rebus and Holmes also visit west-central Fife where both the Inspector and I grew up. It's noticeable to me now that Rebus in particular is not as cynical about his old hunting-ground as he was when paying his respects in *Knots & Crosses*. Maybe enough of my spleen had been vented. London was the enemy now; London, and the harsh materialism I seemed to have found there.

Besides, I had many happy memories of my childhood, memories rekindled by the death of my father in February 1990, while I was in the midst of proofreading *Hide & Seek*. By the time the book was ready for publication, Miranda and I had decidedly had enough of London and Mrs Thatcher. We were making plans to live in France, praying that my writing would start earning enough to turn the dream into a reality. And once we'd left Tottenham behind, I'd be able to put some of my own feelings about the capital into words, by taking John Rebus to London on a case.

A case that would become *Tooth & Nail*.

April 2005

'Hide!'

He was shrieking now, frantic, his face drained of all colour. She was at the top of the stairs, and he stumbled towards her, grabbing her by the arms, propelling her downstairs with unfocussed force, so that she feared they would both fall. She cried out.

'Ronnie! Hide from who?'

'Hide!' he shrieked again. 'Hide! They're coming! They're coming!'

He had pushed her all the way to the front door now. She'd seen him pretty strung out before, but never this bad. A fix would help him, she knew it would. And she knew, too, that he had the makings upstairs in his bedroom. The sweat trickled from his chilled rat's-tails of hair. Only two minutes ago, the most important decision in her life had been whether or not to dare a trip to the squat's seething lavatory. But now. . . .

'They're coming,' he repeated, his voice a whisper now. 'Hide.'

'Ronnie,' she said, 'you're scaring me.'

He stared at her, his eyes seeming almost to recognise her. Then he looked away again, into a distance all of his own. The word was a snakelike hiss.

'Hide.' And with that he yanked open the door. It was raining outside, and she hesitated. But then fear took her, and she made to cross the threshold. But his hand grabbed at her arm, pulling her back inside. He embraced her, his sweat sea-salty, his body throbbing. His mouth was close to her ear, his breath hot.

'They've murdered me,' he said. Then with sudden ferocity he pushed her again, and this time she was outside, and the door was slamming shut, leaving him alone in the house. Alone with himself. She stood on the garden path, staring at the door, trying to decide whether to knock or not.

It wouldn't make any difference. She knew that. So instead she started to cry. Her head slipped forward in a rare show of self-pity and she wept for a full minute, before, breathing hard three times, she turned and walked quickly down the garden path (such as it was). Someone would take her in. Someone would comfort her and take away the fear and dry her clothes.

Someone always did.

John Rebus stared hard at the dish in front of him, oblivious to the conversation around the table, the background music, the flickering candles. He didn't really care about house prices in Barnton, or the latest delicatessen to be opened in the Grassmarket. He didn't much want to speak to the other guests – a female lecturer to his right, a male bookseller to his left – about . . . well, whatever they'd just been discussing. Yes, it was the perfect dinner party, the conversation as tangy as the starter course, and he was glad Rian had invited him. Of course he was. But the more he stared at the half lobster on his plate, the more an unfocussed despair grew within him. What had he in common with these people? Would they laugh if he told the story of the police alsatian and the severed head? No, they would not. They would smile politely, then bow their heads towards their plates, acknowledging that he was . . . well, *different* from them.

'Vegetables, John?'

It was Rian's voice, warning him that he was not 'taking part', was not 'conversing' or even looking interested. He accepted the large oval dish with a smile, but avoided her eyes.

She was a nice girl. Quite a stunner in an individual sort of way. Bright red hair, cut short and pageboyish. Eyes deep, striking green. Lips thin but promising. Oh yes, he liked her. He wouldn't have accepted her invitation otherwise. He fished about in the dish for a piece of broccoli that wouldn't break into a thousand pieces as he tried to manoeuvre it onto his plate.

'Gorgeous food, Rian,' said the bookseller, and Rian smiled, accepting the remark, her face reddening slightly. That was all it took, John. That was all you had to say to make this girl happy. But in his mouth he knew it would come out sounding sarcastic. His tone of voice was not something he could suddenly throw off like a piece of clothing. It was a part of him, nurtured over a course of years. So when the lecturer agreed with the bookseller, all John Rebus did was smile and nod, the smile too fixed, the nod going on a second or two too long, so that they were all looking at him again. The piece of broccoli snapped into two neat halves above his plate and splattered onto the tablecloth.

'Shite!' he said, knowing as the word escaped his lips that it was not quite appropriate, not quite the *right* word for the occasion. Well, what was he, a man or a thesaurus?

'Sorry,' he said.

'Couldn't be helped,' said Rian. My God, her voice was cold.

It was the perfect end to a perfect weekend. He'd gone shopping on Saturday, ostensibly for a suit to wear tonight. But had baulked at the prices, and bought some books instead, one of which was intended as a gift to Rian: *Doctor Zhivago*. But then he'd decided he'd like to read it himself first, and so had brought flowers and chocolates instead, forgetting her aversion to lilies (*had he known in*

3

the first place?) and the diet she was in the throes of starting. Damn. And to cap it all, he'd tried a new church this morning, another Church of Scotland offering, not too far from his flat. The last one he'd tried had seemed unbearably cold, promising nothing but sin and repentance, but this latest church had been the oppressive opposite: all love and joy and what was there to forgive anyway? So he'd sung the hymns, then buggered off, leaving the minister with a handshake at the door and a promise of future attendance.

'More wine, John?'

This was the bookseller, proffering the bottle he'd brought himself. It wasn't a bad little wine, actually, but the bookseller had talked about it with such unremitting pride that Rebus felt obliged to decline. The man frowned, but then was cheered to find this refusal left all the more for himself. He replenished his glass with vigour.

'Cheers,' he said.

The conversation returned to how busy Edinburgh seemed these days. Here was something with which Rebus could agree. This being the end of May, the tourists were almost in season. But there was more to it than that. If anyone had told him five years ago that in 1989 people would be emigrating north from the south of England to the Lothians, he'd have laughed out loud. Now it was fact, and a fit topic for the dinner table.

Later, much later, the couple having departed, Rebus helped Rian with the dishes.

'What was wrong with you?' she said, but all he could think about was the minister's handshake, that confident grip which bespoke assurances of an afterlife.

'Nothing,' he said. 'Let's leave these till morning.'

Rian stared at the kitchen, counting the used pots, the half-eaten lobster carcasses, the wine glasses smudged with grease.

'Okay,' she said. 'What did you have in mind instead?'

He raised his eyebrows slowly, then brought them down low over his eyes. His lips broadened into a smile which had about it a touch of the leer. She became coy.

'Why, Inspector,' she said. 'Is that supposed to be some kind of a clue?'

'Here's another,' he said, lunging at her, hugging her to him, his face buried in her neck. She squealed, clenched fists beating against his back.

'Police brutality!' she gasped. 'Help! Police, help!'

'Yes, madam?' he inquired, carrying her by the waist out of the kitchen, towards where the bedroom and the end of the weekend waited in shadow.

Late evening at a building site on the outskirts of Edinburgh. The contract was for the construction of an office development. A fifteen-foot-high fence separated the works from the main road. The road, too, was of recent vintage, built to help ease traffic congestion around the city. Built so that commuters could travel easily from their country-side dwellings to jobs in the city centre.

There were no cars on the road tonight. The only sound came from the slow chug-chugging of a cement mixer on the site. A man was feeding it spadefuls of grey sand and remembering the far distant days when he had laboured on a building site. Hard graft it had been, but honest.

Two other men stood above a deep pit, staring down into it.

'Should do it,' one said.

'Yes,' the other agreed. They began walking back to the car, an ageing purple Mercedes.

'He must have some clout. I mean, to get us the keys to this place, to set all this up. Some clout.'

'Ours is not to ask questions, you know that.' The man who spoke was the oldest of the three, and the only Calvinist. He opened the car boot. Inside, the body of a frail teenager lay crumpled, obviously dead. His skin was the colour of pencil shading, darkest where the bruises lay.

'What a waste,' said the Calvinist.

'Aye,' the other agreed. Together they lifted the body from the boot, and carried it gently towards the hole. It dropped softly to the bottom, one leg wedging up against the sticky clay sides, a trouser leg slipping to show a naked ankle.

'All right,' the Calvinist said to the cement man. 'Cover it, and let's get out of here. I'm starving.'

Monday

For close on a generation, no one had appeared to drive away
these random visitors or to repair their ravages

What a start to the working week.

The housing estate, what he could see of it through the rain-lashed windscreen, was slowly turning back into the wilderness that had existed here before the builders had moved in many years ago. He had no doubt that in the 1960s it, like its brethren clustered around Edinburgh, had seemed the perfect solution to future housing needs. And he wondered if the planners ever learned through anything other than hindsight. If not, then perhaps today's 'ideal' solutions were going to turn out the same way.

The landscaped areas comprised long grass and an abundance of weeds, while children's tarmacadamed playgrounds had become bombsites, shrapnel glass awaiting a tripped knee or stumbling hand. Most of the terraces boasted boarded-up windows, ruptured drainpipes pouring out teeming rainwater onto the ground, marshy front gardens with broken fences and missing gates. He had the idea that on a sunny day the place would seem even more depressing.

Yet nearby, a matter of a few hundred yards or so, some developer had started building private apartments. The hoarding above the site proclaimed this a LUXURY DEVELOPMENT, and gave its address as MUIR VILLAGE. Rebus wasn't fooled, but wondered how many young buyers would be. This was Pilmuir, and always would be. This was the dumping ground.

There was no mistaking the house he wanted. Two

police cars and an ambulance were already there, parked next to a burnt-out Ford Cortina. But even if there hadn't been this sideshow, Rebus would have known the house. Yes, it had its boarded-up windows, like its neighbours on either side, but it also had an open door, opening into the darkness of its interior. And on a day like this, would any house have its door flung wide open were it not for the corpse inside, and the superstitious dread of the living who were incarcerated with it?

Unable to park as close to this door as he would have liked, Rebus cursed under his breath and pushed open the car door, throwing his raincoat over his head as he made to dash through the stiletto shower. Something fell from his pocket onto the verge. Scrap paper, but he picked it up anyway, screwing it into his pocket as he ran. The path to the open door was cracked and slick with weeds, and he almost slipped and fell, but reached the threshold intact, shaking the water from him, awaiting the welcoming committee.

A constable put his head around a doorway, frowning.

'Detective Inspector Rebus,' said Rebus by way of introduction.

'In here, sir.'

'I'll be there in a minute.'

The head disappeared again, and Rebus looked around the hall. Tatters of wallpaper were the only mementoes of what had once been a home. There was an overpowering fragrance of damp plaster, rotting wood. And behind all that, a sense of this being more of a cave than a house, a crude form of shelter, temporary, unloved.

As he moved further into the house, passing the bare stairwell, darkness embraced him. Boards had been hammered into all the window-frames, shutting out light. The intention, he supposed, had been to shut out squatters, but Edinburgh's army of homeless was too great and too wise. They had crept in through the fabric of the

10

place. They had made it their den. And one of their number had died here.

The room he entered was surprisingly large, but with a low ceiling. Two constables held thick rubber torches out to illuminate the scene, casting moving shadows over the plasterboard walls. The effect was of a Caravaggio painting, a centre of light surrounded by degrees of murkiness. Two large candles had burnt down to the shapes of fried eggs against the bare floorboards, and between them lay the body, legs together, arms outstretched. A cross without the nails, naked from the waist up. Near the body stood a glass jar, which had once contained something as innocent as instant coffee, but now held a selection of disposable syringes. Putting the fix into crucifixion, Rebus thought with a guilty smile.

The police doctor, a gaunt and unhappy creature, was kneeling next to the body as though about to offer the last rites. A photographer stood by the far wall, trying to find a reading on his light meter. Rebus moved in towards the corpse, standing over the doctor.

'Give us a torch,' he said, his hand commanding one from the nearest constable. He shone this down across the body, starting at the bare feet, the bedenimed legs, a skinny torso, ribcage showing through the pallid skin. Then up to the neck and face. Mouth open, eyes closed. Sweat looked to have dried on the forehead and in the hair. But wait. . . . Wasn't that moisture around the mouth, on the lips? A drop of water suddenly fell from nowhere into the open mouth. Rebus, startled, expected the man to swallow, to lick his parched lips and return to life. He did not.

'Leak in the roof,' the doctor explained, without looking up from his work. Rebus shone the torch against the ceiling, and saw the damp patch which was the source of the drip. Unnerving all the same.

11

'Sorry I took so long to get here,' he said, trying to keep his voice level. 'So what's the verdict?'

'Overdose,' the doctor said blandly. 'Heroin.' He shook a tiny polythene envelope at Rebus. 'The contents of this sachet, if I'm not mistaken. There's another full one in his right hand.' Rebus shone his torch towards where a lifeless hand was half clutching a small packet of white powder.

'Fair enough,' he said. 'I thought everyone chased the dragon these days instead of injecting.'

The doctor looked up at him at last.

'That's a very naive view, Inspector. Go talk to the Royal Infirmary. They'll tell you how many intravenous abusers there are in Edinburgh. It probably runs into hundreds. That's why we're the AIDS capital of Britain.'

'Aye, we take pride in our records, don't we? Heart disease, false teeth, and now AIDS.'

The doctor smiled. 'Something you might be interested in,' he said. 'There's bruising on the body. Not very distinct in this light, but it's there.'

Rebus squatted down and shone the torch over the torso again. Yes, there was bruising all right. A lot of bruising.

'Mainly to the ribs,' the doctor continued. 'But also some to the face.'

'Maybe he fell,' Rebus suggested.

'Maybe,' said the doctor.

'Sir?' This from one of the constables, his eyes and voice keen. Rebus turned to him.

'Yes, son?'

'Come and look at this.'

Rebus was only too glad of the excuse to move away from the doctor and his patient. The constable was leading him to the far wall, shining his torch against it as he went. Suddenly, Rebus saw why.

On the wall was a drawing. A five-pointed star,

12

encompassed by two concentric circles, the largest of them some five feet in diameter. The whole had been well drawn, the lines of the star straight, the circles almost exact. The rest of the wall was bare.

'What do you think, sir?' asked the constable.

'Well, it's not just your usual graffiti, that's for sure.'

'Witchcraft?'

'Or astrology. A lot of druggies go in for all sorts of mysticism and hoodoo. It goes with the territory.'

'The candles. . . .'

'Let's not jump to conclusions, son. You'll never make CID that way. Tell me, why are we all carrying torches?'

'Because the electric's been cut off.'

'Right. Ergo, the need for candles.'

'If you say so, sir.'

'I do say so, son. Who found the body?'

'I did, sir. There was a telephone call, female, anonymous, probably one of the other squatters. They seem to have cleared out in a hurry.'

'So there was nobody else here when you arrived?'

'No, sir.'

'Any idea yet who he is?' Rebus nodded the torch towards the corpse.

'No, sir. And the other houses are all squats, too, so I doubt we'll get anything out of them.'

'On the contrary. If anyone knows the identity of the deceased, they're the very people. Take your friend and knock on a few doors. But be casual, make sure they don't think you're about to evict them or anything.'

'Yes, sir.' The constable seemed dubious about the whole venture. For one thing, he was sure to get an amount of hassle. For another, it was still raining hard.

'On you go,' Rebus chided, but gently. The constable shuffled off, collecting his companion on the way.

Rebus approached the photographer.

'You're taking a lot of snaps,' he said.

13

'I need to in this light, to make sure at least a few come out.'

'Bit quick off the mark in getting here, weren't you?'

'Superintendent Watson's orders. He wants pictures of any drugs-related incidents. Part of his campaign.'

'That's a bit gruesome, isn't it?' Rebus knew the new Chief Superintendent, had met him. Full of social awareness and community involvement. Full of good ideas, and lacking only the manpower to implement them. Rebus had an idea.

'Listen, while you're here, take one or two of that far wall, will you?'

'No problem.'

'Thanks.' Rebus turned to the doctor. 'How soon will we know what's in that full packet?'

'Later on today, maybe tomorrow morning at the latest.'

Rebus nodded to himself. What was his interest? Maybe it was the dreariness of the day, or the atmosphere in this house, or the positioning of the body. All he knew was that he felt something. And if it turned out to be just a damp ache in his bones, well, fair enough. He left the room and made a tour of the rest of the house.

The real horror was in the bathroom.

The toilet must have blocked up weeks before. A plunger lay on the floor, so some cursory attempt had been made to unblock it, but to no avail. Instead, the small, splattered sink had become a urinal, while the bath had become a dumping ground for solids, upon which crawled a dozen large and jet-black flies. The bath had also become a skip, filled with bags of refuse, bits of wood. . . . Rebus didn't stick around, pulling the door tight shut behind him. He didn't envy the council workmen who would eventually have to come and fight the good fight against all this decay.

One bedroom was completely empty, but the other

boasted a sleeping bag, damp from the drips coming through the roof. Some kind of identity had been imposed upon the room by the pinning of pictures to its walls. Up close, he noticed that these were original photographs, and that they comprised a sort of portfolio. Certainly they were well taken, even to Rebus's untrained eye. A few were of Edinburgh Castle on damp, misty days. It looked particularly bleak. Others showed it in bright sunshine. It still looked bleak. One or two were of a girl, age indeterminate. She was posing, but grinning broadly, not taking the event seriously.

Next to the sleeping bag was a bin-liner half filled with clothes, and next to this a small pile of dog-eared paperbacks: Harlan Ellison, Clive Barker, Ramsey Campbell. Science fiction and horror. Rebus left the books where they were and went back downstairs.

'All finished,' the photographer said. 'I'll get those photos to you tomorrow.'

'Thanks.'

'I also do portrait work, by the way. A nice family group for the grandparents? Sons and daughters? Here, I'll give you my card.'

Rebus accepted the card and pulled his raincoat back on, heading out to the car. He didn't like photographs, especially of himself. It wasn't just that he photographed badly. No, there was more to it than that.

The sneaking suspicion that photographs really could steal your soul.

On his way back to the station, travelling through the slow midday traffic, Rebus thought about how a group photograph of his wife, his daughter and him might look. But no, he couldn't visualise it. They had grown so far apart, ever since Rhona had taken Samantha to live in London. Sammy still wrote, but Rebus himself was slow at responding, and she seemed to take umbrage at this,

15

writing less and less herself. In her last letter she had hoped Gill and he were happy.

He hadn't the courage to tell her that Gill Templer had left him several months ago. Telling Samantha would have been fine: it was the idea of Rhona's getting to hear of it that he couldn't stand. Another notch in his bow of failed relationships. Gill had taken up with a disc jockey on a local radio station, a man whose enthusing voice Rebus seemed to hear whenever he entered a shop or a filling station, or passed the open window of a tenement block.

He still saw Gill once or twice a week of course, at meetings and in the station-house, as well as at scenes of crimes. Especially now that he had been elevated to her rank.

Detective Inspector John Rebus.

Well, it had taken long enough, hadn't it? And it was a long, hard case, full of personal suffering, which had brought the promotion. He was sure of that.

He was sure, too, that he wouldn't be seeing Rian again. Not after last night's dinner party, not after the fairly unsuccessful bout of lovemaking. *Yet another* unsuccessful bout. It had struck him, lying next to Rian, that her eyes were almost identical to Inspector Gill Templer's. A surrogate? Surely he was too old for that.

'Getting old, John,' he said to himself.

Certainly he was getting hungry, and there was a pub just past the next set of traffic lights. What the hell, he was entitled to a lunch break.

The Sutherland Bar was quiet, Monday lunchtime being one of the lowest points of the week. All money spent, and nothing to look forward to. And of course, as Rebus was quickly reminded by the barman, the Sutherland did not exactly cater for a lunchtime clientele.

'No hot meals,' he said, 'and no sandwiches.'

'A pie then,' begged Rebus, '*any*thing. Just to wash down the beer.'

'If it's food you want, there's plenty of cafes around here. This particular pub happens to sell beers, lagers and spirits. We're not a chippie.'

'What about crisps?'

The barman eyed him for a moment. 'What flavour?'

'Cheese and onion.'

'We've run out.'

'Well, ready salted then.'

'No, they're out too.' The barman had cheered up again.

'Well,' said Rebus in growing frustration, 'what in the name of God *have* you got?'

'Two flavours. Curry, or egg, bacon and tomato.'

'*Egg?*' Rebus sighed. 'All right, give me a packet of each.'

The barman stooped beneath the counter to find the smallest possible bags, past their sell-by dates if possible.

'Any nuts?' It was a last desperate hope. The barman looked up.

'Dry roasted, salt and vinegar, chilli flavour,' he said.

'One of each then,' said Rebus, resigned to an early death. 'And another half of eighty-shillings.'

He was finishing this second drink when the bar door shuddered open and an instantly recognisable figure entered, his hand signalling for refreshment before he was even halfway through the door. He saw Rebus, smiled, and came to join him on one of the high stools.

'Hello, John.'

'Afternoon, Tony.'

Inspector Anthony McCall tried to balance his prodigious bulk on the tiny circumference of the bar stool, thought better of it, and stood instead, one shoe on the foot-rail, and both elbows on the freshly wiped surface of the bar. He stared hungrily at Rebus.

17

'Give us one of your crisps.'

When the packet was offered, he pulled out a handful and stuffed them into his mouth.

'Where were you this morning then?' said Rebus. 'I'd to take one of your calls.'

'The one at Pilmuir? Ach, sorry about that, John. Heavy night last night. I had a bit of a hangover this morning.' A pint of murky beer was placed in front of him. 'Hair of the dog,' he said, and took four slow gulps, reducing it to a quarter of its former size.

'Well, I'd nothing better to do anyway,' said Rebus, sipping at his own beer. 'Christ, those houses down there are a mess though.'

McCall nodded thoughtfully. 'It wasn't always like that, John. I was born there.'

'Really?'

'Well, to be exact, I was born on the estate that was there before this one. It was so bad, so they said, that they levelled it and built Pilmuir instead. Bloody hell on earth it is now.'

'Funny you should say that,' said Rebus. 'One of the young uniformed kids thought there might be some kind of occult tie-in.' McCall looked up from his drink. 'There was a black-magic painting on the wall,' Rebus explained. 'And candles on the floor.'

'Like a sacrifice?' McCall offered, chuckling. 'My wife's dead keen on all those horror films. Gets them out of the video library. I think she sits watching them all day when I'm out.'

'I suppose it must go on, devil worship, witchcraft. It can't *all* be in the imagination of the Sunday newspaper editors.'

'I know how you might find out.'

'How?'

'The university,' said McCall. Rebus frowned, disbelieving. 'I'm serious. They've got some kind of department

18

that studies ghosts and all that sort of thing. Set up with money from some dead writer.' McCall shook his head. 'Incredible what people will do.'

Rebus was nodding. 'I *did* read about that, now you mention it. Arthur Koestler's money, wasn't it?'

McCall shrugged.

'Arthur Daley's more my style,' he said, emptying his glass.

Rebus was studying the pile of paperwork on his desk when the telephone rang.

'DI Rebus.'

'They said you were the man to talk to.' The voice was young, female, full of unfocussed suspicion.

'They were probably right. What can I do for you, miss . . .?'

'Tracy. . . .' The voice fell to a whisper on the last syllable of the name. She had already been tricked into revealing herself. 'Never mind who I am!' She had become immediately hysterical, but calmed just as quickly. 'I'm phoning about that squat in Pilmuir, the one where they found. . . .' The voice trailed off again.

'Oh yes.' Rebus sat up and began to take notice. 'Was it you who phoned the first time?'

'What?'

'To tell us that someone had died there.'

'Yes, it was me. Poor Ronnie. . . .'

'Ronnie being the deceased?' Rebus scribbled the name onto the back of one of the files from his in-tray. Beside it he wrote 'Tracy – caller'.

'Yes.' Her voice had broken again, near to tears this time.

'Can you give me a surname for Ronnie?'

'No.' She paused. 'I never knew it. I'm not sure Ronnie was even his real name. Hardly anyone uses their real name.'

'Tracy, I'd like to talk to you about Ronnie. We can do it over the telephone, but I'd rather it was face to face. Don't worry, you're not in any trouble –'

'But I *am*. That's why I called. Ronnie told me, you see.'

'Told you what, Tracy?'

'Told me he'd been murdered.'

The room around Rebus seemed suddenly to vanish. There was only this disconnected voice, the telephone, and him.

'He said that to you, Tracy?'

'Yes.' She was crying now, sniffing back the unseen tears. Rebus visualised a frightened little girl, just out of school, standing in a distant callbox. 'I've got to hide,' she said at last. 'Ronnie said over and over that I should hide.'

'Shall I bring my car and fetch you? Just tell me where you are.'

'No!'

'Then tell me how Ronnie was killed. You know how we found him?'

'Lying on the floor by the window. That's where he was.'

'Not quite.'

'Oh yes, that's where he was. By the window. Lying wrapped up into a little ball. I thought he was just sleeping. But when I touched his arm he was cold. . . . I went to find Charlie, but he'd gone. So I just panicked.'

'You say Ronnie was lying in a ball?' Rebus had begun to draw pencilled circles on the back of the file.

'Yes.'

'And this was in the living room?'

She seemed confused. 'What? No, not in the living room. He was upstairs, in his bedroom.'

'I see.' Rebus kept on drawing effortless circles. He was trying to imagine Ronnie dying, but not really dead, crawling downstairs after Tracy had fled, ending up in the living room. That might explain those bruises. But the candles. . . . He had been so perfectly positioned between them. . . . 'And when was this?'

'Late last night, I don't know exactly when. I panicked. When I calmed down, I phoned for the police.'

'What time was it when you phoned?'

She paused, thinking. 'About seven this morning.'

'Tracy, would you mind telling this to some other people?'

'Why?'

'I'll tell you when I pick you up. Just tell me where you are.'

There was another pause while she considered this. 'I'm back in Pilmuir,' she said finally. 'I've moved into another squat.'

'Well,' said Rebus, 'you don't want me to come down there, do you? But you must be quite close to Shore Road. What about us meeting there?'

'Well. . . .'

'There's a pub called the Dock Leaf,' continued Rebus, giving her no time to debate. 'Do you know it?'

'I've been kicked out of it a few times.'

'Me too. Okay, I'll meet you outside it in an hour. All right?'

'All right.' She didn't sound over-enthusiastic, and Rebus wondered if she would keep the appointment. Well, what of it? She sounded straight enough, but she might just be another casualty, making it up to draw attention to herself, to make her life seem more interesting than it was.

But then he'd had a feeling, hadn't he?

'All right,' she said, and the connection was severed.

Shore Road was a fast road around the north coast of the city. Factories, warehouses, and vast DIY and home furnishing stores were its landmarks, and beyond them lay the Firth of Forth, calm and grey. On most days, the coast of Fife was visible in the distance, but not today, with a cold mist hanging low on the water. On the other side of the road from the warehouses were the tenements, four-storey predecessors of the concrete high-rise. There was a smattering of corner shops, where neighbour met neighbour, and information was passed on, and a few small unmodernised pubs, where strangers did not go unnoticed for long.

The Dock Leaf had shed one generation of low-life drinkers, and discovered another. Its denizens now were young, unemployed, and living six to a three-bedroom rented flat along Shore Road. Petty crime though was not a problem: you didn't mess your own nest. The old community values still held.

Rebus, early for the meeting, just had time for a half in the saloon bar. The beer was cheap but bland, and everyone seemed to know if not who he was then certainly *what* he was, their voices turned down to murmurs, their eyes averted. When, at three thirty, he stepped outside, the sudden daylight made him squint.

'Are you the policeman?'

'That's right, Tracy.'

She had been standing against the pub's exterior wall. He shaded his eyes, trying to make out her face, and was surprised to find himself looking at a woman of between twenty and twenty-five. Her age was transparent in her face, though her style marked her out as the perennial rebel: cropped peroxide hair, two stud earrings in her left ear (but none in the right), tie-dye T-shirt, tight, faded denims, and red basketball boots. She was tall, as tall as Rebus. As his eyes adjusted to the light, he saw the tear-tracks on either cheek, the old acne scars. But there were also crow's-feet around her eyes, evidence of a life used to laughter. There was no laughter in those olive-green eyes though. Somewhere in Tracy's life a wrong turning had been made, and Rebus had the idea that she was still trying to reverse back to that fork in the road.

The last time he had seen her she had been laughing. Laughing as her semblance curled from the wall of Ronnie's bedroom. She was the girl in the photographs.

'Is Tracy your real name?'

'Sort of.' They had begun to walk. She crossed the road at a zebra crossing, not bothering to check whether any cars were approaching, and Rebus followed her to a wall, where she stopped, staring out across the Forth. She wrapped her arms around herself, examining the lifting mist.

'It's my middle name,' she said.

Rebus leaned his forearms against the wall. 'How long have you known Ronnie?'

'Three months. That's how long I've been in Pilmuir.'

'Who else lived in that house?'

She shrugged. 'They came and went. We'd only been in there a few weeks. Sometimes I'd go downstairs in the morning, and there'd be half a dozen strangers sleeping on the floor. Nobody minded. It was like a big family.'

'What makes you think somebody killed Ronnie?'

She turned towards him angrily, but her eyes were liquid. 'I told you on the phone! He *told* me. He'd been off somewhere and come back with some stuff. He didn't look right though. Usually, when he's got a little smack, he's like a kid at Christmas. But he wasn't. He was scared, acting like a robot or something. He kept telling me to hide, telling me they were coming for him.'

'Who were?'

'I don't know.'

'Was this after he'd taken the stuff?'

'No, that's what's really crazy. This was *before*. He had the packet in his hand. He pushed me out of the door.'

'You weren't there while he was fixing?'

'God no. I hated that.' Her eyes drilled into his. 'I'm not

23

a junkie, you know. I mean, I smoke a little, but never. . . . You know. . . .'

'Was there anything else you noticed about Ronnie?'

'Like what?'

'Well, the state he was in.'

'You mean the bruises?'

'Yes.'

'He often came back looking like that. Never talked about it.'

'Got in a lot of fights, I suppose. Was he short-tempered?'

'Not with me.'

Rebus sunk his hands into his pockets. A chill wind was whipping up off the water, and he wondered whether she was warm enough. He couldn't help noticing that her nipples were very prominent through the cotton of her T-shirt.

'Would you like my jacket?' he asked.

'Only if your wallet's in it,' she said with a quick smile.

He smiled back, and offered a cigarette instead, which she accepted. He didn't take one for himself. There were only three left out of the day's ration, and the evening stretched ahead of him.

'Do you know who Ronnie's dealer was?' he asked casually, helping her to light the cigarette. With her head tucked into his open jacket, the lighter shaking in her hand, she shook her head. Eventually, the windbreak worked, and she sucked hard at the filter.

'I was never really sure,' she said. 'It was something else he didn't talk about.'

'What did he talk about?'

She thought about this, and smiled again. 'Not much, now you mention it. That was what I liked about him. You always felt there was more to him than he was letting on.'

'Such as?'

24

She shrugged. 'Might have been anything, might have been nothing.'

This was harder work than Rebus had anticipated, and he really was getting cold. It was time to speed things up.

'He was in the bedroom when you found him?'

'Yes.'

'And the squat was empty at the time?'

'Yes. Earlier on, there'd been a few people there, but they'd all gone. One of them was up in Ronnie's room, but I didn't know him. Then there was Charlie.'

'You mentioned him on the telephone.'

'Yes, well, when I found Ronnie, I went looking for him. He's usually around somewhere, in one of the other squats or in town doing a bit of begging. Christ, he's strange.'

'In what way?'

'Didn't you see what was on the living-room wall?'

'You mean the star?'

'Yes, that was Charlie. He painted it.'

'He's keen on the occult then?'

'Mad keen.'

'What about Ronnie?'

'Ronnie? Jesus, no. He couldn't even stand to watch horror films. They scared him.'

'But he had all those horror books in his bedroom.'

'That was Charlie, trying to get Ronnie interested. All they did was give him more nightmares. And all those did was push him into taking more smack.'

'How did he finance his habit?' Rebus watched a small boat come gliding through the mist. Something fell from it into the water, but he couldn't tell what.

'I wasn't his accountant.'

'Who was?' The boat was turning in an arc, slipping further west towards Queensferry.

'Nobody wants to know where the money comes from, that's the truth. It makes you an accessory, doesn't it?'

25

'That depends.' Rebus shivered.

'Well, *I* didn't want to know. If he tried to tell me, I put my hands over my ears.'

'He's never had a job then?'

'I don't know. He used to talk about being a photographer. That's what he'd set his heart on when he left school. It was the only thing he wouldn't pawn, even to pay for his habit.'

Rebus was lost. 'What was?'

'His camera. It cost him a small fortune, every penny saved out of his social security.'

Social security: now there was a phrase. But Rebus was sure there had been no camera in Ronnie's bedroom. So add robbery to the list.

'Tracy, I'll need a statement.'

She was immediately suspicious. 'What for?'

'Just so I've got it on record, so we can do something about Ronnie's death. Will you help me do that?'

It was a long time before she nodded. The boat had disappeared. There was nothing floating in the water, nothing left in its wake. Rebus put a hand on Tracy's shoulder, but gently.

'Thanks,' he said. 'The car's this way.'

After she had made her statement, Rebus insisted on driving her home, dropping her several streets from her destination but knowing her address now.

'Not that I can swear to be there for the next ten years,' she had said. It didn't matter. He had given her his work and home telephone numbers. He was sure she would keep in touch.

'One last thing,' he said, as she was about to close the car door. She leaned in from the pavement. 'Ronnie kept shouting "They're coming." Who do you think he meant?'

She shrugged. Then froze, remembering the scene. 'He

26

was strung out, Inspector. Maybe he meant the snakes and spiders.'

Yes, thought Rebus, as she closed the door and he started the car. And then maybe he meant the snakes and spiders who'd supplied him.

Back at Greater London Road station, there was a message that Chief Superintendent Watson wanted to see him. Rebus called his superior's office.

'I'll come along now, if I may.'

The secretary checked, and confirmed that this would be okay.

Rebus had come across Watson on many occasions since the superintendent's posting had brought him from the far north to Edinburgh. He seemed a reasonable man, if just a little, well, agricultural for some tastes. There were a lot of jokes around the station already about his Aberdonian background, and he had earned the whispered nickname of 'Farmer' Watson.

'Come in, John, come in.'

The Superintendent had risen from behind his desk long enough to point Rebus in the vague direction of a chair. Rebus noticed that the desk itself was meticulously arranged, files neatly piled in two trays, nothing in front of Watson but a thick, newish folder and two sharp pencils. There was a photograph of two young children to one side of the folder.

'My two,' Watson explained. 'They're a bit older than that now, but still a handful.'

Watson was a large man, his girth giving truth to the phrase 'barrel-chested'. His face was ruddy, hair thin and silvered at the temples. Yes, Rebus could picture him in galoshes and a trout-fishing hat, stomping his way across a moor, his collie obedient beside him. But what did he want with Rebus? Was he seeking a human collie?

'You were at the scene of a drugs overdose this morning.' It was a statement of fact, so Rebus didn't bother to answer. 'It should have been Inspector McCall's call, but he was . . . well, wherever he was.'

'He's a good copper, sir.'

Watson stared up at him, then smiled. 'Inspector McCall's qualities are not in question. That's not why you're here. But your being on the scene gave me an idea. You probably know that I'm interested in this city's drugs problem. Frankly, the statistics appal me. It's not something I'd encountered in Aberdeen, with the exception of some of the oil workers. But then it was mostly the executives, the ones they flew in from the United States. They brought their habits, if you'll pardon the pun, with them. But here –' He flicked open the folder and began to pick over some of the sheets. 'Here, Inspector, it's Hades. Plain and simple.'

'Yes, sir.'

'Are you a churchgoer?'

'Sir?' Rebus was shifting uncomfortably in his chair.

'It's a simple enough question, isn't it? Do you go to church?'

'Not regularly, sir. But sometimes I do, yes.' Like yesterday, Rebus thought. And here again he felt like fleeing.

'Someone said you did. Then you should know what I'm talking about when I say that this city is turning into Hades.' Watson's face was ruddier than ever. 'The Infirmary has treated addicts as young as eleven and twelve. Your own brother is serving a prison sentence for dealing in drugs.' Watson looked up again, perhaps expecting Rebus to look shamed. But Rebus's eyes were a fiery glare, his cheeks red not with embarrassment.

'With respect, sir,' he said, voice level but as taut as a wire, 'what has this got to do with me?'

'Simply this.' Watson closed the folder and settled back in his chair. 'I'm putting into operation a new anti-drugs campaign. Public awareness and that sort of thing, coupled with funding for discreet information. I've got the backing, and what's more I've got the *money*. A group of the city's businessmen are prepared to put fifty thousand pounds into the campaign.'

'Very public-spirited of them, sir.'

Watson's face became darker. He leaned forward in his chair, filling Rebus's vision. 'You better bloody believe it,' he said.

'But I still don't see where I –'

'John.' The voice was anodyne now. 'You've had . . . experience. Personal experience. I'd like you to help me front our side of the campaign.'

'No, sir, really –'

'Good. That's agreed then.' Watson had already risen. Rebus tried to stand, too, but his legs had lost all power. He pushed against the armrests with his hands and managed to heave himself upright. Was this the price they were demanding? Public atonement for having a rotten brother? Watson was opening the door. 'We'll talk again, go through the details. But for now, try to tie up whatever you're working on, casenotes up to date, that sort of thing. Tell me what you can't finish, and we'll find someone to take it off your hands.'

'Yes, sir.' Rebus clutched at the proffered hand. It was like steel, cool, dry and crushing.

'Goodbye, sir,' Rebus said, standing in the corridor now, to a door that had already closed on him.

That evening, still numb, he grew bored with television and left his flat, planning to drive around a bit, no real destination in mind. Marchmont was quiet, but then it always was. His car sat undisturbed on the cobbles outside his tenement. He started it up and drove, entering the centre of town, crossing to the New Town. At Canonmills he stopped in the forecourt of a petrol station and filled the car, adding a torch, some batteries, and several bars of chocolate to his purchases, paying by credit card.

He ate the chocolate as he drove, trying not to think of the next day's cigarette ration, and listened to the car radio. Gill Templer's lover, Calum McCallum, began his broadcast at eight thirty, and he listened for a few minutes. It was enough. The mock-cheery voice, the jokes so lame they needed wheelchairs, the predictable mix of old records and telephone-linked chatter. . . . Rebus turned the tuning knob until he found Radio Three. Recognising the music of Mozart, he turned up the volume.

He had always known that it would end here of course. He drove through the ill-lit and winding streets, threading his way further into the maze. A new padlock had been fitted to the door of the house, but Rebus had in his pocket a copy of the key. Switching on his torch, he walked quietly into the living room. The floor was bare. There was no sign that a corpse had lain there only ten hours before. The jar of syringes had gone, too, as had the candlesticks. Ignoring the far wall, Rebus left the room and headed upstairs. He pushed open the door of Ronnie's bedroom and walked in, crossing to the window. This was where Tracy said she had found the body. Rebus squatted, resting on his toes, and shone the torch carefully over the floor. No sign of a camera. Nothing. It wasn't going to be made easy for him, this case. Always supposing there *was* a case.

He only had Tracy's word for it, after all.

He retraced his steps, out of the room and towards the stairwell. Something glinted against the top step, right in at the corner of the stairs. Rebus picked it up and examined it. It was a small piece of metal, like the clasp from a cheap brooch. He pushed it into his pocket anyway and took another look at the staircase, trying to imagine

Ronnie regaining consciousness and making his way to the ground floor.

Possible. Just possible. But to end up positioned like that . . .? Much less feasible.

And why bring the jar of syringes downstairs with him? Rebus nodded to himself, sure that he was wandering the maze in something like the right direction. He went downstairs again and into the living room. It had a smell like the mould on an old jar of jam, earthy and sweet at the same time. The earth sterile, the sweetness sickly. He went over to the far wall and shone his torchlight against it.

Then came up short, blood pounding. The circles were still there, and the five-pointed star within them. But there were fresh additions, zodiac signs and other symbols between the two circles, painted in red. He touched the paint. It was tacky. Bringing his fingers away, he shone the torch further up the wall, and read the dripping message:

HELLO RONNIE

Superstitious to his core, Rebus turned on his heels and fled, not bothering to relock the door behind him. Walking briskly towards his car, his eyes turned back in the direction of the house, he fell into someone, and stumbled. The other figure fell awkwardly, and was slow to rise. Rebus switched on his torch, and confronted a teenager, eyes sparkling, face bruised and cut.

'Jesus, son,' he whispered, 'what happened to you?'

'I got beat up,' the boy said, shuffling away on a painful leg.

Rebus made the car somehow, his nerves as thin as old shoelaces. Inside, he locked the door and sat back, closing his eyes, breathing hard. Relax, John, he told himself. Relax. Soon, he was even able to smile at his momentary lapse of courage. Tomorrow he'd come back. In daylight.

He'd seen enough for now.

31

Tuesday

I have since had reason to believe the cause to lie much deeper in the nature of man, and to turn on some nobler hinge than the principle of hatred.

Sleep did not come easy, but eventually, slumped in his favourite chair, a book propped open on his lap, he must have dozed off, because it took a nine o'clock call to bring him to life.

His back, legs and arms were stiff and aching as he scrabbled on the floor for his new cordless telephone.

'Yes?'

'Lab here, Inspector Rebus. You wanted to know first thing.'

'What have you got?' Rebus slumped back into the warm chair, pulling at his eyes with his free hand, trying to engage their cooperation in this fresh and waking world. He glanced at his watch and realised just how late he'd slept.

'Well, it's not the purest heroin on the street.'

He nodded to himself, confident that his next question hardly needed asking. 'Would it kill whoever injected it?'

The reply jolted him upright.

'Not at all. In fact, it's very clean, all things considered. A bit watered down from its pure form, but that's not uncommon. In fact, it's mandatory.'

'But it would be okay to use?'

'I imagine it would be very good to use.'

'I see. Well, thank you.' Rebus pressed the disconnect button. He had been so sure. So sure. . . . He reached into his pocket, found the number he needed, and pushed the seven digits quickly, before the thought of morning coffee could overwhelm him.

'Inspector Rebus for Doctor Enfield.' He waited. 'Doctor? Fine thanks. How about you? Good, good. Listen, that body yesterday, the druggie on the Pilmuir Estate, any news?' He listened. 'Yes, I'll hold.'

Pilmuir. What had Tony McCall said? It had been lovely once, a place of innocence, something like that. The old days always were though, weren't they? Memory smoothed the corners, as Rebus himself knew well.

'Hello?' he said to the telephone. 'Yes, that's right.' Paper was rustling in the background, Enfield's voice dispassionate.

'Bruising on the body. Fairly extensive. Result of a heavy fall or some kind of physical confrontation. The stomach was almost completely empty. HIV negative, which is something. As for the cause of death, well. . . .'

'The heroin?' Rebus prompted.

'Mmm. Ninety-five percent impure.'

'Really?' Rebus perked up. 'What had it been diluted with?'

'Still working on that, Inspector. But an educated guess would be anything from ground-up aspirin to rat poison, with the emphasis strictly on rodent control.'

'You're saying it was lethal?'

'Oh, absolutely. Whoever sold the stuff was selling euthanasia. If there's more of it about . . . well, I dread to think.'

More of it about? The thought made Rebus's scalp tingle. What if someone were going around poisoning junkies? But why the one perfect packet? One perfect, one as rotten as could be. It didn't make sense.

'Thanks, Doctor Enfield.'

He rested the telephone on the arm of the chair. Tracy had been right in one respect at least. They *had* murdered Ronnie. Whoever 'they' were. And Ronnie had known, known as soon as he'd used the stuff. . . . No, wait. . . .

Known *before* he'd used the stuff? Could that be possible? Rebus had to find the dealer. Had to find out why Ronnie had been chosen to die. Been, indeed, sacrificed. . . .

It was Tony McCall's backyard. All right, so he had moved out of Pilmuir, had eventually bought a crippling mortgage which some people called a house. It was a nice house, too. He knew this because his wife told him it was. Told him continually. She couldn't understand why he spent so little time there. After all, as she told him, it was his home too.

Home. To McCall's wife, it was a palace. 'Home' didn't quite cover it. And the two children, son and daughter, had been brought up to tiptoe through the interior, not leaving crumbs or fingerprints, no mess, no breakages. McCall, who had lived a bruising childhood with his brother Tommy, thought it unnatural. His children had grown up in fear and in a swaddling of love – a bad combination. Now Craig was fourteen, Isabel eleven. Both were shy, introspective, maybe even a bit strange. Bang had gone McCall's dream of a professional footballer for a son, an actress for a daughter. Craig played chess a lot, but no physical sports. (He had won a small plaque at school after one tournament. McCall had tried to learn to play after that, but had failed.) Isabel liked knitting. They sat in the too-perfect living room created by their mother, and were almost silent. The clack-clack of needles; the soft movement of chess pieces.

Christ, was it any wonder he kept away?

So here he was in Pilmuir, not checking on anything exactly, just walking. Taking some air. From his own ultra-modern estate, all detached shoeboxes and Volvos, he had to cross some waste ground, avoid the traffic on a busy arterial road, pass a school playing-field and manoeuvre between some factory units to find himself in

Pilmuir. But it was worth the effort. He knew this place; knew the minds that festered here.

He was one of them, after all.

'Hello, Tony.'

He swirled, not recognising the voice, expecting hassle. John Rebus stood there, smiling at him, hands in pockets.

'John! Christ, you made me jump.'

'Sorry. Stroke of luck bumping into you though.' Rebus checked around them, as though looking for someone. 'I tried phoning, but they said it was your day off.'

'Aye, that's right.'

'So what are you doing here?'

'Just walking. We live over that way.' He jerked his head towards the south-west. 'It's not far. Besides, this is my patch, don't forget. Got to keep an eye on the boys and girls.'

'That's why I wanted to speak to you actually.'

'Oh?'

Rebus had begun to walk along the pavement, and McCall, still rattled by his sudden appearance, followed.

'Yes,' Rebus was saying. 'I wanted to ask if you know someone, a friend of the deceased's. The name is Charlie.'

'That's all? Charlie?' Rebus shrugged. 'What does he look like?'

Rebus shrugged again. 'I've no idea, Tony. It was Ronnie's girlfriend Tracy who told me about him.'

'Ronnie? Tracy?' McCall's eyebrows met. 'Who the hell are they?'

'Ronnie is the deceased. That junkie we found on the estate.'

Everything was suddenly clear in McCall's mind. He nodded slowly. 'You work quickly,' he said.

'The quicker the better. Ronnie's girlfriend told me an interesting story.'

'Oh?'

38

'She said Ronnie was murdered.' Rebus kept on walking, but McCall had stopped.

'Wait a minute!' He caught Rebus up. 'Murdered? Come on, John, you saw the guy.'

'True. With a needle's worth of rat poison scuppering his veins.'

McCall whistled softly. 'Jesus.'

'Quite,' said Rebus. 'And now I need to talk to Charlie. He's young, could be a bit scared, and interested in the occult.'

McCall sorted through a few mental files. 'I suppose there are one or two places we could try looking,' he said at last. 'But it'd be a slog. The concept of neighbourhood policing hasn't quite stretched this far yet.'

'You're saying we won't be made very welcome?'

'Something like that.'

'Well, just give me the addresses and point me in the right direction. It's your day off after all.'

McCall looked slighted. 'You're forgetting, John. This is my patch. By rights, this should be my case, if there is a case.'

'It would've been your case if you hadn't had that hangover.' They smiled at this, but Rebus was wondering whether, in Tony McCall's hands, there *would* have been anything to investigate. Wouldn't Tony just have let it slip? Should he, Rebus, let it slip, too?

'Anyway,' McCall was saying on cue, 'surely you must have better things to do?'

Rebus shook his head. 'Nothing. All my work's been farmed out, with the emphasis on "farmed".'

'You mean Superintendent Watson?'

'He wants me working on his anti-drugs campaign. Me, for Christ's sake.'

'That could be a bit embarrassing.'

'I know. But the idiot thinks I've got "personal experience".'

'He's got a point, I suppose.' Rebus was about to argue, but McCall got in first. 'So you've nothing to do?'

'Not until summoned by Farmer Watson, no.'

'You jammy bugger. Well, that does change things a bit, but not enough, I'm sorry to say. You're my guest here, and you're going to have to put up with me. Until I get bored, that is.'

Rebus smiled. 'I appreciate it, Tony.' He looked around them. 'So, where to first?'

McCall inclined his head back the way they had just come. They turned around and walked.

'So tell me,' said Rebus, 'what's so awful at home that you'd think of coming here on your day off?'

McCall laughed. 'Is it so obvious then?'

'Only to someone who's been there himself.'

'Ach, I don't know, John. I seem to have everything I've never wanted.'

'And it's still not enough.' It was a simple statement of belief.

'I mean, Sheila's a wonderful mother and all that, and the kids never get into trouble, but. . . .'

'The grass is always greener,' said Rebus, thinking of his own failed marriage, of the way his flat was cold when he came home, the way the door would close with a hollow sound behind him.

'Now Tommy, my brother, I used to think he had it made. Plenty of money, house with a jacuzzi, automatic-opening garage. . . .' McCall saw that Rebus was smiling, and smiled himself.

'Electric blinds,' Rebus continued, 'personalised number plate, car phone. . .'

'Time share in Malaga,' said McCall, close to laughter, 'marble-topped kitchen units.'

It was too ridiculous. They laughed out loud as they walked, adding to the catalogue. But then Rebus saw where they were, and stopped laughing, stopped walking.

This was where he'd been heading all along. He touched the torch in his jacket pocket.

'Come on, Tony,' he said soberly. 'There's something I want to show you.'

'He was found here,' Rebus said, shining the torch over the bare floorboards. 'Legs together, lying on his back, arms outstretched. I don't think he got into that position by accident, do you?'

McCall studied the scene. They were both professionals now, and acting almost like strangers. 'And the girlfriend says she found him upstairs?'

'That's right.'

'You believe her?'

'Why would she lie?'

'There could be a hundred reasons, John. Would I know the girl?'

'She hasn't been in Pilmuir long. Bit older than you'd imagine, midtwenties, maybe more.'

'So this Ronnie's already dead, and he's brought downstairs and laid out with the candles and everything.'

'That's right.'

'I'm beginning to see why you need to find the friend who's into the occult.'

'Right. Now come and look at this.' Rebus led McCall to the far wall and shone the torch onto the pentagram, then further up the wall.

'"Hello Ronnie",' McCall read aloud.

'And this wasn't here yesterday.'

'Really?' McCall sounded surprised. 'Kids, John, that's all.'

'Kids didn't draw that pentagram.'

'No, agreed.'

'Charlie drew that pentagram.'

'Right.' McCall slipped his hands into his pockets and

41

drew himself upright. 'Point taken, Inspector. Let's go squat hunting.'

But the few people they found seemed to know nothing, and to care even less. As McCall pointed out, it was the wrong time of day. Everyone from the squats was in the city centre, stealing purses from handbags, begging, shoplifting, doing deals. Reluctantly, Rebus agreed that they were wasting their time.

Since McCall wanted to listen to the tape Rebus had made of his interview with Tracy, they headed back to Great London Road. McCall had the idea that there might be some clue on the tape that would lead them to Charlie, something that would help him place the guy, something Rebus had missed.

Rebus was a weary step or two ahead of McCall as they climbed the front steps to the station's heavy wooden door. A fresh duty officer was beginning his shift at the desk, still fussing with his shirt collar and his clip-on tie. Simple but clever, Rebus thought to himself. Simple but clever. All uniformed officers wore clip-on ties, so that in a clinch, if the attacker tried to yank the officer's head forwards, the tie would simply come away in his hands. Likewise, the desk sergeant's glasses had special lenses which, if hit, would slip out of their frame without shattering. Simple but clever. Rebus hoped that the case of the crucified junkie would be simple.

He didn't feel very clever.

'Hello, Arthur,' he said, passing the desk, making towards the staircase. 'Any messages for me?'

'Give me a break, John. I've only been on two minutes.'

'Fair enough.' Rebus pushed his hands deep into his pockets, where the fingers of his right hand touched something alien, metal. He brought the brooch-clip out and studied it. Then froze.

McCall looked at him, puzzled.

'Go on up,' Rebus told him. 'I'll just be a second.'

'Right you are, John.'

Back at the desk, Rebus held his left hand out to the sergeant. 'Do me a favour, Arthur. Give me your tie.'

'What?'

'You heard me.'

Knowing that he would have a story to tell tonight in the canteen, the desk sergeant pulled at his tie. As it came away from his shirt, the clip made a single snapping sound. Simple but clever, thought Rebus, holding the tie between finger and thumb.

'Thanks, Arthur,' he said.

'Anytime, John,' the sergeant called, watching carefully as Rebus walked back towards the stairs. 'Anytime.'

'Know what this is, Tony?'

McCall had seated himself in Rebus's chair, behind Rebus's desk. He had one fist in a drawer, and looked up, startled. Rebus was holding the necktie out in front of him. McCall nodded, then brought his hand out of the drawer. It was curved around a bottle of whisky.

'It's a tie,' he said. 'Got any cups?'

Rebus placed the tie on the desk. He went to a filing cabinet and searched amongst the many cups which sat unloved and uncleaned on top of it. Finally, one seemed to satisfy him, and he brought it to the desk. McCall was studying the cover of a file lying on the desk.

' "Ronnie," ' he read out, ' "Tracy – caller". I see your casenotes are as precise as ever.'

Rebus handed the cup to McCall.

'Where's yours?' asked McCall, pointing to the cup.

'I don't feel like drinking. To tell you the truth, I hardly touch the stuff now.' Rebus nodded at the bottle. 'That's for visitors.' McCall pursed his lips, his eyes opening wide. 'Besides,' Rebus went on, 'I've got the mother and father of a headache. In-laws, too. Kids, neighbours, town and

43

country.' He noticed a large envelope on the desk: PHOTOGRAPHS – DO NOT BEND.

'You know, Tony, when I was a sergeant, this sort of thing would take days to arrive. It's like royalty being an inspector.' He opened the envelope and took out the set of prints, ten by eights, black and white. He handed one to McCall.

'Look,' Rebus said, 'no writing on the wall. And the pentagram's unfinished. Today it was complete.' McCall nodded, and Rebus took back the picture, handing over another in its place. 'The deceased.'

'Poor little sod,' said McCall. 'It could be one of our kids, eh, John?'

'No,' said Rebus firmly. He rolled the envelope into the shape of a tube, and put it in his jacket pocket.

McCall had picked up the tie. He waved it towards Rebus, demanding an explanation.

'Have you ever worn one of those?' Rebus asked.

'Sure, at my wedding, maybe a funeral or a christening. . . .'

'I mean like this. A clip-on. When I was a kid, I remember my dad decided I'd look good in a kilt. He bought me the whole get-up, including a little tartan bow tie. It was a clip-on.'

'I've worn one,' said McCall. 'Everybody has. We all came through the ranks, didn't we?'

'No,' said Rebus. 'Now get out of my bloody chair.'

McCall found another chair, dragging it over from the wall to the desk. Rebus meantime sat down, picking up the tie.

'Police issue.'

'What is?'

'Clip-on ties,' said Rebus. 'Who else wears them?'

'Christ, I don't know, John.'

Rebus threw the clip across to McCall, who was slow to react. It fell to the floor, from where he retrieved it.

44

'It's a clip-on,' he said.

'I found it in Ronnie's house,' said Rebus. 'At the top of the stairs.'

'So?'

'So someone's tie broke. Maybe when they were dragging Ronnie downstairs. Maybe a police constable someone.'

'You think one of our lot . . .?'

'Just an idea,' said Rebus. 'Of course, it could belong to one of the lads who found the body.' He held out his hand, and McCall gave him back the clip. 'Maybe I'll talk to them.'

'John, what the hell. . . .' McCall ended with a sort of choking sound, unable to find words for the question he wanted to ask.

'Drink your whisky,' said Rebus solicitously. 'Then you can listen to that tape, see if you think Tracy's telling the truth.'

'What are you going to do?'

'I don't know.' He put the desk sergeant's tie in his pocket. 'Maybe I'll tie up a few loose ends.' McCall was pouring out a measure of whisky as Rebus left, but the parting shot, called from the staircase, was loud enough for him to hear.

'Maybe I'll just go to the devil!'

'Yes, a simple pentangle.'

The psychologist, Dr Poole, who wasn't really a psychologist, but rather, he had explained, a lecturer in psychology, quite a different thing, studied the photographs carefully, bottom lip curling up to cover his top lip in a sign of confident recognition. Rebus played with the empty envelope and stared out of the office window. The day was bright, and some students were lying in George Square Gardens, sharing bottles of wine, their text books forgotten.

45

Rebus felt uncomfortable. Institutes of higher education, from the simplest college up to the present confines of the University of Edinburgh, made him feel stupid. He felt that his every movement, every utterance, was being judged and interpreted, marking him down as a clever man who could have been cleverer, given the breaks.

'When I returned to the house,' he said, 'someone had drawn some symbols between the two circles. Signs of the zodiac, that sort of thing.'

Rebus watched as the psychologist went over to the bookshelves and began to browse. It had been easy to find this man. Making use of him might be more difficult.

'Probably the usual arcana,' Dr Poole was saying, finding the page he wanted and bringing it back to the desk to show Rebus. 'This sort of thing?'

'Yes, that's it.' Rebus studied the illustration. The pentagram was not identical to the one he had seen, but the differences were slight. 'Tell me, are many people interested in the occult?'

'You mean in Edinburgh?' Poole sat down again, pushing his glasses back up his nose. 'Oh yes. Plenty. Look at how well films about the devil do at the box office.'

Rebus smiled. 'Yes, I used to like horror films myself. But I mean an *active* interest.'

The lecturer smiled. 'I know you do. I was being facetious. So many people think that's what the occult is about – bringing Old Nick back to life. There's much more to it, believe me, Inspector. Or much less to it, depending on your point of view.'

Rebus tried to work out what this meant. 'You know occultists?' he said meantime.

'I know *of* occultists, practising covens of white and black witches.'

'Here? In Edinburgh?'

Poole smiled again. 'Oh yes. Right here. There are six working covens in and around Edinburgh.' He paused, and Rebus could almost see him doing a recount. 'Seven, perhaps. Fortunately, most of these practise white magic.'

'That's using the occult as a supposed force for good, right?'

'Quite correct.'

'And black magic . . .?'

The lecturer sighed. He suddenly became interested in the scene from his window. A summer's day. Rebus was remembering something. A long time ago, he'd bought a book of paintings by H.R. Giger, paintings of Satan flanked by vestal whores. . . . He couldn't say why he'd done it, but it must still be somewhere in the flat. He remembered hiding it from Rhona. . . .

'There is one coven in Edinburgh,' Poole was saying. 'A black coven.'

'Tell me, do they . . . do they make sacrifices?'

Dr Poole shrugged. 'We all make sacrifices.' But, seeing that Rebus was not laughing at his little joke, he straightened in his chair, his face becoming more serious. 'Probably they do, some token. A rat, a mouse, a chicken. It may not even go that far. They could use something symbolic, I really don't know.'

Rebus tapped one of the photographs which were spread across the desk. 'In the house where we found this pentagram, we also found a body. A dead body, in case you were wondering.' He brought these photographs out now. Dr Poole frowned as he glanced at them. 'Dead from a heroin overdose. Laid out with legs together, arms apart. The body was lying between two candles, which had burned down to nothing. Mean anything to you?'

Poole looked horror-struck. 'No,' he said. 'But you think that Satanists. . . .'

'I don't think anything, sir. I'm just trying to piece things together, going through all the possibilities.'

Poole thought for a moment. 'One of our students *might*

47

be of more use to you than I can. I'd no idea we were talking about a death. . . .'

'A student?'

'Yes. I only know him vaguely. He seems very interested in the occult, wrote rather a long and knowledgeable essay this term. Wants to do some project on demonism. He's a second-year student. They have to do a project over the summer. Yes, maybe he can give you more help than I'm able to.'

'And his name is . . .?'

'Well, his surname escapes me for the moment. He usually just calls himself by his first name. Charles.'

'Charles?'

'Or maybe Charlie. Yes, Charlie, that's it.'

Ronnie's friend's name. The hair on Rebus's neck began to prickle.

'That's right, Charlie,' Poole confirmed to himself, nodding. 'Bit of an eccentric. You can probably find him in one of the student union buildings. I believe he's addicted to these video machines. . . .'

No, not video machines. Pinball machines. The ones with all the extras, all the little tricks and treats that made a game a game. Charlie loved them with a vengeance. It was the kind of love which was all the more fervent for having come to him late in life. He was nineteen after all, life was streaming past, and he wanted to hang on to any piece of driftwood he could. Pinball had played no part in his adolescence. That had belonged to books and music. Besides, there had been no pinball machines at his boarding school.

Now, released into university, he wanted to live. And to play pinball. And do all the other things he had missed out on during the years of prep, sensitive essay-writing, and introspection. Charlie wanted to run faster than anyone had ever run, to live not one life, but two or three

48

or four. As the silver ball made contact with the left flipper, he threw it back up the table with real ferocity. There was a pause while the ball sat in one of the bonus craters, collecting another thousand points. He picked up his lager, took a gulp of it, and then returned his fingers to the buttons. In another ten minutes, he'd have the day's high score.

'Charlie?'

He turned at the sound of his name. A bad mistake, a naive mistake. He turned back to the game again, but too late. The man was striding towards him. The serious man. The unsmiling man.

'I'd like a word, Charlie.'

'Okay, how about carbohydrate. That was always one of my favourites.'

John Rebus's smile lasted less than a second.

'Very clever,' he said. 'Yes, that's what we call a smart answer.'

'We?'

'Lothian CID. My name's Inspector Rebus.'

'Pleased to meet you.'

'Likewise, Charlie.'

'No, you're mistaken. My name's not Charlie. He comes in here sometimes though. I'll tell him you called.'

Charlie was just about to hit the high score, five minutes ahead of schedule, when Rebus gripped his shoulder and spun him around. There were no other students in the games room, so he kept squeezing the shoulder while he spoke.

'You're about as funny as a maggot sandwich, Charlie, and patience isn't my favourite card game. So you'll excuse me if I become irritable, short-tempered, that sort of thing.'

'Hands off.' Charlie's face had taken on a new sheen, but not of fear.

49

'Ronnie,' Rebus said, calmly now, releasing his grip on the young man's shoulder.

The colour drained from Charlie's face. 'What about him?'

'He's dead.'

'Yes.' Charlie's voice was quiet, his eyes unfocussed. 'I heard.'

Rebus nodded. 'Tracy tried to find you.'

'Tracy.' There was venom in the word. 'She's no idea, no idea at all. Have you seen her?' Rebus nodded. 'Yeah, what a loser that woman is. She never understood Ronnie. Never even tried.'

As Charlie spoke, Rebus was learning more about him. His accent was Scottish private school, which was the first surprise. Rebus didn't know what he had expected. He knew he hadn't expected this. Charlie was well built, too, a product of the rugby-playing classes. He had curly dark brown hair, cut not too long, and was dressed in traditional student summer wear: training shoes, denims, and a T-shirt. The T-shirt was black, torn loose at the arms.

'So,' Charlie was saying, 'Ronnie did the big one, eh? Well, it's a good age to die. Live fast, die young.'

'Do you want to die young, Charlie?'

'Me?' Charlie laughed, a high-pitched squeal like a small animal. 'Hell, I want to live to be a hundred. I never want to die.' He looked at Rebus, something sparkling in his eyes. 'Do you?'

Rebus considered the question, but wasn't about to answer. He was here on business, not to discuss the death instinct. The lecturer, Dr Poole, had told him about the death instinct.

'I want to know what you know about Ronnie.'

'Does that mean you're going to take me away for questioning?'

'If you like. We can do it here if you'd prefer. . . .'

'No, no. I *want* to go to the police station. Come on, take me there.' There was a sudden eagerness about Charlie which made him seem much younger than his years. Who the hell wanted to *go* to a police station for questioning?

On the route to the car park and Rebus's car, Charlie insisted on walking a few paces ahead of Rebus, and with his hands behind his back, head slumped. Rebus saw that Charlie was pretending to be handcuffed. He was doing a good impersonation too, drawing attention to Rebus and himself. Someone even called out 'bastard' in Rebus's direction. But the word had lost all meaning over the years. They would have disturbed him more by wishing him a pleasant trip.

'Can I buy a couple of these?' Charlie asked, examining the photographs of his work, his pentagram.

The interview room was bleak. It was its purpose to be bleak. But Charlie had settled in like he was planning to rent it.

'No,' Rebus said, lighting a cigarette. He didn't offer one to Charlie. 'So, why did you paint it?'

'Because it's beautiful.' He still studied the photographs. 'Don't you think? So full of meaning.'

'How long had you known Ronnie?'

Charlie shrugged. For the first time, he looked in the direction of the cassette recorder. Rebus had asked if he minded having the dialogue recorded. He had shrugged. Now he seemed a little pensive. 'Maybe a year,' he said. 'Yes, a year. I met him around the time of my first-year exams. That was when I started to get interested in the *real* Edinburgh.'

'The real Edinburgh?'

'Yes. Not just the piper on the ramparts, or the Royal Mile, or the Scott Monument.' Rebus recalled Ronnie's photographs of the Castle.

51

'I saw some photos on Ronnie's wall.' Charlie screwed up his face.

'God, those. He had the idea he was going to be a professional photographer. Taking bloody tourist snaps for postcards. That didn't last long. Like most of Ronnie's schemes.'

'Nice camera he had though.'

'What? Oh, yes, his camera. Yes, it was his pride and joy.' Charlie crossed his legs. Rebus continued to stare into the young man's eyes, but Charlie was busily studying the photographs of the pentagram.

'So what was that you were telling me about the "real" Edinburgh?'

'Deacon Brodie,' said Charlie, suddenly interested again, 'Burke and Hare, justified sinners, the lot. But it's all been cleaned up for the tourists, you see. And I thought, hang on, all this Lowland low-life still exists. That was when I started touring the housing estates, Wester Hailes, Oxgangs, Craigmillar, Pilmuir. And sure enough, it's all still here, the past replaying itself in the present.'

'So you started hanging around Pilmuir?'

'Yes.'

'In other words, you became a tourist yourself?' Rebus had seen Charlie's kind before, though usually the older model, the prosperous businessman debasing himself for kicks, visiting sleazy rooms for a dry cough of pleasure. He didn't like the species.

'I wasn't a tourist!' Charlie's anger rose, a trout snapping a hooked worm. 'I was there because I wanted to be there, and they wanted me there.' His voice began to sound sulky. 'I belong there.'

'No you don't, son, you belong in a big house somewhere with parents interested in your university career.'

'Crap.' Charlie pushed back his chair and walked to the wall, resting his head against it. Rebus thought for a moment that he might be about to beat himself senseless, then claim police brutality. But he seemed merely to need something cool against his face.

The interview room was stifling. Rebus had removed his jacket. Now he rolled up his sleeves before stubbing out the cigarette.

'Okay, Charlie.' The young man was soft now, pliable. It was time to ask some questions. 'The night of the overdose, you were in the house with Ronnie, right?'

'That's right. For a little while.'

'Who else was there?'

'Tracy was there. She was there when I left.'

'Anyone else?'

'Some guy visited earlier in the evening. He didn't stay long. I'd seen him with Ronnie before a couple of times. When they were together, they kept to themselves.'

'Was this person his dealer, do you think?'

'No. Ronnie could always get stuff. Well, up until recently. Past couple of weeks, he found it tough. They seemed pretty close, though. Really close, if you get my meaning.'

'Go on.'

'Close as in loving. As in gay.'

'But Tracy . . .?'

'Yeah, yeah, but what's that supposed to prove, huh? You know how most addicts make their money.'

'How? Theft?'

'Yeah, theft, muggings, whatever. And doing a bit of business over by Calton Hill.'

Calton Hill, large, sprawling, lying to the east of Princes Street. Yes, Rebus knew all about Calton Hill, and about the cars which sat much of the night at the foot of it, along Regent Road. He knew about Calton Cemetery, too, about what went on there. . . .

'You're saying Ronnie was a rent boy?' The phrase sounded ridiculous out loud. It was tabloid talk.

53

'I'm saying he used to hang around there with a load of other guys, and I'm saying he always had money at the end of the night.' Charlie swallowed. 'Money and maybe a few bruises.'

'Jesus.' Rebus added this information to what was becoming a very grubby little dossier in his head. How far would you sink for a fix? The answer was: all the way. And then a little lower. He lit another cigarette.

'Do you know this for a fact?' he asked.

'No.'

'Was Ronnie from Edinburgh, by the way?'

'Stirling.'

'And his surname was –'

'McGrath, I think.'

'What about this guy he was so chummy with? Have you a name for him?'

'He called himself Neil. Ronnie called him Neilly.'

'Neilly? Did you get the impression they'd known one another for a while?'

'Yeah, a goodish while. A nickname like that's a sign of affection, right?' Rebus studied Charlie with new admiration. 'I don't do psychology for nothing, Inspector.'

'Right.' Rebus checked that the small cassette recorder still had some tape left to run. 'Give me a physical description of this Neil character, will you?'

'Tall, skinny, short brown hair. Kind of spotty face, but always clean. Usually wore jeans and a denim jacket. Carried a big black holdall with him.'

'Any idea what was in it?'

'I got the feeling it was just clothes.'

'Okay.'

'Anything else?'

'Let's talk about the pentagram. Someone has been back to the house and added to it since these photographs were taken.'

Charlie said nothing, but did not look surprised.

'It was you, wasn't it?'

Charlie nodded.

'How did you get in?'

'Through the downstairs window. Those wooden slats couldn't keep out an elephant. It's like an extra door. Lots of people used to come into the house that way.'

'Why did you go back?'

'It wasn't finished, was it? I wanted to add the symbols.'

'And the message.'

Charlie smiled to himself. 'Yes, the message.'

'"Hello Ronnie",' Rebus quoted. 'What's that all about?'

'Just what it says. His spirit's still in the house, his soul's still there. I was just saying hello. I had some paint left. Besides, I thought it might give somebody a fright.'

Rebus remembered his own shock at seeing the scrawl. He felt his cheeks redden slightly, but covered the fact with a question.

'Do you remember the candles?'

Charlie nodded, but was becoming restless. Helping police with their inquiries was not as much fun as he had hoped.

'What about your project?' said Rebus, changing tack.

'What about it?'

'It's on demonism, isn't it?'

'Maybe. I haven't decided yet.'

'What aspect of demonism?'

'I don't know. Maybe the popular mythology. How old fears become new fears, that sort of thing.'

'Do you know any of the covens in Edinburgh?'

'I know people who claim to be in some of them.'

'But you've never been along to one?'

'No, worse luck.' Charlie seemed suddenly to come to life. 'Look, what is all this? Ronnie OD'd. He's history. Why all the questions?'

'What can you tell me about the candles?'

Charlie exploded. 'What *about* the candles?'

Rebus was all calmness. He exhaled smoke before responding. 'There were candles in the living room.' He was getting close to telling Charlie something Charlie didn't seem to know. All during the interview, he had been spiralling inwards towards this moment.

'That's right. Big candles. Ronnie got them from some shop that specialises in candles. He *liked* candles. They gave the place *ambience*.'

'Tracy found Ronnie in his bedroom. She thinks he was already dead.' Rebus's voice became lower still, and as flat as the desktop. 'But by the time she'd phoned us, and an officer had turned up at the house, Ronnie's body had been moved downstairs. It was laid out between two candles, which had been burnt down to nothing.'

'There wasn't much left of those candles anyway, not when I left.'

'You left when?'

'Just before midnight. There was supposed to be a party somewhere on the estate. I thought I might get invited in.'

'How long would the candles have burned for?'

'An hour, two hours. God knows.'

'How much smack did Ronnie have?'

'Christ, I don't know.'

'Well, how much would he normally use at any one time?'

'I really don't know. I'm not a user, you know. I hate all that stuff. I've got two friends who were in my sixth form. They're both in private clinics.'

'That's nice for them.'

'Like I said, Ronnie hadn't been able to find any stuff for days. He was a bit whacked out, just about to fall right over the edge. Then he came back with some. End of story.'

'Isn't there much about then?'

'So far as I know, there's plenty, but don't bother asking for names.'

'So if there's plenty, how come Ronnie was finding it so hard?'

'God knows. He didn't know himself. It was like he'd suddenly become bad news. Then he was good news again, and he got that packet.'

It was time. Rebus picked an invisible thread from his shirt.

'He was murdered,' he said. 'Or as good as.'

Charlie's mouth opened. The blood drained from his face, as though a tap had been opened somewhere. 'What?'

'He was murdered. His body was full of rat poison. Self-inflicted, but supplied by someone who probably knew it was lethal. A lot of work was then done to manoeuvre his body into some kind of ritualistic position in the living room. Where your pentagram is.'

'Now wait –'

'How many covens are there in Edinburgh, Charlie?'

'What? Six, seven, I don't know. Look –'

'Do you know them? Any of them? I mean know them personally?'

'Christ, man, you're not going to pin this on me!'

'Why not?' Rebus stubbed out his cigarette.

'Because it's crazy.'

'Seems to me it all fits, Charlie.' String him out, Rebus was thinking. He's already stretched to snapping point. 'Unless you can convince me otherwise.'

Charlie walked to the door purposefully, then paused.

'Go on,' Rebus called, 'it's not locked. Walk out of here if you like. Then I'll *know* you had something to do with it.'

Charlie turned. His eyes seemed moist in the hazy light. A sunbeam from the barred window, penetrating the frosted glass, caught motes of dust and turned them into slow-motion dancers. Charlie moved through them as he returned to the desk.

'I didn't have anything to do with it, honest.'

'Sit down,' said Rebus, a kindly uncle now. 'Let's talk some more.'

But Charlie didn't like uncles. Never had. He placed his hands on the desk and leaned down, looming over Rebus. Something had hardened somewhere within him. His teeth when he spoke glistened with venom.

'Go to hell, Rebus. I see what you're up to, and I'm damned if I'm going to play along. Arrest me if you like, but don't insult me with cheap tricks. I did those in my first term.'

Then he walked, and this time opened the door, and left it open behind him. Rebus got up from the desk, switched off the recorder, took out the tape and, pushing it into his pocket, followed. By the time he reached the entrance hall, Charlie had gone. He approached the desk. The duty sergeant looked up from his paperwork.

'You just missed him,' he said.

Rebus nodded. 'It doesn't matter.'

'He didn't look too happy.'

'Would I be doing my job if they all left here laughing and holding their sides?'

The sergeant smiled. 'I suppose not. So what can I do for you?'

'The Pilmuir overdose. I've got a name for the corpse. Ronnie McGrath. Originally from Stirling. Let's see if we can find his parents, eh?'

The sergeant scribbled the name onto a pad. 'I'm sure they'll be delighted to hear how their son is doing in the big city.'

'Yes,' said Rebus, staring towards the front door of the police station. 'I'm sure they will.'

John Rebus's flat was his castle. Once through the door, he would pull up the drawbridge and let his mind go blank, emptying himself of the world for as long as he could. He would pour himself a drink, put some tenor sax music on the cassette machine, and pick up a book. Many weeks ago, in a crazed state of righteousness, he had put up shelves along one wall of the living room, intending his sprawling collection of books to rest there. But somehow they managed to crawl across the floor, getting under his feet, so that he used them like stepping-stones into the hallway and the bedroom.

He walked across them now, on his way to the bay window where he pulled down the dusty venetian blinds. The slats he left open, so that strawberry slants of evening light came pouring through, reminding him of the interview room. . . .

No, no, no, that wouldn't do. He was being sucked back into work again. He had to clear his mind, find some book which would pull him into its little universe, far away from the sights and smells of Edinburgh. He stepped firmly on the likes of Chekhov, Heller, Rimbaud and Kerouac as he made his way to the kitchen, seeking out a bottle of wine.

There were two cardboard boxes beneath the kitchen worktop, taking up the space where the washing machine had once been. Rhona had taken the washing machine, which was fair enough. He called the resultant space his wine cellar, and now and then would order a mixed case from a good little shop around the corner from his flat. He put a hand into one of the boxes and brought out something called Château Potensac. Yes, he'd had a bottle of this before. It would do.

He poured a third of the bottle into a large glass and returned to the living room, plucking one of the books from the floor as he went. He was seated in his armchair before he looked at its cover: *The Naked Lunch*. No, bad choice. He threw the book down again and groped for another. *Dr Jekyll and Mr Hyde*. Fair enough, he'd been meaning to reread it for ages, and it was blissfully short.

He took a mouthful of wine, sloshed it around before swallowing, and opened the book.

With the timing of a stage-play, there was a rapping at the front door. The noise Rebus made was somewhere between a sigh and a roar. He balanced the book, its covers open, on the arm of the chair, and rose to his feet. Probably it was Mrs Cochrane from downstairs, telling him that it was his turn to wash the communal stairwell. She would have the large, imperative card with her: IT IS YOUR TURN TO WASH THE STAIRS. Why she couldn't just hang it on his door like everyone else seemed to do . . .?

He tried to arrange a neighbourly smile on his face as he opened the door, but the actor in him had left for the evening. So there was something not unlike pain rippling his lips as he stared at the visitor on his doormat.

It was Tracy.

Her face was red, and there were tears in her eyes, but the redness was not from crying. She looked exhausted, her hair cloying with sweat.

'Can I come in?' There was an all too visible effort in her voice. Rebus hadn't the heart to say no. He pushed the door open wide and she stumbled in past him, walking straight through to the living room as though she'd been here a hundred times. Rebus checked that the stairwell was empty of inquisitive neighbours, then closed the door. He was tingling, not a pleasant feeling: he didn't like people visiting him here.

Especially, he didn't like work following him home.

By the time he reached the living room, Tracy had drained the wine and was exhaling with relief, her thirst quenched. Rebus felt the discomfort in him increase until it was almost unbearable.

'How the hell did you find this place?' he asked, standing in the doorway as though waiting for her to leave.

'Not easy,' she said, her voice a little more calm. 'You told me you lived in Marchmont, so I just wandered around looking for your car. Then I found your name on the bell downstairs.'

He had to admit it, she'd have made a good detective. Footwork was what it was all about.

'Somebody's been following me,' she said now. 'I got scared.'

'Following you?' He stepped into the room now, curious, his sense of encroachment easing.

'Yes, two men. I think there were two. They've been following me all afternoon. I was up Princes Street, just walking, and they were always there, a little way behind me. They must've known I could see them.'

'What happened?'

'I lost them. Went into Marks and Spencer, ran like hell for the Rose Street exit, then dived into the ladies' in a pub. Stayed in there for an hour. That seemed to do the trick. Then I headed here.'

'Why didn't you telephone me?'

'No money. That's why I was up Princes Street in the first place.'

She had settled in his chair, her arms hanging over its sides. He nodded towards the empty glass.

'Do you want another?'

'No thanks. I don't really like plonk, but I was thirsty as hell. I could manage a cup of tea though.'

'Tea, right.' Plonk, she had called it! He turned and walked through to the kitchen, his mind half on the idea of tea, half on her story. In one of his sparsely populated cupboards he found an unopened box of teabags. There was no fresh milk in the flat, but an old tin yielded a spoonful or two of powdered substitute. Now, sugar.... Music came suddenly from the living room, a loud rendering of *The White Album*. God, he'd forgotten he still had that old tape. He opened the cutlery drawer, looking

61

for nothing more than a teaspoon, and found several sachets of sugar, stolen from the canteen at some point in his past. Serendipity. The kettle was beginning to boil.

'This flat's huge!'

She startled him, he was so unused to other voices in this place. He turned and watched her lean against the door-jamb, her head angled sideways.

'Is it?' he said, rinsing a mug.

'Christ, yes. Look how high your ceilings are! I could just about touch the ceiling in Ronnie's squat.' She stood on tiptoe and stretched an arm upwards, waving her hand. Rebus feared that she had taken something, some pills or powders, while he'd been on the trail of the furtive teabag. She seemed to sense his thoughts, and smiled.

'I'm just relieved,' she said. 'I feel light-headed from the running. And from being scared, I suppose. But now I feel safe.'

'What did the men look like?'

'I don't know. I think they looked a bit like you.' She smiled again. 'One had a moustache. He was sort of fat, going thin on top, but not old. I can't remember the other one. He wasn't very memorable, I suppose.'

Rebus poured water into the mug and added the teabag. 'Milk?'

'No, just sugar if you've got it.'

He waved one of the sachets at her.

'Great.'

Back in the living room, he went to the stereo and turned it down.

'Sorry,' she said, back in the chair now, sipping tea, her legs tucked under her.

'I keep meaning to find out whether my neighbours can hear the stereo or not,' Rebus said, as if to excuse his action. 'The walls are pretty thick, but the ceiling isn't.'

She nodded, blew onto the surface of the drink, steam covering her face in a veil.

'So,' said Rebus, pulling his director's foldaway chair out from beneath a table and sitting down. 'What can we do about these men who've been following you?'

'I don't know. You're the policeman.'

'It all sounds like something out of a film to me. I mean, *why* should anyone want to follow you?'

'To scare me?' she offered.

'And why should they want to scare you?'

She thought about this, then shrugged her shoulders.

'By the way, I saw Charlie today,' he said.

'Oh?'

'Do you like him?'

'Charlie?' Her laughter was shrill. 'He's horrible. Always hanging around, even when it's obvious nobody wants him anywhere near. Everybody hates him.'

'Everybody?'

'Yes.'

'Did Ronnie hate him?'

She paused. 'No,' she said at last. 'But then Ronnie didn't have much sense that way.'

'What about this other friend of Ronnie's? Neil, or Neilly. What can you tell me about him?'

'Is that the guy who was there last night?'

'Yes.'

She shrugged her shoulders. 'I never saw him before.' She seemed interested in the book on the arm of the chair, picked it up and flipped its pages, pretending to read.

'And Ronnie never mentioned a Neil or a Neilly to you?'

'No.' She waved the book at Rebus. 'But he did talk about someone called Edward. Seemed angry with him about something. Used to shout the name out when he was alone in his room, after a fix.'

Rebus nodded slowly. 'Edward. His dealer maybe?'

'I don't know. Maybe. Ronnie got pretty crazy sometimes after he fixed. He was like a different person. But he

63

was so sweet at times, so gentle. . . .' Her voice died away, eyes glistening.

Rebus checked his watch. 'Okay, what about if I drive you back to the squat now? We can check that there's no one watching.'

'I don't know. . . .' The fear had returned to her face, erasing years from her, turning her into a child again, afraid of shadows and ghosts.

'I'll be there,' Rebus added.

'Well. . . . Can I do something first?'

'What?'

She pulled at her damp clothes. 'Take a bath,' she said. Then she smiled. 'I know it's a bit brassnecked, but I really could use one, and there's no water at all in the squat.'

Rebus smiled too, nodding slowly. 'My bathtub is at your disposal,' he said.

While she was in the bath, he hung her clothes over the radiator in the hall. Turning the central heating on made a sauna of the flat, and Rebus struggled with the sash windows in the living room, trying without success to open them. He made more tea, in a pot this time, and had just carried it into the living room when he heard her call from the bathroom. When he came out into the hall, she had her head around the bathroom door, steam billowing out around her. Her hair, face and neck were gleaming.

'No towels,' she explained.

'Sorry,' said Rebus. He found some in the cupboard in his room, and brought them to her, pushing them through the gap in the door, feeling awkward despite himself.

'Thanks,' she called.

He had swopped *The White Album* for some jazz – barely audible – and was sitting with his tea when she came in. One large red towel was expertly tied around her body, another around her head. He had often wondered how women could be so good at wearing towels. . . . Her arms and legs were pale and thin, but there was no doubting that her shape was pleasing, and the glow from the bath gave her a kind of nimbus. He remembered the photographs of her in Ronnie's room. Then he recalled the missing camera.

'Was Ronnie still keen on photography? I mean, of late.' The choice of words was accidentally unsubtle, and he winced a little, but Tracy appeared not to notice.

'I suppose so. He was quite good, you know. He had a good eye. But he didn't get the breaks.'

'How hard did he try?'

'Bloody hard.' There was resentment in her voice. Perhaps Rebus had allowed too much professional scepticism to creep into his tone.

'Yes, I'm sure. Not an easy profession to get into, I'd imagine.'

'Too true. And there were some who knew how good Ronnie was. They didn't want the competition. Put obstacles in his way whenever and wherever they could.'

'You mean other photographers?'

'That's right. Well, when Ronnie was going through his really keen spell, before disillusionment set in, he didn't know quite how to get the breaks. So he went to a couple of studios, showed some of his work to the guys who worked there. He had some really inspired shots. You know, everyday things seen from weird angles. The Castle, Waverley Monument, Calton Hill.'

'Calton Hill?'

'Yes, the whatsit.'

'The folly?'

'That's it.' The towel was slipping a little from around her shoulders, and as Tracy sat with her legs tucked beneath her, sipping tea, it also fell away to reveal more than enough thigh. Rebus tried to concentrate his eyes on her face. It wasn't easy. 'Well,' she was saying, 'a couple of his ideas got ripped off. He'd see a photo in one of the local rags, and it'd be exactly the angle he'd used, the same time of day, same filters. Those bastards had copied his ideas. He'd see their names beneath the pictures, the same guys he'd shown his portfolio to.'

'What were their names?'

'I don't remember now.' She readjusted the towel. There seemed something defensive in the action. Was it so hard to remember a name? She giggled. 'He tried to get me to pose for him.'

'I saw the results.'

'No, not those ones. You know, nude shots. He said he could sell them for a fortune to some of the magazines. But I wasn't having it. I mean, the money would've been all well and good, but these mags get passed around, don't they? I mean, they never get thrown away. I'd always be wondering if anybody could recognise me on the street.' She waited for Rebus's reaction, and when it was one of thoughtful bemusement, laughed throatily. 'So, it's not true what they say. You *can* embarrass a copper.'

'Sometimes.' Rebus's cheeks were tingling. He put a hand self-consciously to one of them. He had to do something about this. 'So,' he said, 'was Ronnie's camera worth much then?'

She seemed nonplussed by this turn in the conversation, and pulled the towel even tighter around her. 'Depends. I mean, worth and value, they're not the same thing, are they?'

'Aren't they?'

'Well, he might have paid only a tenner for the camera, but that doesn't mean it was only *worth* a tenner to him. Do you see?'

'So he paid a tenner for the camera?'

'No, no, no.' She shook her head, dislodging the towel. 'I thought you had to be brainy to get in the CID? What I mean is . . .' She raised her eyes to the ceiling, and the towel slipped from her head, so that bedraggled rat's-tails of hair strung themselves out across her forehead. 'No, never mind. The camera cost about a hundred and fifty quid. Okay?'

'Fine.'

'Interested in photography are you?'

'Only since recently. More tea?'

He poured from the teapot, then added a sachet of sugar. She liked lots of sugar.

'Thanks,' she said, cradling the mug. 'Listen.' She was bathing her face in the steam from the surface of the tea. 'Can I ask you a favour?'

Here it comes, thought Rebus: money. He had already made a mental note to check whether anything in the flat was missing before letting her leave. 'What?'

Her eyes were on his now. 'Can I stay the night?' Her words came out in a torrent. 'I'll sleep on the couch, on the floor. I don't mind. I just don't want to go back to the squat, not tonight. It's been getting pretty crazy lately, and those men following me. . . .' She shivered, and Rebus had to admit that if this were all an act, she was a top-of-the-form drama student. He shrugged, was about to speak, but rose and went to the window instead, deferring a decision.

The orange street lamps were on, casting a Hollywood film-set glow over the pavement. There was a car outside, directly opposite the flat. Being two floors up, Rebus couldn't quite see into the car, but the driver's side window had been rolled down, and smoke oozed from it.

'Well?' the voice said behind him. It had lost all confidence now.

'What?' Rebus said distractedly.

'Can I?' He turned towards her. 'Can I stay?' she repeated.

'Sure,' Rebus said, making for the door. 'Stay as long as you like.'

*

He was halfway down the curving stairwell before he realised that he was not wearing any shoes. He paused, considering. No, to hell with it. His mother had always warned him about catching chilblains, and he never had. Now was as good a time as any to find out whether his medical luck was holding.

He was passing a door on the first floor when it rattled open and Mrs Cochrane thrust her whole frame out, blocking Rebus's path.

'Mrs Cochrane,' he said after the initial shock had passed.

'Here.' She shoved something towards him, and he could do nothing but take it from her. It was a piece of card, about ten inches by six. Rebus read it: IT IS YOUR TURN TO WASH THE STAIRS. By the time he looked up again, Mrs Cochrane's door was already closing. He could hear her carpet slippers shuffling back towards her TV and her cat. Smelly old thing.

Rebus carried the card downstairs with him, the cold steps penetrating his stockinged soles. The cat didn't smell too good either, he thought maliciously.

The front door was on the latch. He eased it open, trying to keep the aged mechanism as silent as possible. The car was still there. Directly opposite him as he stepped outside. But the driver had already seen him. The cigarette stub was flicked onto the road, and the engine started. Rebus moved forward on his toes. The car's headlamps came on suddenly, their beam as full as a Stalag searchlight. Rebus paused, screwing his eyes, and the car started forward, then swerved to the left, racing downhill to the end of the street. Rebus stared after it, trying to make out the number plate, but his eyes were full of white fuzziness. It had been a Ford Escort. Of that much he was sure.

Looking down the road, he realised that the car had stopped at the junction with the main road, waiting for a space in the traffic. It was less than a hundred yards away. Rebus made up his mind. He had been a handy sprinter in his youth, good enough for the school team when they had been a man short. He ran now with a kind of drunken euphoria, and remembered the wine he had opened. His stomach turned sour at the mere thought, and he slowed. Just then he slipped, skidding on something on the pavement, and, brought up short, he saw the car slip across the junction and roar away.

Never mind. That first glimpse as he'd opened the door had been enough. He'd seen the constabulary uniform. Not the driver's face, but the uniform for sure. A policeman, a constable, driving an Escort. Two young girls were approaching along the pavement. They giggled as they passed Rebus, and he realised that he was standing panting on the pavement, without any shoes but holding a sign telling him it was his turn to WASH THE STAIRS. When he looked down, he saw what it was he had skidded on.

Cursing silently, he removed his socks, tossed them into the gutter, and walked back on bare feet towards the flat.

Dectective Constable Brian Holmes was drinking tea. He had turned this into something of a ritual, holding the cup to his face and blowing on it, then sipping. Blowing then sipping. Swallowing. Then releasing a steamy breath of air. He was chilled tonight, as cold as any tramp on any park bench bed. He didn't even have a newspaper, and the tea tasted revolting. It had come out of one or other of the thermos flasks, piping hot and smelling of plastic. The milk wasn't of the freshest, but at least the brew was warming. Not warming enough to touch his toes, supposing he still had toes.

'Anything happening?' he hissed towards the SSPCA officer, who held binoculars to his eyes as though to hide his embarrassment.

'Nothing,' the officer whispered. It had been an anonymous tip-off. The third this month and, to be fair, the first non-starter. Dog fighting was back in vogue. Several 'arenas' had been found in the past three months, small dirt pits enclosed by lengths of sheet tin. Scrap yards seemed the main source of these arenas, which gave an added meaning to the term 'scrap yard'. But tonight they were watching a piece of waste ground. Goods trains clattered past nearby, heading towards the centre of the city, but apart from that and the low hum of distant traffic, the place was dead. Yes, there was a makeshift pit all right. They'd taken a look at it in daylight, pretending to walk their own alsatian dogs, which were in fact police dogs. Pit bull terriers: that was what they used in the arenas. Brian Holmes had seen a couple of ex-combatants, their eyes maddened with pain and fear. He hadn't stuck around for the vet with his lethal injection.

'Hold on.'

Two men were walking, hands in pockets, across the wilderness, picking their way carefully over the uneven surface, wary of sudden craters. They seemed to know where they were headed: straight towards the shallow pit. Once there, they took a final look around. Brian Holmes stared directly back at them, knowing he could not be seen. Like the SSPCA officer, he was crouching behind thick bracken, behind him one remaining wall of what had been a building of sorts. Though there was some light over towards the pit itself, there was precious little here, and so, as with a two-way mirror, he could see without being seen.

'Got you,' said the SSPCA man as the two men jumped down into the pit.

'Wait . . .' said Holmes, suddenly getting a funny feeling about all of this. The two men had begun to embrace, and their faces merged in a slow, lingering kiss as they sank down towards the ground.

'Christ!' exclaimed the SSPCA man.

Holmes sighed, staring down at the damp, rock-hard earth beneath his knees.

'I don't think pit bulls enter the equation,' he said. 'Or if they do, bestiality rather than brutality might be the charge.'

The SSPCA officer still held his binoculars to his eyes, horror-struck and riveted.

'You hear stories,' he said, 'but you never ... well ... you know.'

'Get to watch?' Holmes suggested, getting slowly, painfully to his feet.

He was talking with the night duty officer when the message came through. Inspector Rebus wanted a word.

'Rebus? What does he want?' Brian Holmes checked his watch. It was two fifteen a.m. Rebus was at home, and he had been told to phone him there. He used the duty officer's telephone.

'Hello?' He knew John Rebus of course, had worked with him on several cases. Still, middle-of-the-night calls were something else entirely.

'Is that you, Brian?'

'Yes, sir.'

'Have you a sheet of paper? Write this down.' Fumbling with pad and biro, Holmes thought he could hear music playing on the line. Something he recognised. The Beatles' *White Album*. 'Ready?'

'Yes, sir.'

'Right. There was a junkie found dead in Pilmuir yesterday, or a couple of days ago now, strictly speaking. Overdose. Find out who the constables who found him were. Get them to come into my office at ten o'clock. Got that?'

'Yes, sir.'

'Good. Now, when you've got the address where the

71

body was found, I want you to pick up the keys from whoever's got them and go to the house. Upstairs in one of the bedrooms there's a wall covered in photographs. Some are of Edinburgh Castle. Take them with you and go to the local newspaper's office. They'll have files full of photographs. If you're lucky they might even have a little old man on duty with a memory like an elephant. I want you to look for any photographs that have been published in the newspaper recently and look to have been taken from the same angle as the ones on the bedroom wall. Got that?'

'Yes, sir,' said Holmes, scribbling furiously.

'Good. I want to know who took the newspaper photographs. There'll be a sticker or something on the back of each print giving a name and address.'

'Anything else, sir?' It came out as sarcasm, meant or not.

'Yes.' Rebus seemed to drop his voice a decibel. 'On the bedroom wall you'll also find some photos of a young lady. I'd like to know more about her. She says her middle name is Tracy. That's what she calls herself. Ask around, show the picture to anyone you think might have an inkling.'

'Right, sir. One question.'

'Go ahead.'

'Why me? Why now? What's all this in aid of?'

'That's three questions. I'll answer as many of them as I can when I see you tomorrow afternoon. Be in my office at three.'

And with that, the line went dead on Brian Holmes. He stared at the drunken rows of writing on his pad, his own shorthand of a week's worth of work, delivered to him in a matter of minutes. The duty officer was reading it over his shoulder.

'Rather you than me,' he said with sincerity.

*

John Rebus had chosen Holmes for a whole bundle of reasons, but mostly because Holmes didn't know much about him. He wanted someone who would work efficiently, methodically, without raising too much fuss. Someone who didn't know Rebus well enough to complain about being kept in the dark, about being used as a shunting engine. A message boy and a bloodhound and a dogsbody. Rebus knew that Holmes was gaining a reputation for efficiency and for not being a complaining sod. That was enough to be going on with.

He carried the telephone back from the hall into the living room, placed it on the bookshelves, and went across to the hi-fi, where he switched off the tape machine, then the amplifier. He went to the window and looked out on an empty street whose lamplight was the colour of Red Leicester cheese. The image reminded him of the midnight snack he had promised himself a couple of hours ago, and he decided to make himself something in the kitchen. Tracy wouldn't be wanting anything. He was sure of that. He stared at her as she lay along the settee, her head at an angle towards the floor, one hand across her stomach, the other hanging down to touch the wool carpet. Her eyes were unseeing slits, her mouth open in a pout, revealing a slight gap between her two front teeth. She had slept soundly as he had thrown a blanket over her, and was sleeping still, her breathing regular. Something niggled him, but he couldn't think what it was. Hunger perhaps. He hoped the freezer would yield a pleasant surprise. But first he went to the window and looked out again. The street was absolutely dead, which was just how Rebus himself was feeling: dead but active. He picked *Dr Jekyll and Mr Hyde* from the floor and carried it through to the kitchen.

Wednesday

The more it looks like Queer Street, the less I ask.

Police Constables Harry Todd and Francis O'Rourke were standing outside Rebus's office when he arrived next morning. They had been leaning against the wall, enjoying a lazy conversation, seemingly unconcerned that Rebus was twenty minutes late. He was damned if he was going to apologise. He noted with satisfaction that as he reached the top of the stairs they pulled themselves up straight and shut their mouths.

That was a good start.

He opened the door, walked into the room, and closed the door again. Let them stew for another minute. Now they'd have something really to talk about. He had checked with the desk sergeant, and Brian Holmes wasn't in the station. He took a slip of paper from his pocket and rang Holmes's house. The telephone rang and rang. Holmes must be out working.

The good run was continuing.

There was mail on his desk. He flipped through it, stopping only to extract a note from Superintendent Watson. It was an invitation to lunch. Today. At twelve thirty. Hell. He was meeting Holmes at three. The lunch was with some of the businessmen who were putting up the hard cash for the drugs campaign. Hell. And it was in The Eyrie, which meant wearing a tie and a clean shirt. Rebus looked down at his shirt. It would do. But the tie would not. Hell.

The smile left his soul.

It had been too good to last. Tracy had woken him with breakfast on a tray. Orange juice, toast and honey, strong coffee. She'd gone out early, she explained, taking with her a little money she found on the shelves in the living room. She hoped he didn't mind. She had found a corner shop open, made the purchases, come back to the flat, and made him breakfast.

'I'm surprised the smell of burning toast didn't wake you,' she had said.

'You're looking at the man who slept through *Towering Inferno*,' he had replied. And she had laughed, sitting on the bed taking dainty bites of toast with her exposed teeth, while Rebus chewed his slices slowly, thoughtfully. Luxuriously. How long had it been since he'd been brought breakfast in bed? It frightened him to think. . . .

'Come in!' he roared now, though no one had knocked.

Tracy had left without complaint, too. She felt all right, she said. She couldn't stay cooped up forever, could she? He had driven her back towards Pilmuir, then had done something stupid. Given her ten pounds. It wasn't just money, as he realised a second after handing it over. It was a bond between them, a bond he shouldn't be making. It lay there in her hand, and he felt the temptation to snatch it back. But then she was out of the car and walking away, her body fragile as bone china, her gait determined, full of strength. Sometimes she reminded him of his daughter Sammy, other times. . . .

Other times of Gill Templer, his ex-lover.

'Come in!' he roared again. This time the door opened an inch, then another ten or eleven. A head looked into the room.

'Nobody's been knocking, sir,' the head said nervously.

'Is that so?' said Rebus in his best stage voice. 'Well, in that case I'd better just speak to you two instead. So why don't you *come in!*'

A moment later, they shuffled through the doorway, a

bit less cocky now. Rebus pointed to the two chairs on the other side of his desk. One of them sat immediately, the other stood to attention.

'I'd rather stand, sir,' he said. The other one looked suddenly fearful, terrified that he had broken some rule of protocol.

'This isn't the bloody army,' Rebus said to the standing one, just as the sitting one was rising. 'So sit down!'

They both sat. Rebus rubbed his forehead, pretending a headache. Truth be told, he had almost forgotten who these constables were and why they were here.

'Right,' he said. 'Why do you think I've called you here this morning?' Corny but effective.

'Is it to do with the witches, sir?'

'Witches?' Rebus looked at the constable who had said this, and remembered the keen young man who had shown him the original pentagram. 'That's right, witches. And overdoses.'

They blinked at him. He sought frantically for a route into the interrogation, if interrogation this was to be. He should have thought more about it before coming in.

He should have at least remembered that it had been arranged. He saw a ten-pound note, a smile, could smell burning toast. . . . He looked at the pentagram constable's tie.

'What's your name, son?'

'Todd, sir.'

'Todd? That's German for dead, did you know that, Todd?'

'Yes, sir. I did German at school up to Highers.'

Rebus nodded, pretending to be impressed. Damn, he *was* impressed. They all had Highers these days, it seemed, all these extraordinarily young-looking constables. Some had gone further: college, university. He had the feeling Holmes had been to university. He hoped he hadn't enlisted the aid of a smart arse. . . .

Rebus pointed to the tie.

'That looks a bit squint, Todd.'

Todd immediately looked down towards his tie, his head angled so sharply Rebus feared the neck would snap.

'Sir?'

'That tie. Is it your usual one?'

'Yes, sir.'

'So you haven't broken a tie recently?'

'Broken a tie, sir?'

'Broken the clip,' explained Rebus.

'No, sir.'

'And what's your name, son?' Rebus said quickly, turning to the other constable, who looked completely stunned by proceedings so far.

'O'Rourke, sir.'

'Irish name,' Rebus commented.

'Yes, sir.'

'What about your tie, O'Rourke? Is that a new tie?'

'Not really, sir. I mean, I've got about half a dozen of these things kicking around.'

Rebus nodded. He picked up a pencil, examined it, set it down again. He was wasting his time.

'I'd like to see the reports you made of finding the deceased.'

'Yes, sir,' they said.

'Nothing unusual in the house, was there? I mean, when you first arrived? Nothing out of the ordinary?'

'Only the dead man, sir,' said O'Rourke.

'And the painting on the wall,' said Todd.

'Did either of you bother to check upstairs?'

'No, sir.'

'The body was where, when you arrived?'

'In the downstairs room, sir.'

'And you didn't go upstairs?'

Todd looked towards O'Rourke. 'I think we shouted to see if anyone was up there. But no, we didn't go up.'

So how could the tie clip have got upstairs? Rebus exhaled, then cleared his throat. 'What kind of car do you drive, Todd?'

'Do you mean police car, sir?'

'No I bloody well don't!' Rebus slapped the pencil down against the desk. 'I mean for private use.'

Todd seemed more confused now than ever. 'A Metro, sir.'

'Colour?'

'White.'

Rebus turned his gaze to O'Rourke.

'I don't have a car,' O'Rourke admitted. 'I like motorbikes. Just now I've got a Honda seven-fifty.'

Rebus nodded. No Ford Escorts then. Nobody hurtling away from his road at midnight.

'Well, that's all right then, isn't it?' And with a smile he dismissed them, picked up the pencil again, examined its point, and very deliberately broke it against the edge of his desk.

Rebus was thinking of Charlie as he stopped his car in front of the tiny old-fashioned men's-wear shop off George Street. He was thinking of Charlie as he grabbed the tie and paid for it. Back in the car, he thought of Charlie as he knotted the tie, started the ignition, and drove off. Heading towards lunch with some of the wealthiest businessmen in the city, all he could think of was Charlie, and how Charlie could probably still choose to be like those businessmen one day. He'd leave university, use his family connections to land a good job, and progress smoothly through to upper management in the space of a year or two. He would forget all about his infatuation with decadence, and would become decadent himself, the way only the rich and successful ever can. . . . True decadence, not the second-hand stuff of witchcraft and demonism, drugs and violence. That bruising on Ronnie's body: could it really have been rough trade? A sadomasochistic game gone wrong? A game played, perhaps, with the mysterious Edward, whose name Ronnie had screamed?

Or a ritual carried too far?

Had he dismissed the Satanism angle too readily? Wasn't a policeman supposed to keep an open mind? Perhaps, but Satanism found him with his mind well and truly closed. He was a Christian, after all. He might not attend church often, detesting all the hymn-singing and the bald sermonising, but that didn't mean he didn't believe in that small, dark personal God of his. Everyone had a God tagging along with them. And the God of the Scots was as ominous as He came.

Midday Edinburgh seemed darker than ever, reflecting his mood perhaps. The Castle appeared to be casting a shadow across the expanse of the New Town, but that shadow did not, could not reach as high as The Eyrie. The Eyrie was the city's most expensive restaurant, and also the most exclusive. Rumour had it that lunchtime was solidly booked twelve months in advance, while dinner entailed the small wait of eight to ten weeks. The restaurant itself was situated on the entire top floor of a Georgian hotel in the heart of the New Town, away from the city centre's human bustle.

Not that the streets here were exactly quiet, a steady amount of through traffic pausing long enough to make parking a problem. But not to a detective. Rebus stopped his car on a double yellow line directly outside the hotel's main door, and, despite the doorman's warnings about wardens and fines, left it there and entered the hotel. He squeezed his stomach as the lift carried him four floors high, and was satisfied that he felt hungry. These businessmen might well bore the pants off him, and the thought of spending two hours with Farmer Watson was almost too much to bear, but he would eat well. Yes, he would eat exceedingly well.

And, given his way with the wine list, he'd bankrupt the buggers to boot.

Brian Holmes left the snack bar carrying a polystyrene cup of grey tea, and studied it, trying to remember when he had last had a cup of good tea, of real tea, of tea he had brewed himself. His life seemed to revolve around polystyrene cups and thermos flasks, unexciting sandwiches and chocolate biscuits. Blow, sip Blow, sip. Swallow.

For this he had given up an academic career.

Which was to say that he had careered around academia for some eight months, studying History at the University of London. The first month he had spent in awe of the city itself, trying to come to terms with its size, the complexities of actually trying to live and travel and survive with dignity. The second and third months he had spent trying to come to terms with university life, with new friends, the persistent openings for discussion, argument, for inclusion in this or that group. He tested the water each time before joining in, all of them nervous as children learning to swim. By months four and five, he had become a Londoner, commuting to the University every day from his digs in Battersea. Suddenly his life had come to be ruled by numbers, by the times of trains and buses and tube connections, the times, too, of late buses and tubes which would whisk him away from coffee-bar politics towards his noisy single room again. Missing a train connection began to be agony, suffering the rush-hour tube, a season spent in hell. Months six and seven he spent isolated in Battersea, studying from his room, hardly attending lectures at all. And in month eight, May, with the sun warming his back, he left London and returned north, back to old friends and a sudden emptiness in his life that had to be filled by work.

But why in the name of God had he chosen the police? He screwed up the now empty polystyrene cup and threw it towards a nearby bin. It missed. So what, he thought. Then caught himself, went to the cup, stooped, picked it up, and deposited it in the bin. You're not in London now, Brian, he told himself. An elderly woman smiled at him.

So shines a good deed in a naughty world.

A naughty world all right. Rebus had landed him in a soup of melted humanity. Pilmuir, Hiroshima of the soul; he couldn't escape quickly enough. Fear of radiation. He had a little list with him, copied down neatly from last night's scrawled telephone conversation, and he took this from his pocket now to examine it. The constables had been easy to locate. Rebus would have seen them by now. Then he had gone to the house in Pilmuir. In his inside pocket he had the photographs. Edinburgh Castle. Good shots, too. Unusual angles. And the girl. She looked quite pretty, he supposed. Hard to tell her age, and her face seemed tempered by hard living, but she was bonny enough in a rough and ready way. He had no idea how he would find out anything about her. All he had to go on was that name, Tracy. True, there were people he could ask. Edinburgh was his home turf, an enormous advantage in this particular line of work. He had contacts all right, old friends, friends of friends. He'd re-established contact after the London fiasco. They'd all told him not to go. They'd all been pleased to see him again so soon after their warnings, pleased because they could boast of their foresight. That had only been five years ago. . . . It seemed longer somehow.

Why had he joined the force? His first choice had been journalism. That went way back, back to his schooldays. Well, childhood dreams could come true, if only momentarily. His next stop would be the offices of the local daily. See if he could find some more unusual angles on the Castle. With any luck, he'd get a decent cup of tea, too.

He was about to walk on when he saw an estate agent's

84

window across the street. He had always assumed that this particular agency would, because of its name, be expensive. But what the hell: he was a desperate man. He manoeuvred his way through the queue of unmoving traffic and stopped in front of the window of Bowyer Carew. After a minute, his shoulders slightly more hunched than before, he turned away again and stalked towards the Bridges.

'And this is James Carew, of Bowyer Carew.'

James Carew lifted his well-upholstered bottom a millimetre off his well-upholstered chair, shook Rebus's hand, then sat again. Throughout the introduction, his eyes had not left Rebus's tie.

'Finlay Andrews,' continued Superintendent Watson, and Rebus shook another firm masonic hand. He didn't need to know the secret pressure spots to be able to place a freemason. The grip itself told you everything, lasting as it did a little longer than normal, the extra time it took the shaker to work out whether you were of the brotherhood or not.

'You might know Mr Andrews. He has a gaming establishment in Duke Terrace. What's it called again?' Watson was trying too hard: too hard to be the host, too hard to get along with these men, too hard for everyone's comfort.

'It's just called Finlay's,' Finlay Andrews supplied, releasing his grip on Rebus.

'Tommy McCall,' said the final luncheon guest, making his own introduction, and giving Rebus's hand a quick, cool shake. Rebus smiled, and sat down, joining them at the table, thankful to be sitting down at last.

'Not Tony McCall's brother?' he asked conversationally.

'That's right.' McCall smiled. 'You know Tony then?'

'Pretty well,' said Rebus. Watson was looking bemused.

'Inspector McCall,' Rebus explained. Watson nodded vigorously.

'So,' said Carew, shifting in his seat, 'what will you have to drink, Inspector Rebus?'

'Not while on duty, sir,' said Rebus, unfolding his prettily arranged napkin. He saw the look on Carew's face and smiled. 'Just a joke. I'll have a gin and tonic, please.'

They all smiled. A policeman with a sense of humour: it usually surprised people. It would have surprised them even more had they known how seldom Rebus made jokes. But he felt the need to conform here, to 'mix', in that unhappy phrase.

There was a waiter at his shoulder.

'Another gin and tonic, Ronald,' Carew told the waiter, who bowed and moved off. Another waiter replaced him, and started handing out huge leather-bound menus. The thick cloth napkin was heavy on Rebus's lap.

'Where do you live, Inspector?' The question was Carew's. His smile seemed more than a smile, and Rebus was cautious.

'Marchmont,' he said.

'Oh,' Carew enthused, 'that's always been a very good area. Used to be a farming estate back in the old days, you know.'

'Really?'

'Mmm. Lovely neighbourhood.'

'What James means,' interrupted Tommy McCall, 'is that the houses are worth a few bob.'

'So they are,' Carew answered indignantly. 'Handy for the centre of town, close to The Meadows and the University. . . .'

'James,' Finlay Andrews warned, 'you're talking shop.'

'Am I?' Carew seemed genuinely surprised. He gave Rebus that smile again. 'Sorry.'

'I recommend the sirloin,' said Andrews. When the

waiter returned to take their order, Rebus made a point of ordering sole.

He tried to be casual, not to stare at the other diners, not to examine the minutiae of the tablecloth, the implements unknown to him, the finger bowls, the hallmarked cutlery. But then this was one of those once-in-a-lifetime things, wasn't it? So why not stare? He did, and saw fifty or so well-fed, happy faces, mostly male, with the occasional decorative female for the sake of decency, of elegance. Prime fillet. That's what everyone else seemed to be having. And wine.

'Who wants to choose the wine?' said McCall, flourishing the list. Carew looked eager to snatch, and Rebus held back. It wouldn't do, would it? To grab the list, to say me, me, me. To look with hungry eyes at the prices, wishing. . . .

'If I may,' said Finlay Andrews, lifting the wine list from McCall's hand. Rebus studied the hallmark on his fork.

'So,' said McCall, looking at Rebus, 'Superintendent Watson has roped you in on our little mission, eh?'

'I don't know that any rope was needed,' said Rebus. 'I'm glad to help if I can.'

'I'm sure your experience will be invaluable,' Watson said to Rebus, beaming at him. Rebus stared back evenly, but said nothing.

As luck would have it, Andrews seemed to know a bit about wine himself, and ordered a decent '82 claret and a crisp Chablis. Rebus perked up a bit as Andrews did the ordering. What was the name of the gaming club again? Andrews? Finlay's? Yes, that was it. Finlay's. He'd heard of it, a small casino, quiet. There had never been any cause for Rebus to go there, either on business or for pleasure. What pleasure was there in losing money?

'Is your Chinaman still haunting the place, Finlay?' asked McCall now, while two waiters ladled a thin covering of soup into wide-circumferenced Victorian soup plates.

'He won't get in again. Management reserves the right to refuse entry, et cetera.'

McCall chuckled, turned to Rebus.

'Finlay had a bad run back there. The Chinese are terrible for gambling, you know. Well, this one Chinaman was taking Finlay for a ride.'

'I had an inexperienced croupier,' Andrews explained. 'The experienced eye, and I do mean *experienced*, could tell pretty much where the ball was going to land on the roulette wheel, just by watching carefully how this youngster was flicking the ball.'

'Remarkable,' said Watson, before blowing on a spoonful of soup.

'Not really,' said Andrews. 'I've seen it before. It's simply a matter of spotting the type before they manage to lay on a really heavy bet. But then, you have to take the rough with the smooth. This has been a good year so far, a lot of money moving north, finding there's not so much to do up here, so why not simply gamble it away?'

'Money moving north?' Rebus was interested.

'People, jobs. London executives with London salaries and London habits. Haven't you noticed?'

'I can't say I have,' Rebus confessed. 'Not around Pilmuir at any rate.'

There were smiles at this.

'My estate agency has certainly noticed it,' said Carew. 'Larger properties are in great demand. Corporate buyers in some cases. Businesses moving north, opening offices. They know a good thing when they see it, and Edinburgh is a good thing. House prices have gone through the roof. I see no reason for them to stop.' He caught Rebus's eye. 'They're even building new homes in Pilmuir.'

'Finlay,' McCall interrupted, 'tell Inspector Rebus where the Chinese players keep their money.'

'Not while we're eating, please,' said Watson, and when McCall, chuckling to himself, looked down at his soup plate, Rebus saw Andrews flash the man a hateful look.

The wine had arrived, chilled and the colour of honey. Rebus sipped. Carew was asking Andrews about some planning permission to do with an extension to the casino.

'It seems to be all right.' Andrews tried not to sound smug. Tommy McCall laughed.

'I'll bet it does,' he said. 'Would your neighbours find the going as smooth if they tried to stick a big bloody extension on the back of *their* premises?'

Andrews gave a smile as cold as the Chablis. 'Each case is considered individually and scrupulously, Tommy, so far as I know. Maybe you know better?'

'No, no.' McCall had finished his first glass of wine, and was reaching for a second. 'I'm sure it's all totally above board, Finlay.' He looked conspiratorially at Rebus. 'I hope you're not going to tell tales, John.'

'No.' Rebus glanced towards Andrews, who was finishing his soup. 'Over lunch, my ears are closed.'

Watson nodded agreement.

'Hello there, Finlay.' A large man, heavily built but with the accent on muscularity, was standing by the table. He was wearing the most expensive-looking suit Rebus had ever seen. A silken sheen of blue with threads of silver running through it. The man's hair was silvered, too, though his face looked to be fortyish, no more. Beside him, leaning in towards him, stood a delicate Oriental woman, more girl than woman. She was exquisite, and everyone at the table rose in a kind of awe. The man waved an elegant hand, demanding they be seated. The woman hid her pleasure beneath her eyelashes.

'Hello, Malcolm.' Finlay Andrews gestured towards the man. 'This is Malcolm Lanyon, the advocate.' The last two words were unnecessary. Everyone knew Malcolm Lanyon, the gossip column's friend. His very public lifestyle provoked either hatred or envy. He was at the same time all that was most despised about the law profession, and a walking TV mini-series. If his lifestyle occasionally scandalised the prurient, it also satisfied a deep need in the readers of Sunday tabloids. He was also, to Rebus's sure knowledge, an extraordinarily good lawyer. He had to be, otherwise the rest of his image would have been wallpaper, nothing more. It wasn't wallpaper. It was bricks and mortar.

'These,' Andrews said, gesturing now to the occupants of the table, 'are the working members of that committee I was telling you about.'

'Ah.' Lanyon nodded. 'The campaign against drugs. An excellent idea, Superintendent.'

Watson almost blushed at the compliment: the compliment was that Lanyon knew who Watson was.

'Finlay,' Lanyon continued, 'you've not forgotten tomorrow night?'

'Firmly etched in my diary, Malcolm.'

'Excellent.' Lanyon glanced over the table. 'In fact, I'd like you all to come. Just a little gathering at my house. No real reason for it, I just felt like having a party. Eight o'clock. Very casual.' He was already moving off, an arm around the porcelain waist of his companion. Rebus caught his final words: his address. Heriot Row. One of the most exclusive streets in the New Town. This was a new world. Although he couldn't be sure that the invitation was serious, Rebus was tempted to take it up. Once in a lifetime, and all that.

A little later, conversation moved to the anti-drugs campaign itself and the waiter brought more bread.

'Bread,' the nervous young man said, carrying another bound file of newspapers over to the counter where

Holmes stood. 'That's what worries me. Everybody's turning into a bread head. You know, nothing matters to them except getting more than anyone else. Guys I went to school with, knew by the age of fourteen that they wanted to be bankers or accountants or economists. Lives were over before they'd begun. These are May.'

'What?' Holmes was shifting his weight from one leg to another. Why couldn't they have chairs in this place? He had been here over an hour, his fingers blackened by old newsprint as he flicked through each day's editions, one daytime, one evening. Now and then, a headline or some football story he'd missed first time around would attract his attention. But soon enough he had tired, and now it was merely routine. What's more, his arms were aching from all that page turning.

'May,' the youth explained. 'These are the May editions.'

'Right, thanks.'

'Finished with June?'

'Yes, thanks.'

The youth nodded, buckled shut two leather straps on the open end of the bound file, and heaved the whole up into his arms, shuffling out of the room. Here we go again, thought Holmes, unbuckling this latest batch of old news and space fillers.

Rebus had been wrong. There had been no old retainer to act as a computer memory, and no computer either. So it was down to hard graft and page turning, looking for photographs of familiar places, made fresh through the use of odd camera angles. Why? He didn't know even that yet, and the thought frustrated him. He'd find out later this afternoon hopefully, when he met with Rebus. There was a shuffling sound again as the youth re-entered, arms dangling now, jaw hanging.

'So why didn't you do the same as your friends?' Holmes said conversationally.

'You mean go in for banking?' The youth wrinkled his nose. 'Wanted something different. I'm learning journalism. Got to start somewhere, haven't you?'

Indeed you have, thought Holmes, turning another page. Indeed you have.

'Well, it's a start,' said McCall, rising. They were crumpling their used napkins, tossing them onto the dishevelled tablecloth. What had once been pristine was now covered with breadcrumbs and splashes of wine, a dark patch of butter, a single dripped coffee stain. Rebus felt woozy as he pulled himself out of the chair. And full. His tongue was furred from too much wine and coffee, and that cognac – Christ! Now these men were about to go back to work, or so they claimed. Rebus, too. He had a meeting at three with Holmes, didn't he? But it was already gone three. Oh well, Holmes wouldn't complain. Couldn't complain, thought Rebus smugly.

'Not a bad spread that,' said Carew, patting his girth. Rebus couldn't be sure whether this, or the food itself, was the spread he meant.

'And we covered a lot of ground,' said Watson, 'let's not forget that.'

'Indeed not,' said McCall. 'A very useful meeting.'

Andrews had insisted on paying the bill. A good three figures' worth by Rebus's hasty calculation. Andrews was studying the bill now, lingering over each item as though checking it against his own mental price list. Not only a businessman, thought Rebus unkindly, but a bloody good Scot. Then Andrews called over the brisk maitre d' and told him quietly about one item for which they had been overcharged. The maitre d' took Andrews' word for it, and altered the bill there and then with his own ballpoint pen, apologising unreservedly.

The restaurant was just beginning to empty. A nice lunch hour over for all the diners. Rebus felt sudden guilt

92

overwhelm him. He had just eaten and drunk his share of about two hundred pounds. Forty quid's worth, in other words. Some had dined better, and were noisily, laughingly making their way out of the dining room. Old stories, cigars, red faces. McCall put an unwelcome arm around Rebus's back, nodding towards the leavetaking.

'If there were only fifty Tory voters left in Scotland, John, they'd all be in this room.'

'I believe it,' said Rebus.

Andrews, turning from the maitre d', had heard them. 'I thought there *were* only fifty Tories left up here,' he said.

There, Rebus noted, were those quiet, confident smiles again. I have eaten ashes for bread, he thought. Ashes for bread. Cigar ash burned red all around him, and for a moment he thought he might be sick. But then McCall stumbled, and Rebus had to hold him up until he found his balance.

'Bit too much to drink, Tommy?' said Carew.

'Just need a breath of air,' said McCall. 'John'll help me, won't you, John?'

'Of course,' said Rebus, glad of this excuse for the very thing he needed.

McCall turned back towards Carew. 'Got your new car with you?'

Carew shook his head. 'I left it in the garage.'

McCall, nodding, turned to Rebus. 'The flash bugger's just bought himself a V-Twelve Jag,' he explained. 'Nearly forty thousand, and I'm not talking about miles on the clock.'

One of the waiters was standing by the lift.

'Nice to have seen you gentlemen again,' he said, his voice as automatic as the lift doors which closed when Rebus and McCall stepped inside.

'I must have arrested him some time,' Rebus said, 'because I've never been here before, so he can't have seen me here before.'

'This place is nothing,' said McCall, screwing up his face. 'Nothing. You want some fun, you should come to the club one night. Just say you're a friend of Finlay's. That'll get you in. Great place it is.'

'I might do that,' said Rebus as the lift doors opened. 'Just as soon as my cummerbund comes back from the dry cleaners.'

McCall laughed all the way out of the building.

Holmes was stiff as he left the building by its staff entrance. The youth, having shown him through the maze of corridors, had already turned back inside, hands in pockets, whistling. Holmes wondered if he really would end up with a career in journalism. Stranger things had happened.

He had found the photographs he wanted, one in each of three consecutive Wednesday daytime's editions. From these, the photographic library had traced the originals, and on the backs of the originals was the same golden rectangular sticker, denoting that the photos were the property of Jimmy Hutton Photographic Studios. The stickers, bless them, even mentioned an address and phone number. So Holmes allowed himself the luxury of a stretch, cracking his spine back into some semblance of shape. He thought about treating himself to a pint, but after leaning over the study table for the best part of two hours the last thing he wanted to do was lean against a bar as he drank. Besides, it was three fifteen. He was already, thanks to a quick-witted but slow-moving photo library, late for his meeting – his *first* – with Inspector Rebus. He didn't know how Rebus stood on the issue of punctuality; he feared the stand would be hard. Well, if the day's work so far didn't cheer him up, he wasn't human.

But then that was the rumour anyway.

Not that Holmes believed rumours. Well, not always.

As it turned out, Rebus was the later of the two for the meeting, though he had phoned ahead to apologise, which was something. Holmes was seated in front of Rebus's desk when Rebus finally arrived, pulling off rather a gaudy tie and dumping it into a drawer. Only then did he turn to Holmes, stare at him, smile, and stretch out a hand, which Holmes accepted.

Well that's something, thought Rebus; he's not a mason either.

'Your first name is Brian, isn't it?' said Rebus sitting down.

'That's right, sir.'

'Good. I'll call you Brian, and you can keep on calling me sir. That seem fair enough?'

Holmes smiled. 'Very fair, sir.'

'Right, any progress?'

So Holmes started at the beginning. As he spoke, he noticed that Rebus, though trying his damnedest to be attentive, was drowsy. His breath across the table was strong-smelling. Whatever he'd had for lunch had agreed with him too well. Finishing his report, he waited for Rebus to speak.

Rebus merely nodded, and was silent for some time. Collecting his thoughts? Holmes felt the need to fill the vacuum.

'What's the problem, sir, if you don't mind my asking?'

'You've every right to ask,' said Rebus at last. But he stopped at that.

'Well, sir?'

'I'm not sure, Brian. That's the truth. Okay, here's what I know – and I stress *know*, because there's plenty I *think*, which isn't quite the same thing in this case.'

'There is a case then?'

'You tell me, as soon as you've listened.' And it was Rebus's turn to make his 'report' of sorts, fixing it again in his mind as he told the story. But it was too fragmented, too speculative. He could see Holmes struggling with the pieces, trying to see the whole picture. Was there a picture there to see?

'So you see,' Rebus ended, 'we've got a junkie full of poison, self-inflicted. Someone who supplied the poison. Bruising on the body, and the hint of a witchcraft connection. We've got a missing camera, a tie clip, some photographs, and a girlfriend being followed. You see my problem?'

'Too much to go on.'

'Exactly.'

'So what do we do now?'

That 'we' caught Rebus's attention. For the first time, he realised that he was no longer in this alone, whatever 'this' was. The thought cheered him a little, though the hangover was starting now, the sleepy slow thumping either side of his forehead.

'I'm going to see a man about a coven,' he said, sure now of the next steps. 'And you're going to visit Hutton's Photographic Studios.'

'That sounds reasonable,' said Holmes.

'So it bloody well should,' said Rebus. 'I'm the one with the brains, Brian. You're the one with the shoeleather. Call me later on to let me know how you get on. Meantime, bugger off.'

Rebus didn't mean to be unkind. But there had been something just too cosy and conspiratorial in the younger man's tone towards the end, and he'd felt the need to re-establish boundaries. His own mistake, he realised as the door closed behind Holmes. His own mistake, for coming on so chattily, for telling all, for confiding, and for using Holmes's first name. That bloody lunch had been to blame. Call me Finlay, call me James, call me Tommy. . . . Never mind, it would all work out. They had begun well,

96

then less well. Things could only get worse, which was fine by Rebus. He enjoyed a measure of antagonism, of competition. They were distinct bonuses in this line of work.

So Rebus was a bastard after all.

Brian Holmes stalked out of the station with hands in pockets tightened to fists. Knuckles red. *You're the one with the shoeleather.* That had really brought him down with a thump, just when he'd thought they were getting on so well. Almost like human beings rather than coppers. Should've known better, Brian. And as for the reason behind all this work. . . . Well, it hardly bore thinking about. It was so flimsy, so personal to Rebus. It wasn't police work at all. It was an inspector with nothing to do for a while, trying to fill the time by playing at being Philip Marlowe. Jesus, they both had better things they could be doing. Well, Holmes did anyway. He wasn't about to head some cushy anti-drugs campaign. And what a choice Rebus was for that! Brother inside Peterhead, doing time for pushing. Biggest dealer in Fife, he'd been. That should have screwed up Rebus's career forever and anon, but instead they'd given him promotion. A naughty world, all right.

He had to visit a photographer. Maybe he could get some passport shots done at the same time. Pack his bags and fly off to Canada, Australia, the States. Sod his flat hunting. Sod the police force. And sod Detective Inspector John Rebus and his witch hunt.

There, it was done.

Rebus found some aspirin in one of his chaotic drawers, and crunched them to a bitter powder as he made his way downstairs. Bad mistake. They removed every fleck of saliva from his mouth, and he couldn't even swallow, couldn't speak. The desk sergeant was sipping a polystyrene beaker of tea. Rebus grabbed it from him and gulped at the tepid liquid. Then squirmed.

'How much sugar did you put in that, Jack?'

'If I'd known you were coming to tea, John, I'd have made it just the way you like it.'

The desk sergeant always had a smart answer, and Rebus could never think of a smarter rejoinder. He handed back the cup and walked away, feeling the sugar cloy inside him.

I'll never touch another drop, he was thinking as he started his car. Honest to God, only the occasional glass of wine. Allow me that. But no more indulgence, and no more mixing wine and spirits. Okay? So give me a break, God, and lift this hangover. I only drank the one glass of cognac, maybe two glasses of claret, one of Chablis. One gin and tonic. It was hardly the stuff of legend, hardly a case for the detox ward.

The roads were quiet though, which was a break. Not enough of a break, but a break. So he made good time to Pilmuir, and then remembered that he didn't know where Charlie boy lived. Charlie, the person he needed to talk to if he was going to find an address for a coven. A white coven. He wanted to double-check the witchcraft story. He wanted to double-check Charlie, too, come to that. But he didn't want Charlie to know he was being checked.

The witchcraft thing niggled. Rebus believed in good and evil, and believed stupid people could be attracted towards the latter. He understood pagan religions well enough, had read about them in books too thick and intense for their own good. He didn't mind people worshipping the Earth, or whatever. It all came down to the same thing in the end. What he did mind was people worshipping Evil as a force, and as *more* than a force: as an entity. Especially, he disliked the idea of people doing it for 'kicks' without knowing or caring what it was they were involved in.

People like Charlie. He remembered that book of Giger prints again. Satan, poised at the centre of a pair of scales, flanked by a naked woman left and right. The women were being penetrated by huge drills. Satan was a goat's head in a mask. . . .

But where would Charlie be now? He'd find out. Stop and ask. Knock on doors. Hint at retribution should information be withheld. He'd act the big bad policeman if that was what it took.

He didn't need to do anything, as it happened. He just had to find the police constables who were loitering outside one of the boarded-up houses, not too far from where Ronnie had died. One of the constables held a radio to his mouth. The other was writing in a notebook. Rebus stopped his car, stepped out. Then remembered something, leaned back into the car and drew his keys from out of the ignition. You couldn't be too careful around here. A second later, he actually locked his driver's side door, too.

He knew one of the constables. It was Harry Todd, one of the men who had found Ronnie. Todd straightened when he saw Rebus, but Rebus waved this acknowledgment aside, so Todd continued with his radio conversation. Rebus concentrated on the other officer instead.

'What's the score here?' The constable turned from his writing to give Rebus that suspicious, near-hostile look almost unique to the constabulary. 'Inspector Rebus,' Rebus explained. He was wondering where Todd's Irish sidekick O'Rourke was.

'Oh,' said the constable. 'Well . . .' He started to put away his pen. 'We were called to a domestic, sir. In this house. A real screaming match. But by the time we got here, the man had fled. The woman is still inside. She's got herself a black eye, nothing more. Not really your territory, sir.'

'Is that right?' said Rebus. 'Well, thank you for telling me, sonny. It's nice to be told what is and isn't my "territory". Thank you so much. Now, may I have your permission to enter the premises?'

The constable was blushing furiously, his cheeks an almighty red against his bloodless face and neck. No: even his *neck* was blushing now. Rebus enjoyed that. He didn't even mind that behind the constable, but in full view of Rebus himself, Todd was smirking at this encounter.

'Well?' Rebus prompted.

'Sorry, sir,' said the constable.

'Right,' said Rebus, walking towards the door. But before he reached it, it was opened from the inside, and there stood Tracy, both eyes reddened from crying, one eye bruised a deep blue. She didn't seem surprised to see Rebus standing in front of her; she seemed relieved, and threw herself at him, hugging him, her head against his chest, the tears beginning all over again.

Rebus, startled and embarrassed, returned the embrace only lightly, with a patting of his hands on her back: a father's 'there, there' to a frightened child. He turned his head to look at the constables, who were pretending to have noticed nothing. Then a car drew up beside his own, and he saw Tony McCall put on his handbrake before pushing open the driver's door, stepping out and seeing Rebus there, and the girl.

Rebus laid his hands on Tracy's arms and pushed her away from him a little, but still retaining that contact between them. His hands, her arms. She looked at him, and began to fight against the tears. Finally, she pulled one arm away so that she could wipe her eyes. Then the other arm relaxed and Rebus's hand fell from it, the contact broken. For now.

'John?' It was McCall, close behind him.

'Yes, Tony?'

'Why is it my patch has suddenly become your patch?'

'Just passing,' said Rebus.

The interior of the house was surprisingly neat and tidy. There were numerous, if uncoordinated, sticks of furniture – two well-worn settees, a couple of dining chairs, trellis table, half a dozen pouffes, burst at the seams and oozing stuffing – and, most surprising of all, the electricity was connected.

'Wonder if the electric board know about that,' said McCall as Rebus switched on the downstairs lights.

For all its trappings, the place had an air of impermanence. There were sleeping bags laid out on the living-room floor, as though ready for any stray waifs and passers-by. Tracy went to one of the settees and sat down, wrapping her hands around her knees.

'Is this your place, Tracy?' said Rebus, knowing the answer.

'No. It's Charlie's.'

'How long have you known?'

'I only found out today. He moves around all the time. It wasn't easy tracking him down.'

'It didn't take you long.' She shrugged her shoulders. 'What happened?'

'I just wanted to talk to him.'

'About Ronnie?' McCall watched Rebus as he said this. McCall was concentrating now, aware that Rebus was trying to fill him in on the situation while at the same time questioning Tracy. Tracy nodded.

'Stupid, maybe, but I needed to talk to someone.'

'And?'

'And we got into an argument. He started it. Told me I was the cause of Ronnie's death.' She looked up at them; not pleadingly, but just to show that she was sincere. 'It's not true. But Charlie said I should have looked after Ronnie, stopped him taking the stuff, got him away from Pilmuir. How could I have done that? He wouldn't have

101

listened to me. I thought he knew what he was doing. Nobody could tell him otherwise.'

'Is that what you told Charlie?'

She smiled. 'No. I only thought of it just now. That's what always happens, isn't it? You only think of the clever comeback after the argument's finished.'

'I know what you mean, love,' said McCall.

'So you started a slanging match –'

'I never started the slanging match!' she roared at Rebus.

'Okay,' he said quietly, 'Charlie started shouting at you, and you shouted back, then he hit you. Yes?'

'Yes.' She seemed subdued.

'And maybe,' Rebus prompted, 'you hit him back?'

'I gave as good as I got.'

'That's my girl,' said McCall. He was touring the room, turning up cushions on the settees, opening old magazines, crouching to pat each sleeping bag.

'Don't patronise me, you bastard,' said Tracy.

McCall paused, looked up, surprised. Then smiled, and patted the next sleeping bag along. 'Ah-ha,' he said, lifting the sleeping bag and shaking it. A small polythene bag fell out onto the floor. He picked it up, satisfied. 'A little bit of blaw,' he said. 'Makes a house into a home, eh?'

'I don't know anything about that,' said Tracy, looking at the bag.

'We believe you,' said Rebus. 'Charlie did a runner then?'

'Yes. The neighbours must've phoned for the pigs . . . I mean, the police.' She averted her eyes from them.

'We've been called worse,' said McCall, 'haven't we, John?'

'That's for sure. So the constables arrived at one door, and Charlie left by another, right?'

'Out of the back door, yes.'

102

'Well,' said Rebus, 'while we're here we might as well have a look at his room, if such a thing exists.'

'Good idea,' said McCall, pocketing the polythene bag. 'There's no smoke without fire.'

Charlie had a room all right. It consisted of a single sleeping bag, a desk, anglepoise lamp, and more books than Rebus had ever seen in such an enclosed space. They were piled against the walls, reaching in precarious pillars from floor to ceiling. Many were library books, well overdue.

'Must owe the City Fathers a small fortune,' said McCall.

There were books on economics, politics and history, as well as learned and not so learned tomes on demonism, devil worship and witchcraft. There was little fiction, and most of the books had been read thoroughly, with much underlining and pencilled marginalia. On the desk sat a half-completed essay, part of Charlie's university course work no doubt. It seemed to be trying to link 'magick' to modern society, but was mostly, to Rebus's eye, rambling nonsense.

'Hello!'

This was shouted from downstairs, as the two constables started to climb the staircase.

'Hello yourselves,' McCall called back. Then he shook the contents of a large supermarket carrier bag onto the floor, so that pens, toy cars, cigarette papers, a wooden egg, a spool of cotton, a personal cassette player, a Swiss army knife, and a camera fell out. McCall stooped to pick up the camera between thumb and middle finger. Nice model, thirty-five-millimetre SLR. Good make. He gestured with it towards Rebus, who took it from him, having first produced a handkerchief from his pocket, with which he held it. Rebus turned towards Tracy who was standing

103

against the door with her arms folded. She nodded back at him.

'Yes,' she said. 'That's Ronnie's camera.'

The constables were at the top of the stairs now. Rebus accepted McCall's offer of the supermarket carrier and dropped the camera into it, careful not to mess up any prints.

'Todd,' he said to the constable he knew, 'take this young lady down to Great London Road station.' Tracy's mouth opened. 'It's for your own protection,' Rebus said. 'Go on with them. I'll see you later, soon as I can.'

She still seemed ready to voice a complaint, but thought better of it, nodded and turned, leaving the room. Rebus listened as she went downstairs, accompanied by the officers. McCall was still searching, though without real concern. Two finds were quite enough to be going on with.

'No smoke without fire,' he said.

'I had lunch with Tommy today,' said Rebus.

'My brother Tommy?' McCall looked up. Rebus nodded. 'Then that's one up to you. He's never taken me to lunch these past fifteen years.'

'We were at The Eyrie.' Now McCall whistled. 'To do with Watson's anti-drugs campaign.'

'Yes, Tommy's shelling out for it, isn't he? Ach, I shouldn't be hard on him. He's done me a few favours in his time.'

'He had a few too many.'

McCall laughed gently. 'He hasn't changed then. Still, he can afford it. That transport company of his, it runs itself. He used to be there twenty-four hours a day, fifty-two weeks of the year. Nowadays, he can take off as long as he likes. His accountant once told him to take a *year* off. Can you imagine that? For tax purposes. If only we had those kinds of problem, eh, John?'

'You're right there, Tony.' Rebus was still holding the supermarket bag. McCall nodded towards it.

'Does this tie it up?'

'It makes things a bit clearer,' said Rebus. 'I might get it checked for prints.'

'I can tell you what you'll find,' said McCall. 'The deceased's and this guy Charlie's.'

'You're forgetting someone.'

'Who?'

'You, Tony. You picked the camera up with your fingers, remember?'

'Ah, sorry. I didn't think.'

'Never mind.'

'Anyway, it's something, isn't it? Something to celebrate, I mean. I don't know about you, but I'm starved.'

As they left the room, one pillar of books finally gave way, slewing down across the floor like dominoes waiting to be shuffled. Rebus opened the door again to look in.

'Ghosts,' said McCall. 'That's all. Just ghosts.'

It wasn't much to look at. Not what he'd been expecting. Okay, so there was a potted plant in one corner, and black roller blinds over the windows, and even a word processor gathering dust on a newish plastic desk. But it was still the second floor of a tenement, still designed as somebody's home and never meant to be used as office, studio, workplace. Holmes gave the room – the so-called 'front office' – a tour as the cute little school-leaver went off to fetch 'His Highness'. That was what she'd called him. If your staff didn't hold you in esteem, or at the very least in frightened awe, there was something wrong with you. Certainly, as the door opened and 'His Highness' walked in, it was evident to Holmes that there was something wrong with Jimmy Hutton.

For a start, he was the other side of fifty, yet what hair he still had was long, thin strands covering his forehead almost down to his eyes. He was also wearing denims: a mistake easily made by those aspiring to youth from the wrong side. And he was short. Five foot two or three. Now Holmes began to see the relevance of the secretary's pun. His highness, indeed.

He had a harassed look on his face, but had left the camera through in the back bedroom or box room or whichever room of the smallish flat served as his studio. He stuck out a hand, and Holmes shook it.

'Detective Constable Holmes,' he announced. Hutton nodded, took a cigarette from the packet on his secretary's desk and lit it. She frowned openly at this as she sat down again, smoothing her tight skirt beneath her. Hutton had not yet looked at Holmes. His eyes seemed to be mirroring some distraction in his mind. He went to the window, looked out, arched his neck to blow a plume of smoke towards the high, dark ceiling, then let his head go limp, leaning against the wall.

'Get me a coffee, Christine.' His eyes met Holmes's momentarily. 'Do you want one?' Holmes shook his head.

'Sure?' said Christine kindly, rising out of her seat again.

'Okay then. Thanks.'

With a smile she left the room, off to the kitchen or darkroom to fill a kettle.

'So,' said Hutton. 'What can I do for you?'

That was another thing about the man. His voice was high, not shrill or girlish, just high. And slightly rasping, as though he had damaged his vocal cords at some point in his youth and they had never recovered.

'Mr Hutton?' Holmes needed to be sure. Hutton nodded.

'Jimmy Hutton, professional photographer, at your service. You're getting married and you want me to do you a discount?'

'No, nothing like that.'

'A portrait then. Girlfriend perhaps? Mum and dad?'

106

'No, this is business, I'm afraid. *My* business, that is.'

'But no new business for me, right?' Hutton smiled, chanced another glance towards Holmes, drew on his cigarette again. 'I *could* do a portrait of you, you know. Nice strong chin, decent cheekbones. With the proper lighting. . . .'

'No, thanks. I hate having my picture taken.'

'I'm not talking about pictures.' Hutton was moving now, circling the desk. 'I'm talking about art.'

'That's why I came here actually.'

'What?'

'Art. I was impressed by some of your photos I saw in a newspaper. I was wondering whether you might be able to help me.'

'Oh?'

'It's a missing person.' Holmes was not a great liar. His ears tingled when he told a real whopper. Not a great liar, but a good one. 'A young man called Ronnie McGrath.'

'Name doesn't mean anything.'

'He wanted to be a photographer, that's why I was wondering.'

'Wondering what?'

'If he'd ever come to you. You know, asking advice, that sort of thing. You're an established name, after all.' It was almost too blatant. Holmes could sense it: could sense Hutton just about realising what the game was. But vanity won in the end.

'Well,' the photographer said, leaning against the desk, folding his arms, crossing his legs, sure of himself. 'What did he look like, this Ronnie?'

'Tallish, short brown hair. Liked to do studies. You know the sort of thing, the Castle, Calton Hill. . . .'

'Are you a photographer yourself, Inspector?'

'I'm only a constable.' Holmes smiled, pleased by the error. Then caught himself: what if Hutton were trying to play the vanity game with *him*? 'And no, I've never really done much photography. Holiday snaps, that sort of thing.'

'Sugar?' Christine put her head around the door, smiling at Holmes again.

'No thanks,' he said. 'Just milk.'

'Put a drop of whisky in mine,' said Hutton. 'There's a love.' He winked towards the door as it closed again. 'Sounds familiar, I have to admit. Ronnie. . . . Studies of the Castle. Yes, yes. I *do* remember some young guy coming in, bloody pest he was. I was doing a portfolio, some long-term stuff. Mind had to be one hundred percent on the job. He was always coming round, asking to see me, wanting to show me his work.' Hutton raised his hands apologetically. 'I mean, we were all young once. I wish I could have helped him. But I didn't have the time, not right then.'

'You didn't look at his work?'

'No. No time, as I say. He stopped coming by after a few weeks.'

'How long ago was this?'

'Few months. Three or four.'

The secretary appeared with their coffees. Holmes could smell the whisky wafting out of Hutton's mug, and was jealous and repelled in equal measure. Still, the interview was going well enough. Time for a side road.

'Thanks, Christine,' he said, seeming to please her with the familiarity. She sat down, not drinking herself, and lit a cigarette. He thought for a moment of reaching out to light it for her, but held back.

'Look,' said Hutton. 'I'd like to be of assistance, but. . . .'

'You're a busy man.' Holmes nodded agreement. 'I really do appreciate your giving me any time at all. Anyway, that just about wraps it up.' He took a scalding mouthful of coffee, but dared not spit it back into the mug, so swallowed hard instead.

'Right,' said Hutton, rising from the edge of the desk.

'Oh,' said Holmes. 'Just one thing. Curiosity really, but is there any chance I could have a peek at your studio? I've never been in a proper studio before.'

Hutton looked at Christine, who muffled a smile behind her fingers as she pretended to puff on her cigarette.

'Sure,' he said, smiling himself. 'Why not? Come on.'

The room was large, but otherwise pretty much as Holmes had expected, excepting one significant detail. Half a dozen different types of camera stood on half a dozen tripods. There were photographs covering three of the walls, and against the fourth was a large white backcloth, looking suspiciously like a bedsheet. This was all obvious enough. However, in front of the backcloth had been arranged the set for Hutton's present 'portfolio': two large, freestanding sections, painted pink. And in front of these was a chair, against which, arms folded, stood a young, blonde and bored-looking man.

A man who was naked.

'Detective Holmes, this is Arnold,' said Hutton by way of introduction. 'Arnold is a male model. Nothing wrong, is there?'

Holmes, who had been staring, now tried not to. The blood was rising to his face. He turned to Hutton.

'No, no, nothing.'

Hutton went to one camera and bent down to squint through the viewfinder, aiming in Arnold's general direction. Not at head height.

'The male nude can be quite exquisite,' Hutton was saying. 'Nothing photographs quite as well as the human body.' He clicked the shutter, ran the film on, clicked again, then looked up at Holmes, smiling at the police-man's discomfort.

'What will you do with the . . .' Holmes searched for some decorous word. 'I mean, what are they for?'

'My portfolio, I told you. To show to possible future clients.'

'Right.' Holmes nodded, to show he understood.

'I am an artist, you see, as well as a portrait snapper.'

'Right,' Holmes said, nodding again.

'Not against the law, is it?'

'I don't think so.' He went to the heavily draped window and peeked out through a slight opening. 'Not unless it disturbs the neighbours.'

Hutton laughed. Even the sober face of the model opened in a momentary grin.

'They queue up,' said Hutton, coming to the window and peering out. 'That's why I had to put up the curtains. Dirty buggers that they were. Women *and* men, crammed into the width of a window.' He pointed to a top-storey window in the tenement across the way. 'There. I caught them one day, took a couple of quick shots of them with the motor-drive. They didn't like that.' He turned away from the window. Holmes was browsing along the walls, picking out this and that photograph and nodding praise towards Hutton, who lapped it up and began to walk with him, pointing out this or that angle or trick.

'That's good,' said Holmes, gesturing towards one shot of Edinburgh Castle bathed in mist. It was almost identical to the one he had seen in the newspaper, which made it a very near relative to the one in Ronnie's bedroom. Hutton shrugged.

'That's nothing,' he said, resting a hand on Holmes's shoulder. 'Here, have a look at some of my nude work.'

There was a cluster of a dozen black and white ten-by-eights, pinned to the wall in one corner of the room. Men and women, not all of them young or pretty. But well enough taken, artistic even, Holmes supposed.

'These are just the best,' said Hutton.

'The best, or the most tasteful?' Holmes tried not to make the remark sound judgmental, but even so Hutton's good humour vanished. He went to a large chest of drawers and pulled open the bottom one, scooping up an armful of photographs which he threw to the floor.

'Have a look,' he said. 'There's no porn. Nothing sleazy or disgusting or obscene. They're just bodies. Posed bodies.'

Holmes stood over the photographs, not seeming to pay them any attention.

'I'm sorry,' he said, 'if I seemed –'

'Forget it.' Hutton turned away, so that his face was towards the male model. He rubbed at his eyes, shoulders slumped. 'I'm just tired. I didn't mean to snap like that. Just tired.'

Holmes stared at Arnold over Hutton's shoulder, then, because there was no way it could be done stealthily, bent down, picked out a photograph from the selection on the floor, and, coming upright again, stuffed the photo into his jacket. Arnold saw, of course, and Holmes just had time to wink at him conspiratorially before Hutton turned back towards him.

'People imagine it's easy, just taking photos all day,' Hutton said. Holmes risked a look over the man's shoulder and saw Arnold wag an admonitory finger. But he was smiling archly. He wasn't about to tell. 'You're thinking all the time,' Hutton went on. 'Every waking minute of every day, every time you look at something, every time you use your eyes. Everything's material, you see.'

Holmes was at the door now, not about to linger.

'Yes, well, I'd better let you get on,' he said.

'Oh,' said Hutton, as though coming out of a dream. 'Right.'

'Thanks for all your help.'

'Not at all.'

'Bye, Arnold,' Holmes called, then pulled the door shut behind him and was gone.

111

'Back to work,' said Hutton. He stared at the photographs on the floor. 'Give me a hand with these, Arnold.'

'You're the boss.'

As they began to scoop the photos back into the drawer, Hutton commented, 'Nice enough bloke for a copper.'

'Yes,' said Arnold, standing naked with his hands full of paper. 'He didn't look like one of the dirty raincoat brigade, did he?'

And though Hutton asked him what he meant, Arnold just shrugged. It wasn't his business after all. It was a shame though, the policeman being interested in women. A waste of a good-looking man.

Holmes stood outside for a minute. For some reason, he was trembling, as though a small motor had stuck somewhere inside him. He touched a hand to his chest. Slight heart murmur, nothing more. Everybody got them, didn't they? He felt as though he had just committed some petty crime, which he supposed, really, he had. He had taken someone's property away without their knowledge or consent. Wasn't that theft? As a child, he had stolen from shops, always throwing away whatever he stole. Ach, all kids did it, didn't they? . . . Didn't they?

He brought from his pocket the gains from this latest pilfering. The photograph was curled now, but he straightened it between his hands. A woman, pushing a pram past him, glanced at the photograph then hurried on, throwing back a disgusted look towards him. It's all right, madam, I'm a police officer. He smiled at the thought, then studied the nude shot again. It was mildly salacious, nothing more. A young woman, stretched out on what appeared to be silk or satin. Photographed from above, as she lay spreadeagled on this sheet. Her mouth open in an amateur's pout, eyes narrowed to slits of fake

112

ecstasy. All this was common enough. More interesting though was the model's identity.

For Holmes was sure it was the girl Tracy, the one whose photograph he already had from the squat. The one whose background he was trying to ascertain. The girlfriend of the deceased. Posed for the camera, uncovered, not at all shy, and enjoying herself.

What was it that kept bringing him back to this house? Rebus wasn't sure. He turned his torch onto Charlie's wall painting again, trying to make sense of the mind that had created it. But why did he want to try to understand a piece of jetsam like Charlie anyway? Perhaps because of the nagging feeling that he was absolutely integral to the case.

'What case?'

There, he had actually, finally said it aloud. What case? There was no 'case', not in the sense in which any criminal court would understand the term. There were personalities, misdeeds, questions without answers. Illegalities, even. But there was no case. That was the frustrating thing. If there were only a case, only something structured enough, tangible enough for him to hold on to, some casenotes which he could *physically* hold up and say, look, here it is. But there was nothing like that. It was all as insubstantial as candle wax. But candle wax left its mark, didn't it? And nothing ever vanished, not totally. Instead, things altered shape, substance, meaning. A five-pointed star within two concentric circles was nothing in itself. To Rebus it looked like nothing so much as a tin sheriff's badge he'd had as a boy. Lawman of the Texas tin badge state, cap-firing six-gun in his plastic holster.

To others it was evil itself.

He turned his back on it, remembering how proudly he had worn that badge, and went upstairs. Here was where the tie clip had lain. Past it, he entered Ronnie's bedroom

113

and walked over to the window, peering out through a chink in the boards covering the glass. The car had drawn up now, not too far from his own. The car that had followed him from the station. The car he had recognised at once as the Ford Escort which had waited outside his flat, the one which had roared away. Now it was here, parked next to the burnt-out Cortina. It was here. Its driver was here. The car itself was empty.

He heard the floorboard creak just the once, and knew that the man was behind him.

'You must know this place pretty well,' he said. 'You managed to miss most of the noisy ones.'

He turned from the window and shone his torch onto the face of a young man with short dark hair. The man shielded his eyes from the beam, and Rebus angled the light down onto the man's body.

It was dressed in a police constable's uniform.

'You must be Neil,' said Rebus calmly. 'Or do you prefer Neilly?'

He levelled the torch at the floor. There was enough light for him to see and be seen by. The young man nodded.

'Neil's fine. Only my friends call me Neilly.'

'And I'm not your friend,' Rebus said, nodding acquiescence. 'Ronnie was though, wasn't he?'

'He was more than that, Inspector Rebus,' said the constable, moving into the room. 'He was my brother.'

There was nowhere in Ronnie's bedroom for them to sit, but that didn't matter, since neither could have sat still for more than a second or two anyway. They were filled with energy: Neil needing to tell his story, Rebus needing to be told. Rebus chose in front of the window as his territory, and paced backwards and forwards without seeming to, his head down, stopping from time to time to lend more concentration to Neil's words. Neil stayed by the door, swinging the handle to and fro, listening for that moment before the whole door creaked, and then pulling or pushing the door through that slow, rending sound. The torch served the scene well, casting unruly shadows over the walls, making silhouettes of each man's profile, the talker and the listener.

'Sure, I knew what he was up to,' Neil said. 'He may have been older than me, but I always knew him better than he knew me. I mean, I knew how his mind worked.'

'So you knew he was a junkie?'

'I knew he took drugs. He started when we were at school. He was caught once, almost expelled. They let him back in after three months, so he could do his exams. He passed the lot of them. That's more than I did.'

Yes, Rebus thought, admiration could make you turn a blind eye. . . .

'He ran away after the exams. We didn't hear anything from him for months. My mum and dad almost went crazy. Then they just shut him out completely, switched off. It was like he didn't exist. I wasn't supposed to mention him in the house.'

'But he got in touch with you?'

'Yes. Wrote a letter to me care of a pal of mine. Clever move that. So I got the letter without Mum and Dad knowing. He told me he had come to Edinburgh. That he liked it better than Stirling. That he had a job and a girlfriend. That was it, no address or phone number.'

'Did he write often?'

'Now and then. He lied a lot, made things seem better than they were. Said he couldn't come back to Stirling until he had a Porsche and a flat, so he could prove something to Mum and Dad. Then he stopped writing. I left school and joined the police.'

'And came to Edinburgh.'

'Not straight away, but yes, eventually.'

'Specifically to find him?'

Neil smiled.

'Not a bit of it. I was forgetting him, too. I had my own life to think about.'

'So what happened?'

'I caught him one night, out on my regular beat.'

'What beat *is* that exactly?'

'I'm based out at Musselburgh.'

'Musselburgh? Not exactly walking distance of here, is it? So what do you mean "caught him"?'

'Well, not caught, since he wasn't really doing anything. But he was high as a kite, and he'd been bashed up a bit.'

'Did he tell you what he'd been doing?'

'No. I could guess though.'

'What?'

'Acting as a punchbag for some of the rough traders around Calton Hill.'

'Funny, someone else mentioned that.'

'It happens. Quick money for people who don't give a shit.'

'And Ronnie didn't give a shit?'

'Sometimes he did. Other times. . . . I don't know, maybe I didn't know his mind as well as I thought.'

'So you started to visit him?'

'I had to help him home that first night. I came back the next day. He was surprised to see me, didn't even remember that I'd helped him home the previous night.'

'Did you try to get him off drugs?'

Neil was silent. The door creaked on its hinges.

'At the beginning I did,' he said at last. 'But he seemed to be in control. That sounds stupid, I know, after what I've said about finding him in such a state that first night, but it was *his* choice, after all, as he kept reminding me.'

'What did he think of having a brother in the force?'

'He thought it was funny. Mind you, I never came round here with my uniform on.'

'Not till tonight.'

'That's right. Anyway, yes, I visited a few times. We stayed up here mostly. He didn't want the others to see me. He was afraid they'd smell pork.'

It was Rebus's turn to smile. 'You didn't happen to follow Tracy, did you?'

'Who's Tracy?'

'Ronnie's girlfriend. She turned up at my flat last night. Some men had been following her.'

Neil shook his head. 'Wasn't me.'

'But you *were* at my flat last night?'

'Yes.'

'And you were here the night Ronnie died.' It was blunt, but necessarily so. Neil stopped playing with the door handle, was silent this time for twenty or thirty seconds, then took a deep breath.

'For a while I was, yes.'

'You left this behind.' Rebus held out the shiny clip, but Neil couldn't quite make it out in the torchlight. Not that he needed to see it to know what it was.

'My tie clip? I wondered about that. My tie had broken that day, it was in my pocket.'

Rebus made no attempt to hand over the clip. Instead, he put it back in his pocket. Neil just nodded, understanding.

'Why did you start following me?'

'I wanted to talk to you. I just couldn't pluck up the courage.'

'You didn't want news of Ronnie's death getting back to your parents?'

'Yes. I thought maybe you wouldn't be able to trace his identity, but you did. I don't know what it'll do to my mum and dad. I think at worst it'll make them happy, because they'll know they were right all along, right not to give him a second's thought.'

'And at best?'

117

'Best?' Neil stared through the gloom, searching out Rebus's eyes. 'There's no best.'

'I suppose not,' said Rebus. 'But they've still got to be told.'

'I know. I've always known.'

'Then why follow me?'

'Because now you're closer to Ronnie than I am. I don't know why you're so interested in him, but you are. And that interests me. I want you to find whoever sold him that poison.'

'I intend to, son, don't worry.'

'And I want to help.'

'That's the first stupid thing you've said, which isn't bad going for a PC. Truth is, Neil, you'd be the biggest bloody nuisance I could ask for. I've got all the help I need for now.'

'Too many cooks, eh?'

'Something like that.' Rebus decided that the confession was ending, that there was little left to be said. He came away from the window and walked to the door, stopping in front of Neil. 'You've already been a bigger nuisance than I needed. It's not pork I can smell off you, it's fish. Herrings, to be precise. And guess what colour they are.'

'What?'

'Red, son, red.'

There was a noise from downstairs, pressure on floorboards, better than an infra-red alarm anyday. Rebus turned off the torch.

'Stay here,' he whispered. Then he went to the top of the stairs. 'Who's there?' A shadow appeared below him. He switched on the torch, and shone it into Tony McCall's squinting face.

'Christ, Tony.' Rebus started downstairs. 'What a fright.'

'I knew I'd find you here,' said McCall. 'I just knew it.' His voice was nasal, and Rebus reckoned that since the time they'd parted some three hours before, McCall had kept on drinking. He stopped on the staircase, then turned and headed back up.

'Where are you going now?' called McCall.

'Just shutting the door,' said Rebus, closing the bedroom door, leaving Neil inside. 'Don't want the ghosts to catch cold, do we?'

McCall was chuckling as Rebus headed downstairs again.

'Thought we might have a wee snifter,' he said. 'And none of that bloody alcohol-free stuff you were quaffing before.'

'Fair enough,' said Rebus, expertly manoeuvring McCall out of the front door. 'Let's do that.' And he locked the door behind him, figuring that Ronnie's brother would know of the many easy ways in and out of the house. Everybody else seemed to know them, after all.

Everybody.

'Where'll it be?' said Rebus. 'I hope you didn't drive here, Tony.'

'Got a patrol car to drop me off.'

'Fine. We'll take my car then.'

'We could drive down to Leith.'

'No, I fancy something more central. There are a few good pubs in Regent Road.'

'By Calton Hill?' McCall was amazed. 'Christ, John, I can think of better places to go for a drink.'

'I can't,' said Rebus. 'Come on.'

Nell Stapleton was Holmes's girlfriend. Holmes had always preferred tall women, tracing the fixation back to his mother who had been five foot ten. Nell was nearly three quarters of an inch taller than Holmes's mother, but he still loved her.

Nell was more intelligent than Holmes. Or, as he liked to think, they were more intelligent than one another in different ways. Nell could crack the *Guardian* cryptic crossword in under quarter of an hour on a good day. But she had trouble with arithmetic and remembering names: both strengths possessed by Holmes. People said they looked good together in public, looked comfortable with one another, which was probably true. They felt good together, too, living as they did by several simple rules: no talk of marriage, no thoughts of children, no hinting at living together, and definitely no cheating.

Nell worked as a librarian at Edinburgh University, a vocation Holmes found handy. Today, for example, he had asked her to find him some books on the occult. She had done even better, locating a thesis or two which he could read on the premises if he wished. She also had a printed bibliography of relevant materials, which she handed to him in the pub when they met that evening.

The Bridge of Sighs was at a mid-week and mid-evening cusp, as were most of the city centre bars. The just-one-after-work brigade had slung their jackets over their arms and headed off, while the revitalised night-time crowd had yet to catch their buses from the housing estates into the middle of town. Nell and Holmes sat at a corner table, away from the video games, but a bit too close to one of the hi-fi system's loudspeakers. Holmes, at the bar to buy another half for himself, an orange juice and Perrier for Nell, asked if the volume could be turned down.

'Sorry, can't. The customers like it.'

'We *are* the customers,' Holmes persisted.

'You'll have to speak to the manager.'

'Fine.'

'He's not in yet.'

Holmes shot the young barmaid a filthy look before turning towards his table. What he saw made him pause. Nell had opened his briefcase and was examining the photograph of Tracy.

'Who is she?' Nell said, closing the case as he placed her drink on the table.

'Part of a case I'm working on,' he said frostily, sitting down. 'Who said you could open my briefcase?'

'Rule seven, Brian. No secrets.'

'All the same –'

'Pretty, isn't she?'

'What? I haven't really –'

'I've seen her around the university.'

He was interested now. 'You have?'

'Mmm. In the library cafeteria. I remember her because she always seemed a little bit older than the other students she was with.'

'She's a student then?'

'Not necessarily. Anybody can go into the cafe. It's students only in the library itself, but I can't recall having seen her there. Only in the cafe. So what's she done?'

'Nothing, so far as I know.'

'So why is there a nude photo of her in your briefcase?'

'It's part of this thing I'm doing for Inspector Rebus.'

'You're collecting dirty pictures for him.'

She was smiling now, and he smiled too. The smile vanished as Rebus and McCall walked into the pub, laughing at some shared joke as they made for the bar. Holmes didn't want Rebus and Nell to meet. He tried very hard to leave his police life behind him when he was spending the evening with her – favours such as the occult booklist notwithstanding. He was also planning to keep Nell very much up his sleeve, so that he could have a booklist ready to hand should Rebus ever need such a thing.

Now it looked as though Rebus was going to spoil everything. And there was something else, another reason he didn't want Rebus to come sauntering across to their table. He was afraid Rebus would call him 'Shoeleather'.

He kept his eyes to the table as Rebus took in the bar

with a single sweep of his head, and was relieved when
the two senior officers, drinks purchased, wandered off
towards the distant pool table, where they started another
argument about who shouldn't and should provide the
two twenty-pence pieces for the game.

'What's wrong?'

Nell was staring at him. To do so, she had brought
herself to his level, her head resting against the table.

'Nothing.' He turned towards her, offering the rest of
the room a hard profile. 'Are you hungry?'

'I suppose so, yes.'

'Good, me too.'

'I thought you said you'd eaten.'

'Not enough. Come on, I'll treat you to an Indian.'

'Let me finish my drink first.' She did so in three
swallows, and they left together, the door swinging shut
silently behind them.

'Heads or tails?' Rebus asked McCall, flipping a coin.

'Tails.'

Rebus examined the coin. 'Tails it is. You break.'

As McCall angled his cue down onto the table, closing
one eye as he concentrated on the distant triangle of balls,
Rebus stared at the door of the bar. Fair enough, he
supposed. Holmes was off duty, and had a girl with him,
too. He supposed that gave him grounds for ignoring his
senior officer. Perhaps there had been no progress,
nothing to report. Fair enough again. But Rebus couldn't
help thinking that the whole thing was meant to be taken
as a snub. He had given Holmes a mouthful earlier on,
and now Holmes was sulking.

'You to play, John,' said McCall, who had broken
without potting.

'Right you are, Tony,' said Rebus, chalking the tip of his
cue. 'Right you are.'

McCall came to Rebus's side as he was making ready to
play.

'This must be just about the only straight pub in the whole street,' he said quietly.

'Do you know what homophobia means, Tony?'

'Don't get me wrong, John,' said McCall, straightening up and watching Rebus's chosen ball miss the pocket. 'I mean, each to his own and all that. But some of those pubs and clubs. . . .'

'You seem to know a lot.'

'No, not really. It's just what I hear.'

'Who from?'

McCall potted one striped ball, then another. 'Come on, John. You know Edinburgh as well as I do. Everybody knows the gay scene here.'

'Like you said, Tony, each to his own.' A voice suddenly sounded in Rebus's mind: *you're the brother I never had.* No, no, shut that out. He'd been there too often before. McCall missed on his next shot and Rebus approached the table.

'How come,' he said, completely miscuing, 'you can drink so much and play so well?'

McCall chuckled. 'Alcohol cures the shakes,' he said. 'So finish that pint and I'll buy you another. My treat.'

James Carew felt that he deserved his treat. He had sold a substantial property on the outskirts of Edinburgh to the financial director of a company new to Scotland, and a husband and wife architects' partnership – Scottish in origin, but now relocating from Sevenoaks in Kent – had just made a rather better offer than expected for an estate of seven acres in the Borders. A good day. By no means the best, but nevertheless worthy of celebration.

Carew himself owned a *pied à terre* in one of the loveliest of the New Town's Georgian streets, and a farmhouse with some acreage on the Isle of Skye. These were good days for him. London was shifting north, it seemed, the incomers brimming with cash from properties sold in the south-east, wanting bigger and better and prepared to pay.

He left his George Street offices at six thirty, and returned to his split-level flat. Flat? It seemed an insult to term it such: five bedrooms, living room, dining room, two bathrooms, adequate kitchen, walk-in cupboards the size of a decent Hammersmith bedsit. . . . Carew was in the right place, the only place, and the time was right, too. This was a year to be clutched, embraced, a year unlike any other. He removed his suit in the master bedroom, showered, and changed into something more casual, but without shrugging off the mark of wealth. Though he had walked home, he would need the car for tonight. It was garaged in a mews to the rear of his street. The keys were hanging on their appointed hook in the kitchen. Was the Jaguar an indulgence? He smiled, locking the flat as he left. Perhaps it was. But then his list of indulgences was long, and about to grow longer.

Rebus waited with McCall until the taxi arrived. He gave the driver McCall's address, and watched the cab pull away. Damn, he felt a little groggy himself. He went back into the pub and headed for the toilets. The bar was busier now, the jukebox louder. The bar staff had grown in strength from one to three, and they were working hard to cope. The toilets were a cool tiled haven, free from much of the bar's cigarette smoke. Pine disinfectant caught in Rebus's nostrils as he leaned over into one of the sinks. Two fingers sought out his tonsils, pausing there at the back of his throat until he retched, bringing up half a pint of beer, then another half. He breathed deeply, feeling a little better already, then washed his face thoroughly with cold water, drying himself off with a fistful of paper towels.

'You all right?' The voice lacked real sympathy. Its

owner had just pushed open the door to the gents' and was already seeking the closest urinal.

'Never felt better,' said Rebus.

'That's good.'

Good? He didn't know about that, but at least his head was clearer, the world more in focus. He doubted if he'd fail a breathalyser, which was just as well, since his next port of call was his car, parked on a darkened side road. He was still wondering how Tony McCall, shaky on his pins after half a dozen pints, had managed to play pool with such a steady eye and steady hand. The man was miraculous. He'd beaten Rebus six straight games. And Rebus had been trying. By the end he'd *really* been trying. After all, it didn't look good when a man barely able to stand upright could pot ball after ball, cleaning up and roaring to yet another victory. It didn't look good. It hadn't felt good.

It was eleven o'clock, perhaps a little early yet. He allowed himself one cigarette in the stationary car, window open, picking up the sounds from the world around him. The honest sounds of the late evening: traffic, heightened voices, laughter, the clatter of shoes on cobblestones. One cigarette, that was all. Then he started the car, and slowly drove the half mile or so to his destination. There was still some light in the sky, typical of the Edinburgh summer. Further north he knew it never got truly dark at this time of year.

But the night could be dark in other ways.

He spotted the first one on the pavement outside the Scottish Assembly building. There was no reason for the teenager to be standing there. It was an unlikely time of night to have arranged to meet friends, and the nearest bus stop was a hundred yards further up Waterloo Place. The lad stood there, smoking, one foot up behind him resting against the stone wall. He watched Rebus as the car slowly went past, and even lowered his head forward a little so that he could peer in, as though inspecting the driver. Rebus thought there was a smile there, but couldn't be sure. Further along the road, he turned the car and came back. Another car had stopped beside the boy, and a conversation was taking place. Rebus kept driving. Two young men were talking together outside the Scottish Office building on this side of the road. A little way past them, a line of three cars stood outside Calton Cemetery. Rebus cruised one more circuit, then parked near these cars, and walked.

The night was fresh. No cloud cover. There was a slight breeze, nothing more. The lad outside the Assembly building had gone off in the car. No one stood there now. Rebus crossed the road, stopped by the wall, and waited, biding his time. He watched. One or two cars drove past him slowly, the drivers turning to stare at him. But nobody stopped. He tried memorising the number plates, unsure why.

'Got a light, mister?'

He was young, no more than eighteen or nineteen. Dressed in jeans, training shoes, a shapeless T-shirt and denim jacket. His hair had been razored short, face clean-shaven but scarred with acne. There were two gold studs in his left ear.

'Thanks,' he said as Rebus held out a box of matches. Then: 'What's happening then?', with an amused glance towards Rebus before lighting the cigarette.

'Not much,' Rebus said, taking back the matchbox. The young man blew smoke out through his nostrils. He didn't seem about to go. Rebus wondered if there were any codes he should be using. He felt clammy beneath his thin shirt, despite the gooseflesh.

'Nah, there's never much happens around here. Fancy a drink?'

'At this time? Whereabouts?'

The young man nodded a vague direction. 'Calton Cemetery. You can always get a drink there.'

'No, thanks anyway.' Rebus was appalled to find himself blushing. He hoped the street lighting would disguise it.

'Fair enough. See you around then.' The young man was moving off.

'Yes,' Rebus said, relieved. 'See you.'

'And thanks for the light.'

Rebus watched him go, walking slowly, purposefully, turning from time to time at the sign of an approaching car. A hundred yards or so on, he crossed the road and began walking back, paying Rebus no attention, his mind on other things. It struck Rebus that the boy was sad, lonely, certainly no hustler. But no victim either.

Rebus stared at the wall of Calton Cemetery, broken only by its metal gates. He'd taken his daughter in there once to show her the graves of the famous – David Hume, the publisher Constable, the painter David Allan – and the statue of Abraham Lincoln. She'd asked him about the men who walked briskly from the cemetery, their heads bowed down. One older man, two teenagers. Rebus had wondered about them, too. But not too much.

No, he couldn't do it. Couldn't go in there. It wasn't that he was afraid. Jesus, no, not that, not for one minute. He was just . . . he didn't know what. But he was feeling giddy again, unsteady on his pins. I'll go back to the car, he thought.

He went back to the car.

He had been sitting in the driver's seat, smoking another cigarette thoughtfully for about a minute before he caught sight of the figure out of the corner of his eye. He turned and looked towards where the boy was seated; no, not seated, crouching against a low wall. Rebus turned away and resumed smoking. Only then did the boy rise to his feet and walk towards the car. He tapped on the passenger side window. Rebus took a deep breath before unlocking the door. The boy got in without a word, closing the door solidly behind him. He sat there, staring out through the windscreen, silent. Rebus, unable to think of a single sensible thing to say, stayed silent, too. The boy cracked first.

'Hiya.'

It was a man's voice. Rebus turned to examine the boy. He was maybe sixteen. Dressed in leather jacket, open-necked shirt. Torn jeans.

'Hello,' he said in reply.

'Got a cigarette?'

Rebus handed over the packet. The boy took one and swopped the packet for a box of matches. He inhaled the cigarette smoke deeply, holding it for a long time, then exhaling almost nothing of it back into the atmosphere. Take without give, thought Rebus. The creed of the street.

'So what are you up to tonight then?' The question had been on Rebus's own lips, but the boy had given voice to it.

'Just killing time,' said Rebus. 'I couldn't sleep.'

The boy laughed harshly. 'Yeah, couldn't sleep, so you came for a drive. Got tired driving so you just happened to stop here. This particular street. This time of night. Then you went for a walk, a stretch of the legs, and came back to the car. Right?'

'You've been watching me,' Rebus admitted.

'I didn't *need* to watch you. I've seen it all before.'

'How often?'

'Often enough, James.'

The words were tough, the voice was tough. Rebus had no cause to doubt the teenager. Certainly he was as dissimilar to the first boy as chalk to cheese.

'The name's not James,' he said.

'Of course it is. Everybody's called James. Makes it easier to remember a name, even if you can't recall the face.'

128

'I see.'

The boy finished the cigarette in silence, then flicked it out of the window.

'So what's it to be?'

'I don't know,' said Rebus sincerely. 'A drive maybe?'

'Fuck that.' He paused, seeming to change his mind. 'Okay, let's drive to the top of Calton Hill. Take a look out over the water, eh?'

'Fine,' said Rebus, starting the car.

They drove up the steep and winding road to the top of the hill, where the observatory and the folly – a copy of one side of Greece's Parthenon – sat silhouetted against the sky. They were not alone at the top. Other darkened cars had parked, facing across the Firth of Forth towards the dimly lit coast of Fife. Rebus, trying not to look too closely at the other cars, decided to park at a discreet distance from them, but the boy had other ideas.

'Stop next to that Jag,' he ordered. 'What a great-looking car.'

Rebus felt his own car take the insult with as much pride as it could muster. The brakes squealed in protest as he pulled to a halt. He turned off the ignition.

'What now?' he asked.

'Whatever you want,' said the boy. 'Cash on delivery, of course.'

'Of course. What if we just talk?'

'Depends on the kind of talk you want. The dirtier it is, the more it'll cost.'

'I was just thinking about a guy I met here once. Not so long ago. Haven't seen him around. I was wondering what happened to him.'

The boy suddenly placed his hand on Rebus's crotch, rubbing hard and fast against the material. Rebus stared at the hand for a full second before calmly, but with a deliberate grip, removing it. The boy grinned, leaning back in his seat.

'What's his name, James?'

Rebus tried to stop himself trembling. His stomach was filling with bile. 'Ronnie,' he said at last, clearing his throat. 'Not too tall. Dark hair, quite short. Used to take a few pictures. You know, keen on photography.'

The boy's eyebrows rose. 'You're a photographer, are you? Like to take a few snaps? I see.' He nodded slowly. Rebus doubted that he did see, but wasn't about to say more than was necessary. And yes, that Jag was nice. New-looking. Paintwork brightly reflective. Someone with a bit of money. And dear God why did he have an erection?

'I think I know which Ronnie you mean now,' said the boy. 'I haven't seen him around much myself.'

'So what can you tell me about him?'

The boy was staring out of the windscreen again. 'Great view from here, isn't it?' he said. 'Even at night. *Especially* at night. Amazing. I hardly ever come here in the daytime. It all looks so ordinary. You're a copper, aren't you?'

Rebus looked towards him, but the boy was still staring out of the windscreen, smiling, unconcerned.

'Thought you were,' he went on. 'Right from the start.'

'So why did you get in the car?'

'Curious, I suppose. Besides,' and now he looked towards Rebus, 'some of my best customers are officers of the law.'

'Well, that's none of my concern.'

'No? It should be. I'm underage, you know.'

'I guessed.'

'Yeah, well. . . .' The boy slumped in his seat, putting his feet up on the dashboard. For a moment, Rebus thought he was about to do something, and jerked himself upright. But the boy just laughed.

'What did you think? Think I was going to *touch* you again? Eh? No such luck, James.'

130

'So what about Ronnie?' Rebus wasn't sure whether he wanted to punch this rather ugly little kid in the gut, or take him to a good and a caring home. But he knew, above all, that he wanted answers.

'Give me another ciggie.' Rebus obliged. 'Ta. Why are you so interested in him?'

'Because he's dead.'

'Happens all the time.'

'He overdosed.'

'Ditto.'

'The stuff was lethal.'

The boy was silent for a moment.

'Now that *is* bad news.'

'Has there been any poisoned stuff going around recently?'

'No.' He smiled again. 'Only good stuff. Got any on you?' Rebus shook his head, thinking: *I do want to punch him in the gut.* 'Pity,' said the boy.

'What's your name, by the way?'

'No names, James, and no pack drill.' He put out his hand, palm up. 'I need some money.'

'I need some answers first.'

'So give me the questions. But first, a little goodwill, eh?' The hand was still there, expectant as any father-to-be. Rebus found a crumpled tenner in his jacket and handed it over. The boy seemed satisfied. 'This gets you the answers to two questions.'

Rebus's anger ignited. 'It gets me as many answers as I want, or so help me –'

'Rough trade? That your game?' The boy seemed unconcerned. Maybe he'd heard it all before. Rebus wondered.

'Is there much rough stuff goes on?' he asked.

'Not much.' the boy paused. 'But still too much.'

'Ronnie was into it, wasn't he?'

'That's your second question,' stated the boy. 'And the answer is, I don't know.'

'Don't knows don't count,' said Rebus. 'And I've got plenty of questions left.'

'Okay, if that's the way –' The boy was reaching for the door handle, ready to walk away from it all. Rebus grabbed him by the neck and brought his head down against the dashboard, right between where both feet were still resting.

'Jesus Christ!' The boy checked for blood on his forehead. There was none. Rebus was pleased with himself: maximum shock, minimum visible damage. 'You can't –'

'I can do anything I like, son, and that includes tipping you over the edge of the highest point in the city. Now tell me about Ronnie.'

'I can't tell you about Ronnie.' There were tears in his eyes now. He rubbed at his forehead, trying to erase the hurt. 'I didn't know him well enough.'

'So tell me what you *do* know.'

'Okay, okay.' He sniffed, wiping his nose on the sleeve of his jacket. 'All I know is that a few friends of mine have gotten into a scene.'

'What scene?'

'I don't know. Something heavy. They don't talk about it, but the marks are there. Bruises, cuts. One of them ended up in the Infirmary for a week. Said he fell down the stairs. Christ, he looked like he fell down a whole high-rise.'

'But nobody's talking?'

'There must be good money in it somewhere.'

'Anything else?'

'It may not be important. . . .' The kid had broken. Rebus could hear it in his voice. He'd talk from now till judgment day. Good: Rebus didn't have too many ears in

132

this part of the city. A fresh pair might make all the difference.

'What?' he barked, enjoying his role now.

'Photographs. Somebody's putting a whisper around that there's interest in photographs. Not faked ones, either. The real McCoy.'

'Porn shots?'

'I suppose so. The rumours have been a bit vague. Rumours get that way when they've gone past being second-hand.'

'Chinese whispers,' said Rebus. He was thinking: this whole thing is like a game of Chinese whispers, everything at second and third remove, nothing absolutely proof positive.

'What?'

'Never mind. Anything else?'

The boy shook his head. Rebus reached into his pocket and, to his own surprise, found yet another tenner. Then he remembered that he'd visited a cashpoint machine somewhere during the drinking session with McCall. He handed the money over.

'Here. And I'll give you my name and phone number. I'm always open to bits of information, no matter how small. Sorry about your head, by the way.'

The boy took the money. 'That's all right. I've seen worse pay.' Then he smiled.

'Can I give you a lift?'

'The Bridges maybe?'

'No problem. What's your name?'

'James.'

'Really?' Rebus was smiling.

'Yes, really.' The boy was smiling, too. 'Listen, there *is* one other thing.'

'Go ahead, James.'

'It's just a name I've been hearing. Maybe it doesn't mean anything.'

'Yes?'

'Hyde.'

Rebus frowned. 'Hide? Hide what?'

'No, *Hyde*. H-y-d-e.'

'What about Hyde?'

'I don't know. Like I said, it's just a name.'

Rebus gripped the steering wheel. Hyde? *Hyde?* Was that what Ronnie had been telling Tracy? Not just to hide, but to hide from some man called Hyde? Trying to think, he found himself staring at the Jag again. Or rather, staring at the profile of the man in the driver's seat. The man with his hand up around the neck of the much younger occupant of the passenger seat. Stroking, and all the time talking in a low voice. Stroking, talking. All very innocent.

A wonder then that James Carew of Bowyer Carew Estate Agents should look so startled when, being stared at, he returned the stare and found himself eye to eye with Dectective Inspector John Rebus.

Rebus was taking all this in as Carew fumbled with his ignition key, revved up the new V12 engine and reversed out of the car park as though Cutty Sark herself were after him.

'He's in a hurry,' said James.

'Have you seen him before?'

'Didn't really catch his face. Haven't seen the car before though.'

'No, well, it's a new car, isn't it?' said Rebus, lazily starting his own.

The flat was still redolent of Tracy. She lingered in the living room and the bathroom. He saw her with a towel falling down around her head, legs tucked beneath her. . . . Bringing him breakfast: the dirty dishes were still lying beside his unmade bed. She had laughed to find that he slept on a mattress on the floor. 'Just like in a squat,'

134

she had said. The flat seemed emptier now, emptier than it had felt for a while. And Rebus could do with a bath. He returned to the bathroom and turned the hot tap on. He could still feel James's hand on his leg. . . . In the living room, he looked at a bottle of whisky for a full minute, but turned his back on it and fetched a low-alcohol lager from the fridge instead.

The bath was filling slowly. An Archimedean screw would have been more efficient. Still, it gave him time to make another telephone call to the station, to check on how they were treating Tracy. The news was not good. She was becoming irritable, refusing to eat, complaining of pains in her side. Appendicitis? More likely cold turkey. He felt a fair amount of guilt at not having gone to see her before now. Another layer of guilt wouldn't do any harm, so he decided to put off the visit until morning. Just for a few hours he wanted to be away from it all, all the sordid tinkering with other people's lives. His flat didn't feel so secure any more, didn't feel like the castle it had been only a day or two ago. And there was internal damage as well as the structural kind: he was feeling soiled in the pit of his gut, as though the city had scraped away a layer of its surface grime and force-fed him the lot.

To hell with it.

He was caught all right. He was living in the most beautiful, most civilised city in northern Europe, yet every day had to deal with its flipside, with the minor matter of its animus. *Animus?* Now there was a word he hadn't used in a while. He wasn't even sure now what it meant exactly; but it sounded right. He sucked from the beer bottle, holding the foam in his mouth like a child playing with toothpaste. This stuff was all foam. No substance.

All foam. Now there was another idea. He would put some foaming bath oil in the water. Bubblebath. Who the hell had given him this stuff? Oh. Yes. Gill Templer. He remembered now. Remembered the occasion, too. She had been gently chiding him about how he never cleaned the bath. Then had presented him with this bath oil.

'It cleans you *and* your bath,' she had said, reading from the bottle. 'And puts the fun back into bathtime.'

He had suggested that they test this claim together, and they had. . . . Jesus, John, you're getting morbid again. Just because she's gone off with some vacuum-headed disc jockey with the unlikely name of Calum McCallum. It wasn't the end of anybody's world. The bombs weren't falling. There were no sirens in the sky.

Nothing but . . . Ronnie, Tracy, Charlie, James and the rest. And now Hyde. Rebus was beginning to know now the meaning of the term 'dead beat'. He rested his naked limbs in the near-scalding water and closed his eyes.

Thursday

*That house of voluntary bondage . . . with
its inscrutable recluse.*

Dead beat: Holmes yawned again, dead on his feet. For once, he had actually beaten the alarm, so that he was returning to bed with instant coffee when the radio blared into action. What a way to wake up every day. When he had a spare half hour, he'd retune the bloody thing to Radio Three or something. Except he knew Radio Three would send him straight back to sleep, whereas the voice of Calum McCallum and the grating records he played in between hoots and jingles and enthusiastic bad jokes brought him awake with a jolt, ready, teeth gritted, to face another day.

This morning, he had beaten the smug little voice. He switched the radio off.

'Here,' he said. 'Coffee, and time to get up.'

Nell turned her head from the pillow, squinting up at him.

'Has it gone nine?'

'Not quite.'

She turned back into the pillow again, moaning softly.

'Good. Wake me up again when it does.'

'Drink your coffee,' he chided, touching her shoulder. Her shoulder was warm, tempting. He allowed himself a wistful smile, then turned and left the bedroom. He had gone ten paces before he paused, turned, and went back. Nell's arms were long, tanned, and open in welcome.

Despite the breakfast he had brought her in the cell, Tracy

was furious with Rebus, and especially when he explained to her that she could leave whenever she wanted, that she wasn't under arrest.

'This is called *protection*,' he told her. 'Protection from the men who were chasing you. Protection from Charlie.'

'Charlie. . . .' She calmed a little at the sound of his name, and touched her bruised eye. 'But why didn't you come to see me sooner?' she complained. Rebus shrugged.

'Things to do,' he said.

He stared at her photograph now, while Brian Holmes sat on the other side of the desk, warily sipping coffee from a chipped mug. Rebus wasn't sure whether he hated Holmes or loved him for bringing this into the office, for laying it flat on the desktop in front of him. Not saying a word. No good morning, no hail fellow well met. Just this. This photograph, this nude shot. Of Tracy.

Rebus had stared at it while Holmes made his report. Holmes had worked hard yesterday, and had achieved a result. *So why had he snubbed Rebus in the bar?* If he'd seen this picture last night, it would not now be ruining his morning, not now be eroding the memory of a good night's sleep. Rebus cleared his throat.

'Did you find out anything about her?'

'No, sir,' said Holmes. 'All I got was that.' He nodded towards the photograph, his eyes unblinking: *I've given you that. What more do you want from me?*

'I see,' said Rebus, his voice level. He turned the photo over and read the small label on the back. Hutton Studios. A business telephone number. 'Right. Well, leave this with me, Brian. I'll have to give it some thought.'

'Okay,' said Holmes, thinking: *he called me Brian! He's not thinking straight this morning.*

Rebus sat back, sipping from his own mug. Coffee, milk no sugar. He had been disappointed when Holmes had asked for his coffee the same way. It gave them something in common. A taste in coffee.

140

'How's the househunting going?' he said conversationally.

'Grim. How did you . . .?' Holmes remembered the *Houses for Sale* list, folded in his jacket pocket like a tabloid newspaper. He touched it now. Rebus smiled, nodded.

'I remember buying my flat,' he said. 'I scoured those freesheets for weeks before I found a place I liked.'

'Liked?' Holmes snorted. 'That would be a bonus. The problem for me is just finding somewhere I can afford.'

'That bad, is it?'

'Haven't you noticed?' Holmes was slightly incredulous. So involved was he in the game, it was hard to believe that anyone wasn't. 'Prices are going through the roof. In fact, a roof's about all I can afford near the centre of the city.'

'Yes, I remember someone telling me about it.' Rebus was thoughtful. 'At lunch yesterday. You know I was with the people putting up the money for Farmer Watson's drugs campaign? One of them was James Carew.'

'He wouldn't be anything to do with Carew Bowyers?'

'The head honcho. Do you want me to have a word? See about a discount on your house?'

Holmes smiled. Some of the glacier between them had been chipped away. 'That would be great,' he said. 'Maybe he could arrange for a summertime sale, bargains in all departments.' Holmes started this sentence with a grin, but it trailed away with his words. Rebus wasn't listening, was lost somewhere in thought.

'Yes,' Rebus said quietly. 'I've got to have a word with Mr Carew anyway.'

'Oh?'

'To do with some soliciting.'

'Thinking of moving houses yourself?'

Rebus looked at Holmes, not comprehending. 'Anyway,' he said, 'I suppose we need a plan of attack for today.'

'Ah.' Holmes looked uncomfortable. 'I wanted to ask you about that, sir. I had a phone call this morning. I've been working for some months on a dog-fighting ring, and they're about to arrest the gang.'

'Dog fighting?'

'Yes, you know. Put two dogs in a ring. Let them tear each other to shreds. Place bets on the result.'

'I thought that died with the depression.'

'There's been a revival of late. Vicious it is, too. I could show you some photos –'

'Why the revival?'

'Who knows? People looking for kicks, something less tame than a bet at the bookie's.'

Rebus was nodding now, almost lost to his own thoughts again.

'Would you say it was a yuppie pursuit, Holmes?'

Holmes shrugged: *he's getting better. Stopped calling me by my first name.*

'Well, never mind. So you want to be in on the arrest?'

Holmes nodded. 'If possible, sir.'

'Entirely possible,' said Rebus. 'So where's it all happening?'

'I still have to check that out. Somewhere in Fife though.'

'Fife? Home territory for me.'

'Is it? I didn't know. What's that saying again . . .?'

' "Ye need a lang spoon tae sup wi' a Fifer." '

Holmes smiled. 'Yes, that's it. There's a similar saying about the devil, isn't there?'

'All it means is that we're close, Holmes, tightly knit. We don't suffer fools and strangers gladly. Now off you go to Fife and see what I'm on about.'

'Yes, sir. What about you? I mean, what will you do about . . .?' His eyes were on the photograph again. Rebus picked it up and placed it carefully in the inside pocket of his jacket.

'Don't worry about me, son. I've plenty to keep me busy. Just keeping out of range of Farmer Watson is work enough for a day. Maybe I'll take the car out. Nice day for a drive.'

'Nice day for a drive.'

Tracy was doing her best to ignore him. She stared from her passenger side window, seemingly interested in the passing parade of shops and shoppers, tourists, kids with nothing to do now the schools had broken up for summer.

She'd been keen enough to get out of the station though. He'd held the car door open for her, dissuading her from just walking away. And she'd complied, but silently, sullenly. Okay, she was in the huff with him. He'd get over it. So would she.

'Point taken,' he said. 'You're pissed off. But how many times do I have to tell you? It was for your own safety, while I was doing some checking up.'

'Where are we going?'

'Do you know this part of town?'

She was silent. There was to be no conversation. Only questions and answers: *her* questions.

'We're just driving,' he said. 'You must know this side of town. A lot of dealing used to go on around here.'

'I'm not into that!'

It was Rebus's turn to be silent. He wasn't too old to play a game or two himself. He took a left, then another, then a right.

'We've been here already,' she commented. She'd noticed then, clever girl. Still, that didn't matter. All that mattered was that slowly, by degrees, by left and right then left and right again, he was guiding them towards the destination.

He pulled into the kerb abruptly and yanked on the handbrake.

'Right,' he said. 'We're here.'

'Here?' She looked out of the side window, up at the tenement building. The red stone had been cleaned in the past year, giving it the look of a child's plasticine, pinky ochre and malleable. 'Here?' she repeated, the word choking off as she recognised the exact address, and then tried not to let that recognition show.

The photograph was on her lap when she turned from the window. She flicked it from her with a squeal, as though it were an insect. Rebus plucked the photo from the floor of the car and held it out to her.

'Yours, I believe.'

'Where the hell did you get that?'

'Do you want to tell me about it?'

Her face was as red as the stonework now, her eyes flitting in panic like a bird's. She fumbled with the seatbelt, desperate to be out of the car, but Rebus's hand on the catch was rock hard.

'Let me go!' she yelled, thumping down on his fist. Then she pushed open the door, but the camber of the road pulled it shut again. There was not enough give in the seatbelt anyway. She was securely bound.

'I thought we'd pay Mr Hutton a call,' Rebus was saying, his voice like a blade. 'Ask him about this photo. About how he paid you a few quid to model for him. About how you brought him Ronnie's pictures. Looking for a few bob more maybe, or just to spite Ronnie. Is that how it was, Tracy? I'll bet Ronnie was pissed off when he saw Hutton had stolen his ideas. Couldn't prove it though, could he? And how was he to know how the hell Hutton got them in the first place? I suppose you put the blame on Charlie, and that's why the two of you aren't exactly on speaking terms. Some friend to Ronnie you were, sweetheart. Some friend.'

She broke down at that, and gave up trying to free herself from the seatbelt. Her head angled forward into her hands, and she wept, loudly and at length. While Rebus caught his breath. He wasn't proud of himself, but it had needed saying. She had to stop hiding from the truth. It was all conjecture, of course, but Rebus was sure Hutton could confirm the details if pressed. She had modelled for money, maybe happened to mention that her boyfriend was a photographer. Had taken the photos to Hutton, giving away Ronnie's glimmer of a chance, his creativity, for a few more pound notes. If you couldn't trust your friends, who could you trust?

He had left her overnight in the cells to see if she would crack. She hadn't, so he supposed she must be clean. But that didn't mean she didn't have some kind of habit. If not needles, then something else. Everybody needed a little something, didn't they? And the money was needed, too. So she had ripped off her boyfriend. . . .

'Did you plant that camera in Charlie's squat?'

'No!' It was as though, after all that had gone before, the accusation still hurt. Rebus nodded. So Charlie had taken the camera, or someone else had planted it there. For him to find. No . . . not quite, because *he* hadn't found it: McCall had. And very easily at that, the way he had blithely found the dope in the sleeping bag. A true copper's nose? Or something else? A little information perhaps, *inside* information? If you can't trust your friends. . . .

'Did you see the camera the night Ronnie died?'

'It was in his room, I'm sure it was.' She blinked back the tears and wiped her nose on the handkerchief Rebus gave her. Her voice was cracked still, her throat a little clogged, but she was recovering from the shock of the photo, and the greater shock that Rebus knew now of her betrayal.

'That guy who came to see Ronnie, he was in Ronnie's room after me.'

'You mean Neil?'

'I think that was his name, yes.'

Too many cooks, Rebus was thinking. He was going to have to revise his definition of 'circumstantial'. He had very little so far that *wasn't* circumstantial. It felt like the spiral was widening, taking him further and further away from the central, crucial point, the point where Ronnie lay dead on a damp, bare floor, flanked by candles and dubious friends.

'Neil was Ronnie's brother.'

'Really?' Her voice was disinterested. The safety curtain between her and the world was coming down again. The matinee was over.

'Yes, really.' Rebus felt a sudden chill. If nobody, *nobody* cares what happened to Ronnie except Neil and me, why am I bothering?

'Charlie always thought they had some kind of gay thing going. I never asked Ronnie. I don't suppose he would have told me.' She rested her head against the back of the seat, seeming to relax again. 'Oh God.' She released a whistle of breath from her lungs. 'Do we have to stick around here?'

Her hands were rising slowly, ready to clasp her head, and Rebus was beginning to answer in the negative, when he saw those same hands come swiftly down, curling into tiny fists. There was no room to escape them, and so they hit him full in the groin. A flashgun exploded somewhere behind his eyes, the world turning into nothing but sound and blinding pain. He was roaring, doubled up in agony, head coming to rest on the steering wheel, which was also the car's horn. It was blaring lazily as Tracy undid her seatbelt, opened the door, and swivelled out of the car. She left the door wide open as she ran. Rebus watched through eyes brimming with tears, as if he were in a

146

swimming pool, watching her running along the edge of the pool away from him, chlorine stinging his pupils.

'Jesus Almighty Christ,' he gasped, still hunched over the wheel, and not about to move for some considerable time.

Think like Tarzan, his father had told him once: one of the old man's few pieces of advice. He was talking about fights. About one-to-one scrapes with the lads at school. Four o'clock behind the bike shed, and all that. *Think like Tarzan. You're strong, king of the jungle, and above all else you're going to protect your nuts.* And the old boy had raised a bent knee towards young John's crotch. . . .

'Thanks, Dad,' Rebus hissed now. 'Thanks for reminding me.' Then the reaction hit his stomach.

By lunchtime he could just about walk, so long as he kept his feet close to the ground, moving as though he had wet himself. People stared, of course, and he tried to improvise a limp specially for them. Ever the crowd pleaser.

The thought of the stairs to his office was too much, and driving the car had been excruciating, the foot pedals impossible to operate. So he had taken a taxi to the Sutherland Bar. Three quarter-gill measures of whisky later, he felt the pain replaced by a drowsy numbness.

'"As though of hemlock . . .",' he muttered to himself.

He wasn't worried about Tracy. Anyone with a punch like that could look after herself. There were probably kids on the street harder than half the bloody police force. Not that Tracy was a kid. He still hadn't found out anything about her. That was supposed to be Holmes's department, but Holmes was off on a wild dog chase in Fife. No, Tracy would be all right. Probably there had been no men chasing her. But then why come to him that night? There could be a hundred reasons. After all, she'd conned a bed, the best part of a bottle of wine, a hot bath and breakfast out of him. Not bad going that, and him supposed to be a

147

hardened old copper. Too old maybe. Too much the 'copper', not enough the police officer. Maybe.

Where to next? He already had the answer to that, legs permitting and pray God he could drive.

He parked at a distance from the house, not wanting to scare off anyone who might be there. Then he simply walked up to the door and knocked. Standing there, awaiting a response, he remembered Tracy opening that door and running into his arms, her face bruised, her eyes welling with tears. He didn't think Charlie would be here. He didn't think Tracy would be here. He didn't *want* Tracy to be here.

The door opened. A bleary teenage boy squinted up at Rebus. His hair was lank, lifeless, falling into his eyes.

'What is it?'

'Is Charlie in? I've got a bit of business with him.'

'Naw. Havenae seen him the day.'

'All right if I wait a while?'

'Aye.' The boy was already closing the door on Rebus's face. Rebus stuck a hand up against the door and peered round it.

'I meant, wait indoors.'

The boy shrugged, and slouched back inside, leaving the door ajar. He slipped back into his sleeping bag and pulled it over his head. Just passing through, and catching up on lost sleep. Rebus supposed the boy had nothing to lose by letting a stranger into this way station. He left him to his sleep, and, after a cursory check that there was no one else in the downstairs rooms, climbed the steep staircase.

The books were still slewed like so many felled dominoes, the contents of the bag McCall had emptied still lying in a clutter on the floor. Rebus ignored these and went to the desk, where he sat, studying the pieces of paper in front of him. He had flicked on the light switch beside the door of Charlie's room, and now switched on the desk lamp, too. The walls were miraculously free from posters, postcards and the like. It wasn't like a student's room. Its identity had been left suspended, which was probably exactly the way Charlie wanted it. He didn't want to look like a student to his drop-out friends; he didn't want to look like a drop-out to his student friends. He wanted to be all things to all people. Chameleon, then, as well as tourist.

The essay on Magick was Rebus's main interest, but he gave the rest of the desk a good examination while he was here. Nothing out of the ordinary. Nothing to suggest that Charlie was pushing bad drugs around the city streets. So Rebus picked up the essay, opened it, and began to read.

Nell liked the library when it was quiet like this. During term time, a lot of the students used it as a meeting place, a sort of glorified youth club. Then, the first-floor reading room was filled with noise. Books tended to be left lying everywhere, or to go missing, to be shifted out of their proper sections. All very frustrating. But during the summer months, only the most determined of the students came in: the ones with a thesis to write, or work to catch up on, or those precious few who were passionate about their chosen fields, and who were giving up sunshine and freedom to be here, indoors, in studied silence.

She got to know their faces, and then their names. Conversations could be struck up in the deserted coffee shop, authors' names swopped. And at lunchtime, one could sit in the gardens, or walk behind the library building onto The Meadows, where more books were being read, more faces rapt in thought.

Of course, summer was also the time for the library's most tedious jobs. The check on stock, the rebinding of misused volumes. Reclassification, computer updating, and so on. The atmosphere more than made up for all this. All traces of hurry and haste were gone. No more complaints about there being too few copies of this or that title, desperately needed by a class of two hundred for some overdue essay. But after the summer there would be a new intake, and with every year's fresh intake, she felt that whole year older, and more distanced from the students. They already seemed hopelessly young to her, a glow surrounding them, reminding her of something she could never have.

She was sorting through request forms when the commotion began. The guard on the library entrance had stopped someone who was trying to get in without any identification. Normally, Nell knew, the guard wouldn't have worried, but the girl was so obviously distraught, so obviously not a reader, not even a student. She was loudly argumentative, where a real student would have quietly explained that they had forgotten to bring their matriculation card with them. There was something else, too . . . Nell frowned, trying to place the girl. Catching her profile, she remembered the photograph in Brian's briefcase. Yes, it was the same girl. No girl, really, but a fully grown, if youthful, woman. The lines around the eyes were the giveaway, no matter how slender the body, how fashionably young the clothes. But why was she making this fuss? She'd always gone to the coffee shop, had never, to Nell's knowledge, tried to get into the library proper before now. Nell's curiosity was aroused.

The guard was holding Tracy by the arm, and she was shrieking abuse at him, her eyes frantic. Nell tried to be authoritarian in her walk as she approached the pair of them.

'Is there some problem, Mr Clarke?'

'I can handle it, miss.' His eyes betrayed his words. He was sweating, past retirement age, neither used to this sort of physical struggle nor knowing what to do about it. Nell turned to the girl.

'You can't just barge in here, you know. But if you want a message passed on to one of the students inside, I'll see what I can do.'

The girl struggled again. 'I just want to come in!' All reasoning had gone now. She knew only that if someone was stopping her getting in, then she *had* to get in somehow.

'Well you can't,' Nell said angrily. She should not have interfered. She was used to dealing with quiet, sane, rational people. Okay, some of them might lose their tempers momentarily when frustrated in their search for a book. But they would always remember their place. The girl stared at her, and the stare seemed absolutely malevolent. There was no trace of human kindness in it at all. Nell felt the hairs on her neck bristle. Then the girl gave a banshee wail, throwing herself forward, loosing the guard's grip. Her forehead smashed into Nell's face, sending the librarian flying, feet rooted to the spot, so that she fell like so much timber. Tracy stood there for a moment, seeming to come to herself. The guard made to grab her, but she gave another yell, and he backed off. Then she pushed past him out of the library doors and started running again, head down, arms and legs uncoordinated. The guard watched her, fearful still, then turned his attention to the bloody and unconscious face of Nell Stapleton.

The man who answered the door was blind.

'Yes?' he asked, holding the door, sightless eyes discernible behind the dark green lenses of his glasses. The hallway behind him was in deep shadow. What need had it of light?

'Mr Vanderhyde?'

The man smiled. 'Yes?' he repeated. Rebus couldn't take his own eyes off those of the elderly man. Those green lenses reminded him of claret bottles. Vanderhyde would be sixty-five, maybe seventy. His hair was silvery yellow, thick, well groomed. He was wearing an open-necked shirt, brown waistcoat, a watch chain hanging from one pocket. And he was leaning ever so slightly on a silver-topped stick. For some reason, Rebus had the idea that Vanderhyde would be able to handle that cane swiftly and effectively as a weapon, should anyone unpleasant ever come calling.

'Mr Vanderhyde, I'm a police officer.' Rebus was reaching for his wallet.

'Don't bother with identification, unless it's in braille.' Vanderhyde's words stopped Rebus short, his hand frozen in his inside jacket pocket.

'Of course,' he mumbled, feeling ever so slightly ridiculous. Funny how people with disabilities had that special gift of making you seem so much less able than them.

'You'd better come in, Inspector.'

'Thank you.' Rebus was in the hall before it hit him. 'How did you –?'

Vanderhyde shook his head. 'A lucky guess,' he said, leading the way. 'A shot in the dark, you might say.' His laughter was abrasive. Rebus, studying what he could see of the hall, was wondering how even a blind man could make such a botched job of interior decoration. A stuffed owl stared down from its dusty pedestal, next to an umbrella stand which seemed to consist of a hollowed elephant's foot. An ornately carved occasional table boasted a pile of unread mail and a cordless telephone. Rebus gave this latter item most attention.

'Technology has made such progress, don't you agree?' Vanderhyde was saying. 'Invaluable for those of us who have lost one of the senses.'

'Yes,' Rebus replied, as Vanderhyde opened the door to another room, almost as dark to Rebus's eyes as the hall.

'In here, Inspector.'

'Thank you.' The room was musty, and smelled of old people's medicaments. It was comfortably furnished, with a deep sofa and two robust armchairs. Books lay behind glass along one wall. Some uninspired watercolours stopped the other walls from seeming bare. There were ornaments everywhere. Those on the mantelpiece caught Rebus's eye. There wasn't a spare centimetre of space on the deep wooden mantelpiece, and the ornaments were exotic. Rebus could identify African, Caribbean, Asian and Oriental influences, without being able to pinpoint any one country for any one piece.

Vanderhyde flopped into a chair. It struck Rebus that there were no occasional tables scattered through the room, no extraneous furniture into which the blind man might bump.

'Nick-nacks, Inspector. Gewgaws collected on my travels as a younger man.'

'Evidence of a lot of travel.'

'Evidence of a magpie mind,' Vanderhyde corrected. 'Would you care for some tea?'

'No, thank you, sir.'

'Something a little stronger perhaps?'

'Thank you, but no.' Rebus smiled. 'I'd a bit too much last night.'

'Your smile comes over in your voice.'

'You don't seem curious as to why I'm here, Mr Vanderhyde.'

'Perhaps that's because I *know*, Inspector. Or, perhaps it's because my patience is limitless. Time doesn't mean as much to me as to most people. I'm in no hurry for your explanations. I'm not a clock watcher, you see.' He was smiling again, eyes fixed somewhere just right of Rebus and above him. Rebus stayed silent, inviting further speculation. 'Then again,' Vanderhyde continued, 'since I no longer go out, and have few visitors, and since I have never to my knowledge broken the laws of the land, that certainly narrows the possible reasons for your visit. You're sure you won't have some tea?'

'Don't let me stop you making some for yourself.' Rebus had spotted the near-empty mug sitting on the floor beside the old man's chair. He looked down around his own chair. Another mug sat on the muted pattern of the carpet. He reached a silent arm down towards it. There was a slight warmth on the base of the mug, a warmth on the carpet beneath.

'No,' Vanderhyde said. 'I had one just recently. As did my visitor.'

'Visitor?' Rebus sounded surprised. The old man smiled, giving a slight and indulgent shake of his head. Rebus, feeling caught, decided to push on anyway. 'I thought you said you didn't get many visitors?'

'No, I don't recall *quite* saying that. Still, it happens to be true. Today is the exception that proves the rule. Two visitors.'

'Might I ask who the other visitor was?'

'Might *I* ask, Inspector, why you're here?'

It was Rebus's turn to smile, nodding to himself. The blood was rising in the old man's cheeks. Rebus had succeeded in riling him.

'Well?' There was impatience in Vanderhyde's voice.

'Well, sir.' Rebus deliberately pulled himself out of the chair and began to circuit the room. 'I came across your name in an undergraduate essay on the occult. Does that surprise you?'

The old man considered this. 'It pleases me slightly. I do have an ego that needs feeding, after all.'

'But it doesn't surprise you?' Vanderhyde shrugged. 'This essay mentioned you in connection with the workings of an Edinburgh-based group, a sort of coven, working in the nineteen sixties.'

' "Coven" is an inexact term, but never mind.'

'You were involved in it?'

154

'I don't deny the fact.'

'Well, while we're dealing in fact, you were, more correctly, its guiding light. "Light" may be an inexact term.'

Vanderhyde laughed, a piping, discomfiting sound. 'Touché, Inspector. Indeed, touché. Do continue.'

'Finding your address wasn't difficult. Not too many Vanderhydes in the phone book.'

'My kin are based in London.'

'The reason for my visit, Mr Vanderhyde, is a murder, or at the very least a case of tampering with evidence at the scene of a death.'

'Intriguing.' Vanderhyde put his hands together, fingertips to his lips. It was hard to believe the man was sightless. Rebus's movements around the room were failing to have any effect on Vanderhyde at all.

'The body was discovered lying with arms stretched wide, legs together –'

'Naked?'

'No, not quite. Shirtless. Candles had been burning either side of the body, and a pentagram had been painted on one wall.'

'Anything else?'

'No. There were some syringes in a jar by the body.'

'The death was caused by an overdose of drugs?'

'Yes.'

'Hmm.' Vanderhyde rose from his chair and walked unerringly to the bookcase. He did not open it, but stood as though staring at the titles. 'If we're dealing with a sacrifice, Inspector – I take it that's your theory?'

'One of many, sir.'

'Well, *if* we are dealing with a sacrifice, then the means of death are quite unusual. No, more than that, are unheard of. To begin with, very few Satanists would ever contemplate a human sacrifice. Plenty of psychopaths have carried out murder and then excused it as ritual, but

155

that's something else again. But in any case, a human sacrifice – a sacrifice of any kind – requires blood. Symbolic in some rites, as in the blood and body of Christ. Real in others. A sacrifice *without* blood? That would be original. And to administer an overdose. . . . No, Inspector, surely the more plausible explanation is that, as you say, someone muddied the water as it were, after the life had expired.'

Vanderhyde turned into the room again, picking out Rebus's position. He raised his arms high, to signal that this was all he had to offer.

Rebus sat down again. The mug when he touched it was no longer warm. The evidence had cooled, dissipated, vanished.

He picked up the mug and looked at it. It was an innocent thing, patterned with flowers. There was a single crack running downwards from its rim. Rebus felt a sudden surge of confidence in his own abilities. He got to his feet again and walked to the door.

'Are you leaving?'

He did not reply to Vanderhyde's question, but walked smartly to the bottom of the dark oak staircase. Halfway up, it twisted in a ninety-degree angle. From the bottom, Rebus's view was of this halfway point, this small landing. A second before, there had been someone there, someone crouching, listening. He hadn't seen the figure so much as *sensed* it. He cleared his throat, a nervous rather than necessary action.

'Come down here, Charlie.' He paused. Silence. But he could still sense the young man, just beyond that turning on the stairs. 'Unless you want me to come up. I don't think you want that, do you? Just the two of us, up there in the dark?' More silence, broken by the shuffling of Vanderhyde's carpet-slippered feet, the walking cane tapping against the floor. When Rebus looked round, the old man's jaw was set defiantly. He still had his pride. Rebus wondered if he felt any shame.

Then the single creak of a floorboard signalled Charlie's presence on the stair landing.

Rebus broke into a smile: of conquest, of relief. He had trusted himself, and had proved worthy of that trust.

'Hello, Charlie,' he said.

'I didn't mean to hit her. She had a go at me first.'

The voice was recognisable, but Charlie seemed rooted to the landing. His body was slightly hunched, his face in silhouette, his arms hanging by his side. The educated voice seemed discorporate, somehow not part of this shadow-puppet.

'Why don't you join us?'

'Are you going to arrest me?'

'What's the charge?' The question was Rebus's, his voice tinged with amusement.

'That should be *your* question, Charles,' Vanderhyde called out, making it sound like an instruction.

Rebus was suddenly bored with these games. 'Come on down,' he commanded. 'Let's have another mug of Earl Grey.'

Rebus had pulled open the crimson velvet curtains in the living room. The interior seemed less cramped in what was left of the daylight, less overpowering, and certainly a lot less gothic. The ornaments on the mantelpiece were revealed as just that: ornaments. The books in the bookcase were revealed as by and large works of popular fiction: Dickens, Hardy, Trollope. Rebus wondered if Trollope *was* still popular.

Charlie had made tea in the narrow kitchen, while Vanderhyde and Rebus sat in silence in the living room, listening to the distant sounds of cups chinking and spoons ringing.

'You have good hearing,' Vanderhyde stated at last.

Rebus shrugged. He was still assessing the room. No, he couldn't live here, but he could at least imagine visiting some aged relative in such a place.

'Ah, tea,' said Vanderhyde as Charlie brought in the unsteady tray. Placing it on the floor between chairs and sofa, his eyes sought Rebus's. They had an imploring look. Rebus ignored it, accepting his cup with a curt nod of the head. He was just about to say something about how well Charlie seemed to know his way around his chosen bolt-hole, when Charlie himself spoke. He was handing a mug to Vanderhyde. The mug itself was only half filled – a wise precaution – and Charlie sought out the old man's hand, guiding it to the large handle.

'There you go, Uncle Matthew,' he said.

'Thank you, Charles,' said Vanderhyde, and if he had been sighted, his slight smile would have been directed straight at Rebus, rather than a few inches over the detective's shoulder.

'Cosy,' Rebus commented, sipping the dry perfume of Earl Grey.

Charlie sat on the sofa, crossing his legs, almost relaxed. Yes, he knew this room well, was slipping into it the way one slipped into an old, comfortable pair of trousers. He might have spoken, but Vanderhyde seemed to want to put his points forward first.

'Charles has told me all about it, Inspector Rebus. Well, when I say that, I mean he has told me as much as he deems it necessary for me to know.' Charlie glared at his uncle, who merely smiled, knowing the frown was there. 'I've already told Charles that he should talk to you again. He seems unwilling. *Seemed* unwilling. Now the choice has been taken away from him.'

'How did you know?' asked Charlie, so much more at home here, Rebus was thinking, than in some ugly squat in Pilmuir.

'Know?' said Rebus.

'Know where to find me? Know about Uncle Matthew?'

'Oh, that.' Rebus picked at invisible threads on his trousers. 'Your essay. It was sitting on your desk. Handy that.'

'What?'

'Doing an essay on the occult, and having a warlock in the family.'

Vanderhyde chuckled. 'Not a warlock, Inspector. Never that. I think I've only ever met one warlock, one *true* warlock, in my whole life. Local he is, mind.'

'Uncle Matthew,' Charlie interrupted, 'I don't think the Inspector wants to hear –'

'On the contrary,' said Rebus. 'It's the reason I'm here.'

'Oh.' Charlie sounded disappointed. 'Not to arrest me then?'

'No, though you deserve a good slap for that bruise you gave Tracy.'

'She deserved it!' Charlie's voice betrayed petulance, his lower lip filling out like a child's.

'You struck a woman?' Vanderhyde sounded aghast. Charlie looked towards him, then away, as if unable to hold a stare that didn't – couldn't – exist.

'Yes,' Charlie hissed. 'But look.' He pulled the polo-necked jumper down from around his neck. There were two huge weals there, the result of prising fingernails.

'Nice scratches,' Rebus commented for the blind man's benefit. 'You got the scratches, she got a bruise on her eye. I suppose that makes it neck and neck in the eye-for-an-eye stakes.'

Vanderhyde chuckled again, leaning forward slightly on his cane.

'Very good, Inspector,' he said. 'Yes, very good. Now –' he lifted the mug to his lips and blew. 'What can we do for you?'

'I saw your name in Charlie's essay. There was a footnote quoting you as an interview source. I reckoned that made you local and reasonably extant, and there aren't too many –'

'– Vanderhydes in the phone book,' finished the old man. 'Yes, you said.'

'But you've already answered most of my questions. Concerning the black magic connection, that is. However, I would just like to clear up a few points with your nephew.'

'Would you like me to –?' Vanderhyde was already rising to his feet. Rebus waved for him to stay, then realised the gesture was in vain. However, Vanderhyde had already paused, as though anticipating the action.

'No, sir,' Rebus said now, as Vanderhyde seated himself again. 'This'll only take a couple of minutes.' He turned to Charlie, who was almost sinking into the deep padded cushions of the sofa. 'So, Charlie,' Rebus began. 'I've got you down this far as thief, and as accessory to murder. Any comments to make?'

Rebus watched with pleasure as the young man's face lost its tea-like colour and became more like uncooked pastry. Vanderhyde twitched, but with pleasure, too, rather than discomfort. Charlie looked from one man to the other, seeking friendly eyes. The eyes he saw were blind to his pleas.

'I – I –'

'Yes?' Rebus prompted.

'I'll just fill my cup,' Charlie said, as though only these five meagre words were left in his vocabulary. Rebus sat back patiently. Let the bugger fill and refill and boil another brew. But he'd have his answers. He'd make Charlie sweat tannin, and he'd have his answers.

'Is Fife always this bleak?'

'Only the more picturesque bits. The rest's no' bad at a'.'

The SSPCA officer was guiding Brian Holmes across a

twilit field, the area around almost completely flat, a dead tree breaking the monotony. A fierce wind was blowing, and it was a cold wind, too. The SSPCA man had called it an 'aist wind'. Holmes assumed that 'aist' translated as 'east', and that the man's sense of geography was somewhat askew, since the wind was clearly blowing from the west.

The landscape proved deceptive. Seeming flat, the land was actually slanting. They were climbing a slope, not steep but perceptible. Holmes was reminded of some hill somewhere in Scotland, the 'electric brae', where a trick of natural perspective made you think you were going uphill when in fact you were travelling *down*. Or was it vice versa? Somehow, he didn't think his companion was the man to ask.

Soon, over the rise, Holmes could see the black, grainy landscape of a disused mineworking, shielded from the field by a line of trees. The mines around here were all worked out, had been since the 1960s. Now, money had appeared from somewhere, and the long-smouldering bings were being levelled, their mass used to fill the chasms left by surface mining. The mine buildings themselves were being dismantled, the landscape reseeded, as though the history of mining in Fife had never existed.

This much Brian Holmes knew. His uncles had been miners. Not here perhaps, but nevertheless they had been great deep workings of information and anecdote. The child Brian had stored away every detail.

'Grim,' he said to himself as he followed the SSPCA officer down a slight slope towards the trees, where a cluster of half a dozen men stood, shuffling, turning at the sound of approach. Holmes introduced himself to the most senior-looking of the plain-clothes men.

'DC Brian Holmes, sir.'

The man smiled, nodded, then jerked his head in the

direction of a much younger man. Everyone, uniformeds, plain-clothes, even the SSPCA Judas, was smiling, enjoying Holmes's mistake. He felt a rush of blood to his face, and was rooted to the spot. The young man saw his discomfort and stuck out a hand.

'I'm DS Hendry, Brian. Sometimes I'm in charge here.' There were more smiles. Holmes joined in this time.

'Sorry, sir.'

'I'm flattered actually. Nice to think I'm so young-looking, and Harry here's so old.' He nodded towards the man Holmes had mistaken for the senior officer. 'Right, Brian. I'll just tell you what I've been telling the lads. We have a good tip that there's going to be a dog fight here tonight. It's secluded, half a mile from the main road, a mile from the nearest house. Perfect, really. There's a track the lorries take from the main road up to the site here. That's the way they'll come in, probably three or four vans carrying the dogs, and then who knows how many cars with the punters. If it gets to Ibrox proportions, we'll call in reinforcements. As it is, we're not bothered so much about nabbing punters as about catching the handlers themselves. The word is that Davy Brightman's the main man. Owns a couple of scrap yards in Kirkcaldy and Methil. We know he keeps a few pit bulls, and we think he fights them.'

There was a blast of static from one of the radios, then a call sign. DS Hendry responded.

'Do you have a Detective Constable Holmes with you?' came the message. Hendry stared at Holmes as he handed him the radio. Holmes could only look apologetic.

'DC Holmes speaking.'

'DC Holmes, we've a message for you.'

'Go ahead,' said Holmes.

'It's to do with a Miss Nell Stapleton.'

Sitting in the hospital waiting room, eating chocolate

from a vending machine, Rebus went over the day's events in his mind. Remembering the incident with Tracy in the car, his scrotum began to rise up into his body in an act of self-protection. Painful still. Like a double hernia, not that he'd ever had one.

But the afternoon had been very interesting indeed. Vanderhyde had been interesting. And Charlie, well, Charlie had sung like a bird.

'What is it you want to ask me?' he had said, bringing more tea into the living room.

'I'm interested in time, Charlie. Your uncle has already told me that *he's* not interested in time. He isn't ruled by it, but policemen are. Especially in a case like this. You see, the chronology of events isn't quite right in my mind. That's what I want to clear up, if possible.'

'All right,' Charlie said. 'How can I help?'

'You were at Ronnie's that night?'

'Yes, for a while.'

'And you left to look for some party or other?'

'That's right.'

'Leaving Neil in the house with Ronnie?'

'No, he'd left by then.'

'You didn't know, of course, that Neil was Ronnie's brother?'

The look of surprise on Charlie's face seemed authentic, but then Rebus knew him for an accomplished actor, and was taking nothing for granted, not any more.

'No, I didn't know that. Shit, his brother. Why didn't he want any of us to meet him?'

'Neil and I are in the same profession,' Rebus explained. Charlie just smiled and shook his head. Vanderhyde was leaning back thoughtfully in his chair, like a meticulous juror at some trial.

'Now,' Rebus continued, 'Neil says he left quite early. Ronnie was being uncommunicative.'

'I can guess why.'

'Why?'

'Easy. He'd just scored, hadn't he? He hadn't seen any stuff for ages, and suddenly he'd scored.' Charlie suddenly remembered that his aged uncle was listening, and stopped short, looking towards the old man. Vanderhyde, shrewd as ever, seemed to sense this, and waved his hand regally before him, as if to say, I've been too long on this planet and can't be shocked any more.

'I think you're right,' Rebus said to Charlie. 'One hundred percent. So, in an empty house, Ronnie shoots up. The stuff's lethal. When Tracy comes in, she finds him in his room –'

'So *she* says,' interrupted Charlie. Rebus nodded, acknowledging his scepticism.

'Let's accept for the moment that's what happened. He's dead, or seems so to her. She panics, and runs off. Right. So far so good. Now it begins to get hazy, and this is where I need your help, Charlie. Thereafter, someone moves Ronnie's body downstairs. I don't know why. Maybe they were just playing silly buggers, or, as Mr Vanderhyde put it so succinctly, trying to muddy the water. Anyway, around this stage in the chronology, a second packet of white powder appears. Tracy only saw one –' Rebus saw that Charlie was about to interrupt again '– so she says. So, Ronnie had one packet and shot up with it. When he died, his body came downstairs and another packet magically appeared. This new packet contains good stuff, not the poison Ronnie used on himself. And, to add a little more to the concoction, Ronnie's camera disappears, to turn up later in your squat, Charlie, in your room, and in your black polythene bag.'

Charlie had stopped looking at Rebus. He was looking at the floor, at his mug, at the teapot. His eyes still weren't on Rebus when he spoke.

'Yes, I took it.'

'You took the camera?'

'I just said I did, didn't I?'

'Okay.' Rebus's voice was neutral. Charlie's smoulder-ing shame might at any moment catch light and ignite into anger. 'When did you take it?'

'Well, I didn't exactly stop to look at my watch.'

'Charles!' Vanderhyde's voice was loud, the word coming from his mouth like a bite. Charlie took notice. He straightened in his chair, reduced to some childhood fear of this imposing creature, his uncle the magician.

Rebus cleared his throat. The taste of Earl Grey was thick on his tongue. 'Was there anyone in the house when you got back?'

'No. Well, yes, if you're counting Ronnie.'

'Was he upstairs or down?'

'He was at the top of the stairs, if you must know. Just lying there, like he'd been trying to come down them. I thought he was crashed out. But he didn't look right. I mean, when someone's sleeping, there's *some* kind of movement. But Ronnie was . . . rigid. His skin was cold, damp.'

'And he was at the top of the stairs?'

'Yes.'

'What did you do then?'

'Well, I knew he was dead. And it was like I was dreaming. That sounds stupid, but it was like that. I know now that I was just trying to shut it out. I went into Ronnie's room.'

'Was the syringe jar there?'

'I can't remember.'

'Never mind. Go on.'

'Well, I knew that when Tracy got back –'

'Yes?'

'God, this is going to make me sound like a monster.'

'What is it?'

'Well, I knew that when she came back, she'd see

Ronnie was dead and grab what she could of his. I *knew* she would, I just felt it. So I took something I thought he'd have wanted me to have.'

'For sentimental reasons then?' asked Rebus archly.

'Not totally,' Charlie admitted. Rebus had a sudden cooling thought: *this is going too easily*. 'It was the only thing Ronnie had that was worth any money.'

Rebus nodded. Yes, that was more like it. Not that Charlie was short of a few bob; he could always rely on Uncle Matthew. But it was the illicit nature of the act that appealed. Something Ronnie would have wanted him to have. Some chance.

'So you lifted the camera?' Rebus said. Charlie nodded. 'Then you left?'

'Went straight back to my squat. Somebody said Tracy had come looking for me. Said she'd been in a right state. So I assumed she already knew about Ronnie.'

'And she hadn't made off with the camera. She'd come looking for you instead.'

'Yes.' Charlie seemed almost contrite. Almost. Rebus wondered what Vanderhyde was making of all this.

'What about the name Hyde, does it mean anything to you?'

'A character in Robert Louis Stevenson.'

'Apart from that.'

Charlie shrugged.

'What about someone called Edward?'

'A character in Robert Louis Stevenson.'

'I don't understand.'

'Sorry, I'm being facetious. Edward is Hyde's first name in *Jekyll and Hyde*. No, I don't know anyone called Edward.'

'Fair enough. Do you want to know something, Charlie?'

'What?'

Rebus looked to Vanderhyde, who sat impassively.

'Actually, I think your uncle already knows what I'm going to say.'

Vanderhyde smiled. 'Indeed. Correct me if I'm wrong, Inspector Rebus, but you were about to say that, the young man's corpse having moved from the bedroom to the stairs, you can only assume that the person who moved the body was actually in the house when Charles arrived.'

Charlie's jaw dropped open. Rebus had never witnessed the effect in real life before.

'Quite right,' he said. 'I'd say you were lucky, Charlie. I'd say that someone was moving the body downstairs and heard you arrive. Then they hid in one of the other rooms, maybe even that stinking bathroom, until you'd left. They were in the house all the time you were.'

Charlie swallowed. Then closed his mouth. Then let his head fall forward and began to weep. Not quite silently, so that his uncle caught the action, and smiled, nodding towards Rebus with satisfaction.

Rebus finished the chocolate. It had tasted of antiseptic, the same strong flavour of the corridor outside, the wards themselves, and this waiting room, where anxious faces buried themselves in old colour supplements and tried to look interested for more than a second or two. The door opened and Holmes came in, looking anxious and exhausted. He'd had the distance of a forty-minute car journey in which to mentally live his worst fears, and the result was carved into his face. Rebus knew that swift treatment was needed.

'She's fine. You can see her whenever you like. They're keeping her in overnight for no good reason at all, and she's got a broken nose.'

'A broken nose?'

'That's all. No concussion, no blurred vision. A good old broken nose, curse of the bare-knuckle fighter.'

Rebus thought for one moment that Holmes was about to take offence at his levity. But then relief flooded the younger man and he smiled, his shoulders relaxing, head dropping a little as though from a sense of anticlimax, albeit a welcome one.

'So,' Rebus said, 'do you want to see her?'

'Yes.'

'Come on, I'll take you.' He placed a hand on Holmes's shoulder and guided him out of the door again.

'But how did you know?' Holmes asked as they walked up the corridor.

'Know what?'

'Know it was Nell? Know about Nell and me?'

'Well now, you're a detective, Brian. Think about it.'

Rebus could see Holmes's mind take on the puzzle. He hoped the process was therapeutic. Finally, Holmes spoke.

'Nell's got no family, so she asked for me.'

'Well, she *wrote* asking for you. The broken nose makes it hard to understand what she's saying.'

Holmes nodded dully. 'But I couldn't be located, and you were asked if you knew where I was.'

'That's close enough. Well done. How was Fife anyway? I only get back there once a year.' *April 28th*, he thought to himself.

'Fife? It was okay. I'd to leave before the bust. That was a shame. And I don't think I exactly impressed the team I was supposed to be part of.'

'Who was in charge?'

'A young DS called Hendry.'

Rebus nodded. 'I know him. I'm surprised you don't, at least by reputation.'

Holmes shrugged. 'I just hope they nab those bastards.'

Rebus had stopped outside the door of a ward.

'This it?' Holmes asked. Rebus nodded.

'Want me to come in with you?'

168

Holmes stared at his superior with something approaching gratitude, then shook his head.

'No, it's all right. I won't stay if she's asleep. One last thing though.'

'Yes?'

'Who did it?'

Who did it. That was the hardest part to understand. Walking back along the corridor, Rebus saw Nell's puffy face, saw her distress as she tried to talk, and couldn't. She had signalled for some paper. He had taken a notebook from his pocket, and handed her his pen. Then she had written furiously for a full minute. He stopped now and took out the notebook, reading it through for the fourth or fifth time that evening.

'I was working at the library. A woman tried to push her way into the building, past the guard. Talk to him if you want to check. This woman then butted me on the face. I was trying to help, to calm her down. She must have thought I was interfering. But I wasn't. I was trying to help. She was the girl in that photograph, the nude photograph Brian had in his briefcase last night in the pub. You were there, weren't you, in the same pub as us? Not easy not to notice — the place was empty, after all. Where's Brian? Out chasing more salacious pictures for you, Inspector?'

Rebus smiled now, as he had smiled then. She had guts, that one. He rather liked her, her face taped, eyes blackened. She reminded him a lot of Gill.

So, Tracy was leaving a silvery snail's trail of chaos by which to follow her. Little bitch. Had she simply flipped, or was there a real motive for her trip to the University Library? Rebus leaned against the wall of the corridor. God, what a day. He was supposed to be between cases. Supposed to be 'tidying things up' before starting full time on the drugs campaign. He was supposed, for the sake of Christ, to be having things *easy*. That'd be the day.

The ward doors swung shut, alerting him to the figure of Brian Holmes in the corridor. Holmes seemed lacking direction, then spotted his superior and came walking briskly up the hall. Rebus wasn't sure yet whether Holmes was invaluable, or a liability. Could you be both things at once?

'Is she all right?' he asked solicitously.

'Yes. I suppose so. She's awake. Face looks a bit of a mess though.'

'Just bruises. They say the nose will heal. You'll never know it was broken.'

'Yes, that's what Nell said.'

'She talking? That's good.'

'She also told me who did it.' Holmes looked at Rebus, who looked away. 'What's this all about? What's Nell got to do with it?'

'Nothing, so far as I know. She just happened to be in the wrong place, et cetera. Chalk it down to coincidence.'

'Coincidence? That's a nice easy word to say. Put it down to "coincidence" and then we can forget all about it, is that it? I don't know what your game is, Rebus, but I'm not going to play it any longer.'

Holmes turned and stalked off along the hall. Rebus almost warned him that there was no exit at that end of the building, but favours weren't what Holmes wanted. He needed a bit of time, a break. So did Rebus, but he had some thinking to do, and the station was the best place for that.

By taking them slowly, Rebus managed the stairs to his office. He had been at his desk fully ten minutes before a craving for tea had him reaching for the telephone. Then he sat back, holding in front of him a piece of paper on which he had attempted to set out the 'facts' of the 'case'.

He was chilled by the thought that he might be wasting time and effort. A jury would have to work hard to see any crime there at all. There was no suggestion that Ronnie had not injected himself. However, he *had* been starved of his supply, despite there being no shortage of dope in the city, and someone *had* moved his body, and left behind a packet of good heroin, hoping, perhaps, that this would be tested, found clean, and therefore death by misadventure would be recorded: a simple overdose. But the rat poison had been found.

Rebus looked at the paper. Already 'perhapses' and conjecture had entered the picture. Maybe the frame wasn't right. So, turn the picture another way round, John, and start again.

Why had someone gone to the trouble of killing Ronnie? After all, the poor bugger would have topped himself given time. Ronnie had been starved of a fix, then given some, but had known this stuff to be less than pure. So doubtless he had known that the person who supplied it wanted him dead. But he had taken it anyway. . . . No, viewed this way round it was making even less sense. Start again.

Why would someone want Ronnie dead? There were several obvious answers. Because he knew something he shouldn't. Because he possessed something he shouldn't. Because he didn't possess something he should. Which was correct? Rebus didn't know. Nobody seemed to know. The picture still lacked meaning.

There was a knock on the door, and the door itself was pushed open by a constable carrying a mug of tea. The constable was Harry Todd. Rebus recognised him.

'You get around a bit, son.'

'Yes, sir,' said Todd, placing the tea on a corner of the desk, the only three square inches of wood visible from beneath a surface covering of paperwork.

'Is it quiet tonight?'

'The usual, sir. A few drunks. Couple of break-ins. Nasty car crash down near the docks.'

Rebus nodded, reaching for the tea. 'Do you know another constable, name of Neil McGrath?' Raising the mug to his lips, Rebus stared up at Todd, who had begun to blush.

'Yes, sir,' he said. 'I know him.'

'Mm-hm.' Rebus tested the tea, seeming to relish the bland flavour of milk and hot water. 'Told you to keep an eye on me, did he?'

'Sir?'

'If you happen to see him, Todd, tell him everything's fine.'

'Yes, sir.' Todd was turning to leave.

'Oh, and Todd?'

'Yes, sir?'

'Don't let me see you near me again, understood?'

'Yes, sir.' Todd was clearly downhearted. At the door, he paused, seeming to have a sudden plan that would ingratiate himself with his superior. Smiling, he turned back to Rebus.

'Did you hear about the action across in Fife, sir?'

'What action?' Rebus sounded uninterested.

'The dog fight, sir.' Rebus tried hard to still look unmoved. 'They broke up some dog fight. Guess who got arrested?'

'Malcolm Rifkind?' guessed Rebus. This deflated Todd totally. The smile left his face.

'No, sir,' he said, turning again to leave. Rebus's patience was short.

'Well who then?' he snapped.

'That disc jockey, Calum McCallum,' Todd said, closing the door after him. Rebus stared at the door for a count of five before it struck home: Calum McCallum ... Gill Templer's lover!

Rebus raised his head and let out a roar which mixed

172

laughter with a kind of twisted victory cry. And when he had stopped laughing, and was wiping his eyes with a handkerchief, he looked towards the door again and saw that it was open. There was someone standing in the doorway, watching his performance with a look of puzzlement on their face.

It was Gill Templer.

Rebus checked his watch. It was nearly one in the morning.

'Working the late shift, Gill?' he said to cover his confusion.

'I suppose you've heard,' she said, ignoring him.

'Heard what?'

She walked into the room, pushed some papers off the chair onto the floor, and sat down, looking exhausted. Rebus looked at all that paper slewed across the floor.

'The cleaners come in in the morning anyway,' he said. Then: 'I've heard.'

'Is that what all the screaming was about?'

'Oh, that.' Rebus tried to shrug it off, but could feel the blood tingling in his cheeks. 'No,' he said, 'that was just something . . . well, something else. . . .'

'Not very convincing, Rebus, you bastard.' Her words were tired. He wanted to buoy her up, tell her she was looking well or something. But it wouldn't have been true and she would just scowl at him again. So he left it. She *was* looking drawn, not enough sleep and no fun left any more. She'd just had her world locked up in a cell somewhere in Fife. They would be photographing and fingerprinting it perhaps, ready to file it away. Her life, Calum McCallum.

Life was full of surprises.

'So what can I do for you?'

She looked up at him, studying his face as though she wasn't sure who he was or why she was here. Then she shook herself awake with a twitch of the shoulders.

'It sounds corny, but I really was just passing. I dropped into the canteen for a coffee before going home, and then I heard –' She shivered again; the twitch which wasn't quite a twitch. Rebus could see how fragile she was. He hoped she wasn't going to shake apart. 'I heard about Calum. How could he do that to me, John? Keep a secret like that? I mean, where's the fun in watching dogs ripping each other –'

'That's something you'll have to ask him yourself, Gill. Can I get you some more coffee?'

'Christ no, I'm going to find it hard enough getting to sleep as it is. Tell you what I would like though, if it's not too much trouble.'

'Name it.'

'A lift home.' Rebus was already nodding agreement. 'And a hug.'

Rebus got up slowly, donned his jacket, put the pen and piece of paper in his pocket, and met her in the middle of the room. She had already risen from her chair, and, standing on reports to be read, paperwork to be signed, arrest statistics and the rest, they hugged, their arms strong. She buried her head in his shoulder. He rested his chin on her neck, staring at the closed door, rubbing her back with one hand, patting with the other. Eventually, she pulled away, head first, then chest, but still holding him with her arms. Her eyes were moist, but it was over now. She was looking a little better.

'Thanks,' she said.

'I needed it as much as you did,' said Rebus. 'Come on, let's get you home.'

Friday

The inhabitants were all doing well, it seemed, and all emulously hoping to do better still, and laying out the surplus of their grains in coquetry.

Someone was knocking on his door. An authoritarian knock, using the old brass knocker that he never cleaned. Rebus opened his eyes. The sun was streaming into his living room, a record's run-out track crackling. Another night spent in the chair, fully clothed. He'd be as well selling the mattress in the bedroom. Would anyone buy a mattress without a bed-frame?

Knockity knock knock again. Still patient. Still waiting for him to answer. His eyes were gummy, and he pushed his shirt back into his trousers as he walked from the living room to the door. He felt not too bad, considering. Not stiff, no tightness in the neck. A wash and a shave, and he might even feel human.

He opened the door, just as Holmes was about to knock again.

'Brian.' Rebus sounded genuinely pleased.

'Morning. Mind if I come in?'

'Not at all. Is Nell okay?'

'I phoned this morning. They say she had a good night.'

They were walking in the direction of the kitchen, Rebus leading. Holmes had imagined the flat would smell of beer and cigarettes, a typical bachelor pad. In fact, it was tidier than he'd expected, furnished with a modicum of taste. There were a lot of books. Rebus had never struck him as a reader. Mind you, not all the books looked as though they'd been read: bought with a rainy, dead weekend in mind. The weekend that never came.

Rebus pointed vaguely in the direction of kettle and cupboards.

'Make us some coffee, will you? I'll just take a quick shower.'

'Right.' Holmes thought that his news could probably wait. At least until Rebus was fully awake. He sought in vain for instant coffee, but found, in one cupboard, a vacuum pack of ground coffee, several months past its sell-by date. He opened it and spooned some into the teapot while the kettle was boiling. Sounds of running water came from the bathroom, and above these the tinny sound of a transistor radio. Voices. Some talk show, Holmes supposed.

While Rebus was in the bathroom, he took the opportunity to wander through the flat. The living room was huge, with a high corniced ceiling. Holmes felt a pang of jealousy. He'd never be able to buy a place like this. He was looking around Easter Road and Gorgie, near the football grounds of Hibs and Hearts respectively. He could afford a flat in both these parts of the city, a decent-sized flat, too, three bedrooms. But the rooms were small, the areas mean. He was no snob. Hell, yes he was. He wanted to live in the New Town, in Dean Village, here in Marchmont, where students philosophised in pretty coffee shops.

He wasn't overcareful with the stylus when he lifted the arm off the record. The record itself was by some jazz combo. It looked old, and he sought in vain for its sleeve. The noises from the bathroom had stopped. He walked stealthily back to the kitchen and found a tea strainer in the cutlery drawer. So he was able to keep the grounds out of the coffee he now poured into two mugs. Rebus came in, wrapped in a bath-towel, rubbing at his head with another, smaller towel. He needed to lose weight, or to exercise what weight he had. His chest was beginning to hang, pale like a carcass.

He picked up a mug and sipped.

'Mmm. The real McCoy.'

'I found it in the cupboard. No milk though.'

'Never mind. This is fine. You say you found it in the cupboard? We might make a detective of you yet. I'll just put on some togs.' And he was off again, for only two minutes this time. The clothes he came back wearing were clean, but unironed. Holmes noticed that though there was plumbing in the kitchen for a washing machine, there was no machine. Rebus seemed to read his mind.

'My wife took it when she moved out. Took a lot of stuff. That's why the place looks so bare.'

'It doesn't look bare. It looks planned.'

Rebus smiled. 'Let's go into the living room.'

Rebus motioned for Holmes to sit, then sat down himself. The chair was still warm from his night's sleep. 'I see you've already been in here.'

Holmes looked surprised. Caught. He remembered that he'd lifted the stylus off the record.

'Yes,' he said.

'That's what I like to see,' Rebus said. 'Yes, we'll make a detective of you yet, Brian.'

Holmes wasn't sure whether Rebus was being flattering or condescending. He let it go.

'Something I thought you might like to know,' he began.

'I already know,' said Rebus. 'Sorry to spoil the surprise, but I was at the station late last night, and somebody told me.'

'Last night?' Holmes was confused. 'But they only found the body this morning.'

'The body? You mean he's dead?'

'Yes. Suicide.'

'Jesus, poor Gill.'

'Gill?'

179

'Gill Templer. She was going out with him.'

'Inspector Templer?' Holmes was shocked. 'I thought she was living with that disc jockey?'

Now Rebus was confused. 'Isn't that who we're talking about?'

'No,' said Holmes. The surprise was still intact. He felt real relief.

'So who *are* we talking about?' asked Rebus with a growing sense of dread. 'Who's committed suicide?'

'James Carew.'

'Carew?'

'Yes. Found him in his flat this morning. Overdose apparently.'

'Overdose of what?'

'I don't know. Some kind of pills.'

Rebus was stunned. He recalled the look on Carew's face that night atop Calton Hill.

'Damn,' he said. 'I wanted a word with him.'

'I was wondering . . .' said Holmes.

'What?'

'I don't suppose you ever got round to asking him about getting me a flat?'

'No,' said Rebus. 'I never got the chance.'

'I was only joking,' Holmes said, realising that Rebus had taken his comment literally. 'Was he a friend? I mean, I know you met him for lunch, but I didn't realise –'

'Did he leave a note?'

'I don't know.'

'Well who *would* know?'

Holmes thought for a second. 'I think Inspector McCall was at the scene.'

'Right, come on.' Rebus was up on his feet.

'What about your coffee?'

'Sod the coffee. I want to see Tony McCall.'

'What was all that about Calum McCallum?' said Holmes, rising now.

'You mean you haven't heard?' Holmes shook his head. 'I'll tell you on the way.'

And then Rebus was on the move, grabbing jacket, getting out his keys to lock the front door. Holmes wondered what the secret was. What had Calum McCallum done? God, he hated people who hung on to secrets.

Rebus read the note as he stood in Carew's bedroom. It was elegantly written with a proper nib pen, but in one or two of the words fear could be clearly read, the letters trembling uncontrollably, scribbled out to be tried again. Good-quality writing paper too, thick and watermarked. The V12 was in a garage behind the flat. The flat itself was stunning, a museum for art deco pieces, modern art prints, and valuable first editions, locked behind glass.

This is the flipside of Vanderhyde's home, Rebus had thought as he moved through the flat. Then McCall had handed him the suicide note.

'If I am the chief of sinners, I am the chief of sufferers also.' Was that a quote from somewhere? Certainly, it was a bit prolix for a suicide note. But then Carew would have gone through draft upon draft until satisfied. It had to be exact, had to stand as his monument. 'Some day you may perhaps come to learn the right and wrong of this.' Not that Rebus needed to seek too hard. He had the queasy feeling, reading the note, that Carew's words were directed straight at him, that he was saying things only Rebus could fully understand.

'Funny sort of note to leave behind,' said McCall.

'Yes,' said Rebus.

'You met him recently, didn't you?' said McCall. 'I remember you saying. Did he seem okay then? I mean, he wasn't depressed or anything?'

'I've seen him since then.'

'Oh?'

'I was sniffing around Calton Hill a couple of nights back. He was there in his car.'

'Ah-ha.' McCall nodded. Everything was starting to make a little bit of sense.

Rebus handed back the note and went over to the bed. The sheets were rumpled. Three empty pill bottles stood in a neat line on the bedside table. On the floor lay an empty cognac bottle.

'The man went out in style,' McCall said, pocketing the note. 'He'd gone through a couple of bottles of wine before that.'

'Yes, I saw them in the living room. Lafite sixty-one. The stuff of a very special occasion.'

'They don't come more special, John.'

Both men turned as a third presence became evident in the room. It was Farmer Watson, breathing heavily from the effort of the stairs.

'This is bloody awkward,' he said. 'One of the linchpins of our campaign tops himself, and by taking a bloody overdose. How's that going to look, eh?'

'Awkward, sir,' replied Rebus, 'just as you say.'

'I do say. I do say.' Watson thrust a finger out towards Rebus. 'It's up to you, John, to make sure the media don't make a meal of this, or of us.'

'Yes, sir.'

Watson looked over towards the bed. 'Waste of a bloody decent man. What makes someone do it? I mean, look at this place. And there's an estate somewhere on one of the islands. Own business. Expensive car. Things we can only dream about. Makes you wonder, doesn't it?'

'Yes, sir.'

'Right.' Watson took a last glance towards the bed, then slapped a hand on Rebus's shoulder. 'I'm depending on you, John.'

'Yes, sir.'

McCall and Rebus watched their superior go.

'Bloody hell!' whispered McCall. 'He didn't look at me, not once. I might as well have not been there.'

'You should thank your lucky stars, Tony. I wish I had your gift of invisibility.'

Both men smiled. 'Seen enough?' McCall asked.

'Just one more circuit,' said Rebus. 'Then I'll get out of your hair.'

'Whatever you say, John. Just one thing.'

'What's that?'

'What the hell were you doing up Calton Hill in the middle of the night?'

'Don't ask,' said Rebus, blowing a kiss as he headed for the living area.

It *would* be big news locally, of course. There was no getting away from the fact. The radio stations and newspapers would have trouble deciding which headline deserved most prominence: Disc Jockey Arrested at Illegal Dog Fight or Suicide Shock of Estate Agent Giant. Well, something along those lines. Jim Stevens would have loved it, but then Jim Stevens was in London and married, by all accounts, to some girl half his age.

Rebus admired that kind of dangerous move. He had no admiration for James Carew: none. Watson was right in at least one respect: Carew had everything going for him, and Rebus was finding it difficult to believe that he would commit suicide solely because he had been spotted by a police officer on Calton Hill. No, that might have been the trigger, but there *had* to be something more. Something, perhaps, in the flat, or in the offices of Bowyer Carew on George Street.

James Carew owned a lot of books. A quick examination showed that they were for the most part expensive, impressive titles, but unread, their spines crackling as they were opened by Rebus for the first time. The top right hand section of the bookcase held several titles which interested him more than the others. Books by Genet and Alexander Trocchi, copies of Forster's *Maurice* and even *Last Exit to Brooklyn*. Poems by Walt Whitman, the text of *Torchlight Trilogy*. A mixed bag of predominantly gay reading. Nothing wrong in that. But their positioning in the bookshelves – right at the top and separated from the other titles – suggested to Rebus that here was a man ashamed of himself. There was no reason for this, not these days. . . .

Who was he kidding? AIDS had squeezed homosexuality back into the darker corners of society, and by keeping the truth a secret Carew had laid himself open to feelings of shame, and, therefore, to blackmail of all kinds.

Yes, blackmail. Suicides were occasionally victims of blackmail who could see no way out of their dilemma. Just maybe there would be some evidence, a letter or a note or something. *Anything*. Just so Rebus could prove to himself he wasn't completely paranoid.

Then he found it.

In a drawer. A locked drawer, to be sure, but the keys were in Carew's trousers. He had died in his pyjamas, and his other clothes had not been taken away with the corpse. Rebus got the keys from the bedroom and headed back to the desk in the living room. A gorgeous writing desk, antique for sure: its surface was barely large enough to accommodate a sheet of A4 paper and an elbow. What had been once a useful piece of furniture now found itself an ornament in a rich man's apartment. Rebus opened the drawer carefully and drew out a leather-bound desk diary. A page a day, the pages large. Not a diary for appointments, not locked away in darkness like that. A personal diary then. Eagerly, Rebus flipped it open. His disappointment was immediate. The pages were blank for the most part. A line or two of pencil per page was as much as there was.

Rebus cursed.

All right, John. It's better than nothing. He rested at one of the pages with some writing on it. The pencil marking was faint, neatly written. 'Jerry, 4pm'. A simple appointment. Rebus flipped to the day on which they had all met for lunch at The Eyrie. The page was blank. Good. That meant the appointments weren't of the business lunch variety. There weren't many of them. Rebus felt sure that Carew's diary at his office would be crammed. This was a much more private affair.

'Lindsay, 6.30.'

'Marks, 11am.' An early start that day, and what about that name: two individuals, each named Mark? Or one individual whose surname was Marks? Maybe even the department store . . .? The other names – Jerry, Lindsay – were androgynous, anonymous. He needed a telephone number, a location.

He turned another page. And had to look twice at what was written there. His finger ran along the letters.

'Hyde, 10pm.'

Hyde. What had Ronnie said to Tracy the night he'd died? *Hide, he's after me?* Yes, and James had given him the name, too: not hide but H-y-d-e.

Hyde!

Rebus whooped. Here was a connection, no matter how tenuous. A connection between Ronnie and James Carew. Something more than a fleeting business transaction on Calton Hill. A name. He hurried through the other pages. There were three more mentions of Hyde, always in the late evening (when Calton Hill was starting its trade), always on a Friday. Sometimes the second Friday of the month, sometimes the third. Four mentions in the course of six months.

'Anything?' It was McCall, leaning over Rebus's shoulder for a peek.

'Yes,' Rebus said. Then he changed his mind. 'No, not

really, Tony. Just an old diary, but the bugger wasn't much of a writer.'

McCall nodded and moved away. He was more interested in the hi-fi system.

'The old guy had taste,' McCall said, scrutinising it. 'Linn turntable. Know how much one of those costs, John? Hundreds. They're not showy. They're just bloody good at what they do.'

'A bit like us then,' said Rebus. He was thinking of pushing the diary into his trousers. It wasn't allowed, he knew. And what good would it do him? But with Tony McCall's back turned so conveniently. . . . No, no, he couldn't. He threw it noisily back into its drawer, shut the drawer again and locked it. He handed the key to McCall, who was still squatting in front of the hi-fi.

'Thanks, John. Nice piece of equipment this, you know.'

'I didn't know you were interested in all that stuff.'

'Since I was a kid. Had to get rid of my system when we got married. Too noisy.' He straightened. 'Are we going to find any answers here, do you think?'

Rebus shook his head. 'I think he kept all his secrets in his head. He was a very private man, after all. No, I think he's taken the answers with him to the grave.'

'Oh, well. Makes it nice and clear-cut then, doesn't it?'

'Clear as crystal, Tony,' said Rebus.

What was it the old man, Vanderhyde, had said? Something about muddying the water. Rebus had the gnawing feeling that the solution to these many conundrums was a simple one, as crystal clear as one could wish. The problem was that extraneous stories were being woven into the whole. *Do I mix my metaphors? Very well then, I mix my metaphors.* All that counted was getting to the bottom of the pool, muddied or no, and bringing up that tiny cache of treasure called the truth.

He knew, too, that the problem was one of classification. He had to break the interlinked stories into separate threads, and work from those. At the moment, he was guilty of trying to weave them all into a pattern, a pattern that might not be there. By separating them all, maybe he'd be in with a chance of solving each.

Ronnie committed suicide. So did Carew. That gave them a second thing in common to add to the name of Hyde. Some client of Carew's perhaps? Buying a substantial piece of property with money made through the dealing of hard drugs? That would be a link, for sure. Hyde. The name couldn't be real. How many Hydes were there in the Edinburgh directory? It could always be an assumed name. Male prostitutes seldom used their own names, after all. Hyde. Jekyll and Hyde. Another coincidence: Rebus had been reading Stevenson's book the night Tracy had visited. Maybe he should be looking for someone called Jekyll? Jekyll, the respectable doctor, admired by society; Hyde, his alter ego, small and brutish, a creature of the night. He remembered the shadowy forms he'd encountered by Calton Hill. . . . Could the answer be so obvious?

He parked in the only vacant bay left outside Great London Road station and climbed the familiar steps. They seemed to grow larger with the passing years, and he could swear there were more of them now than there had been when he'd first come to this place, all of – what was it? – six years ago? That wasn't so long in the span of a man's life, was it? So why did it feel so bloody Sisyphean?

'Hello, Jack,' he said to the desk sergeant, who watched him walk past without the usual nod of the head. Strange, Rebus thought. Jack had never been a cheery bugger, but he'd usually had the use of his neck muscles. He was famous for his slight bow of the head, which he could make mean anything from approbation to insult.

But today, for Rebus, nothing.

Rebus decided to ignore the slight, and went upstairs. Two constables, in the act of coming down, fell quiet as they passed him. Rebus began to redden, but kept walking, sure now that he had forgotten to zip his fly, or had somehow contrived to get a smudge on his nose. Something like that. He'd check in the privacy of his office.

Holmes was waiting for him, seated in Rebus's chair, at Rebus's desk, some property details spread across the tabletop. He began to rise as Rebus entered, gathering together the sheets of paper like a kid caught with a dirty book.

'Hello, Brian.' Rebus took off his jacket, hanging it on the back of the door. 'Listen, I want you to get me the names and addresses of all Edinburgh inhabitants whose names are Jekyll or Hyde. I know that may sound daft, but just do it. Then –'

'I think you should sit down, sir,' said Holmes tremulously. Rebus stared at him, saw the fear in the young man's eyes, and knew that the worst had happened.

Rebus pushed open the door of the interview room. His face was the colour of pickled beetroot, and Holmes, following, feared that his superior was about to suffer a coronary. There were two CID men in the room, both in their shirtsleeves as though after a hard session. They turned at Rebus's entrance, and the one who was seated rose as if for combat. On the other side of the table, the weasel-faced teenager known to Rebus as 'James' actually squealed, and flew to his feet, knocking the chair with a clatter onto the stone floor.

'Don't let him near me!' he yelled.

'Now, John –' started one detective, a Sergeant Dick. Rebus held up a hand to show that he was not here to cause violence. The detectives eyed one another, not sure whether to believe him. Then Rebus spoke, his eyes on the teenager.

'You're going to get what's coming to you, so help me.' There was calm, lucid anger in Rebus's voice. 'I'm going to have you by your balls for this, son. You better believe that. Really, you better.'

The teenager saw now that the others would restrain Rebus, that the man himself presented an empty physical threat. He sneered.

'Yeah, sure,' he said dismissively. Rebus lurched forward, but Holmes's hand was rigid against his shoulder, pulling him back.

'Leave it be, John,' the other detective, DC Cooper, cautioned. 'Just let the wheels grind round. It won't take long.'

'Too long though,' Rebus hissed, as Holmes pulled him out of the room, closing the door after them. Rebus stood in the shadowy corridor, all rage spent, head bowed. It was so very hard to believe. . . .

'Inspector Rebus!'

Rebus and Holmes both jerked their heads towards the voice. It belonged to a WPC. She looked scared, too.

'Yes?' Rebus managed, swallowing.

'The Super wants to see you in his office. I think it's urgent.'

'I'm sure it is,' said Rebus, walking towards her with such menace that she retreated hurriedly, back towards the reception area and daylight.

'It's a bloody set-up, with all due respect, sir.'

Remember the golden rule, John, Rebus thought to himself: never swear at a superior without adding that 'with all due respect'. It was something he'd learned in the Army. As long as you added that coda, the brass couldn't have you for insubordination.

'John.' Watson interlaced his fingers, studying them as

if they were the latest craze. 'John, we've got to investigate it. That's our duty. *I* know it's daft, and everyone else knows it's daft, but we've got to *show* that it's daft. That's our duty.'

'All the same, sir –'

Watson cut him off with a wave of his hand. Then started twining fingers again.

'God knows, you're already "suspended" from duty as it is, until our little campaign gets into full swing.'

'Yes, sir, but this is just what he wants.'

'He?'

'Some man called Hyde. He wants me to stop poking about in the Ronnie McGrath case. That's what this is all about. That's why it's a set-up job.'

'That's as maybe. The fact remains, a complaint has been made against you –'

'By that little bastard downstairs.'

'He says you gave him money, twenty pounds, I believe.'

'I *did* give him twenty quid, but not for a shag, for Chrissake!'

'For what then?'

Rebus made to answer, but was defeated. Why *had* he handed the teenager called James that money? He'd set himself up, all right. Hyde couldn't have done it better himself. And now James was downstairs, spilling his carefully rehearsed story to CID. And say what you liked, mud stuck. By Christ, it didn't half. No amount of soap and water would clean it off. The little toerag.

'This is playing right into Hyde's hands, sir,' Rebus tried: one last shot. 'If his story's true, why didn't he come in yesterday? Why wait till today?'

But Watson was decided.

'No, John. I want you out of here for a day or two. A week even. Take a break. Do whatever you like, but leave well alone. We'll clear it up, don't worry. We'll break his story down into pieces so small he won't be able to see them any more. One of those pieces will snap, and with it, his whole story. Don't you worry.'

Rebus stared at Watson. What he said made sense; more than that, it was actually fairly subtle and shrewd. Maybe the Farmer wasn't so agricultural in his ways after all. He sighed.

'Whatever you say, sir.'

Watson nodded, smiling.

'By the way,' he said. 'Remember that fellow Andrews, ran a club called Finlay's?'

'We had lunch with him, sir.'

'That's right. He's invited me to apply for membership.'

'Good for you, sir.'

'Apparently the waiting list's about a year long – all these rich Sassenachs coming north – but he said he could do a bit of pruning in my case. I told him not to bother. I seldom drink, and I certainly don't gamble. Still, a nice gesture all the same. Maybe I should ask him to consider you in my place. That'd give you something to do with your time off, eh?'

'Yes, sir.' Rebus seemed to consider the suggestion. Booze and gambling: not a bad combination. His face brightened. 'Yes, sir,' he said. 'That would be very kind of you.'

'I'll see what I can do then. One last thing.'

'Yes, sir?'

'Are you intending to go to Malcolm Lanyon's party tonight? Remember, he invited us at The Eyrie?'

'I'd forgotten all about it, sir. Would it be more . . . proper for me to stay away?'

'Not at all. I may not manage along myself, but I see no reason why you shouldn't attend. But not a word about. . . .' Watson nodded towards the door, and by implication to the interview room beyond.

'Understood, sir. Thank you.'

'Oh, and John?'

'Yes, sir?'

'Don't swear at me. Ever. With respect or otherwise. Okay?'

Rebus felt his cheeks reddening, not in anger but in shame. 'Yes, sir,' he said, making his exit.

Holmes was waiting impatiently in Rebus's office.

'What did he want then?'

'Who?' Rebus was supremely nonchalant. 'Oh, Watson you mean? He wanted to tell me that he's put my name forward for Finlay's.'

'Finlay's Club?' Holmes' face was quizzical; this wasn't what he'd been expecting at all.

'That's right. At my age, I think I deserve a club in town, don't you?'

'I don't know.'

'Oh, and he also wanted to remind me about a party tonight at Malcolm Lanyon's place.'

'The lawyer?'

'That's him.' Rebus had Holmes at a disadvantage, and knew it. 'I hope you've been busy while I've been having a chinwag.'

'Eh?'

'Hydes and Jekylls, Brian. I asked you for addresses.'

'I've got the list here. Not too long, thank the Lord. I suppose I'm going to be Shoeleather on this one?'

Rebus looked flabbergasted. 'Not at all. You've got better things to be doing with your time. No, I think this time the shoeleather ought to be mine.'

'But . . . with respect, shouldn't you be keeping out of things?'

'With respect, Brian, that's none of your bloody business.'

From home, Rebus tried phoning Gill, but she couldn't be reached. Keeping out of things, no doubt. She had been quiet during the drive home last night, and hadn't invited him in. Fair enough, he supposed. He wasn't about to take advantage. . . . So why was he trying to telephone her? Of course he was trying to take advantage! He wanted her back.

He tidied the living room, did some washing up, and took a binbag's-worth of dirty washing to the local laundrette for a service wash. The attendant, Mrs Mackay, was full of outrage about Calum McCallum.

'Yon's a celebrity and a'. They should ken better.'

Rebus smiled and nodded agreement.

Back in the flat, he sat down and picked up a book, knowing he wouldn't be able to keep his mind on it. He didn't want Hyde to win, and, kept away from the case, that's exactly what would happen. He took the slip of paper from his pocket. There were no people with the surname Jekyll in the Lothians, and a scant dozen with the surname Hyde. At least, those were the ones he could be sure about. What if Hyde possessed an unlisted number? He'd get Brian Holmes to check the possibility.

He reached for the telephone and was halfway through the number before he realised he was calling Gill's office. He punched in the rest of the number. What the hell, she wouldn't be there anyway.

'Hello?'

It was Gill Templer's voice, sounding as unflappable as ever. Yes, but that sort of trick was easy by phone. All the oldest tricks were.

'It's John.'

'Hello there. Thanks for the lift home.'

'How are you?'

'I'm fine, honestly. I just feel a bit . . . I don't know, confused doesn't seem to cover it. I feel as though I've been conned. That's as near as I can get to an explanation.'

'Are you going to see him?'

'What? In Fife? No, I don't think so. It's not that I couldn't face *him*. I *want* to see *him*. It's the thought of walking into the station with everyone knowing who I was, why I was there.'

'I'd go with you, Gill, if you wanted.'

'Thanks, John. Maybe in a day or two. But not yet.'

'Understood.' He became aware that he was gripping the receiver too hard, that his fingers were hurting. God, this was hurting him all over. Did she have any inkling of his feelings right this minute? He was sure he couldn't put them into words. The words hadn't been coined. He felt so close to her, and yet so far away, like a schoolkid who'd lost his first girlfriend.

'Thanks for phoning, John. I appreciate it. But I'd better be getting –'

'Oh, right, right you are. Well, you've got my number, Gill. Take care.'

'Bye, J –'

He broke the connection. Don't crowd her, John, he was thinking. That's how you lost her the first time. Don't go making any assumptions. She doesn't like that. Give her space. Maybe he had made a mistake phoning in the first place. Hell and damn.

With respect.

That little weasel called James. That little toerag. He'd rip his head from his shoulders when he got him. He wondered how much Hyde had paid the kid. Considerably more than two ten-pound notes, that was for sure.

The telephone rang.

'Rebus here.'

'John? It's Gill again. I've just heard the news. Why didn't you tell me?'

'Tell you what?' He affected indifference, knowing she'd see through it immediately.

'About this complaint against you.'

194

'Oh, that. Come on, Gill, you know this sort of thing happens from time to time.'

'Yes, but why didn't you *say*? Why did you let me prattle on like that?'

'You weren't prattling.'

'Dammit!' She was almost in tears now. 'Why do you always have to try and hide things from me like that? What's the matter with you?'

He was about to explain, when the line went dead. He stared at the receiver dumbly, wondering just *why* he hadn't told her in the first place. Because she had worries of her own? Because he was embarrassed? Because he hadn't wanted the pity of a vulnerable woman? There were reasons enough.

Weren't there?

Of course there were. It was just that none of them seemed to make him feel any better. *Why do you always have to try and hide things from me?* There was that word again: hide. A verb, an action, and a noun, a place. And a person. Faceless, but Rebus was beginning to know him so well. The adversary was cunning, there was no doubting that. But he couldn't hope to tie up all the loose threads the way he'd tied up Ronnie and Carew, the way he was trying to tie up John Rebus.

The telephone rang again.

'Rebus here.'

'It's Superintendent Watson. I'm glad I caught you at home.'

Because, Rebus added silently, it means I'm not out on the street causing trouble for you.

'Yes, sir. Any problem?'

'Quite the reverse. They're still questioning this male prostitute. Shouldn't be too long now. But meantime, the reason I called is because I've been on to the casino.'

'Casino, sir?'

'You know, Finlay's.'

195

'Oh, yes.'

'And they say that you'll be welcome there anytime, should you wish to pop in. You've just to mention Finlay Andrews' name, and that's your ticket.'

'Right, sir. Well, thanks for that.'

'My pleasure, John. Shame you're having to take it easy, what with this suicide business and all. The press are all over it, sniffing around for any little piece of dirt they can find. What a job, eh?'

'Yes, sir.'

'McCall's fielding their questions. I just hope he doesn't appear on the box. Not exactly photogenic, is he?'

Watson made this sound like Rebus's fault, and Rebus was on the point of apologising when the Superintendent placed a hand over the mouthpiece at his end, while he had a few words with someone. And when he came on again it was to say a hasty goodbye.

'Press conference apparently,' he said. And that was that.

Rebus stared at the receiver for a full minute. If there were to be any more calls, let them come now. They didn't. He threw the instrument onto the floor, where it landed heavily. Secretly, he was hoping to break it one of these days, so he could go back to an old-style handset. But the blasted thing seemed tougher than it looked.

He was opening the book when the door-knocker sounded. Tappity tap tap. A business call then, and not Mrs Cochrane wondering why he hadn't washed the communal stairwell yet.

It was Brian Holmes.

'Can I come in?'

'I suppose so.' Rebus felt no real enthusiasm, but left the door open for the young detective to follow him through to the living room if he so desired. He so desired, following Rebus with mock heartiness.

'I was just looking at a flat near Tollcross, and thought I'd –'

'Skip the excuses, Brian. You're checking up on me. Sit down and tell me what's been happening in my absence.' Rebus checked his watch while Holmes seated himself. 'An absence, for the record, of just under two hours.'

'Ach, I was concerned, that's all.'

Rebus stared at him. Simple, direct, and to the point. Maybe Rebus could learn something from Holmes after all.

'It's not Farmer's orders then?'

'Not at all. And as it happens, I *did* have a flat to look at.'

'What was it like?'

'Ghastly beyond speech. Cooker in the living room, shower in a wee cupboard. No bath, no kitchen.'

'How much did they want for it? No, on second thoughts don't tell me. It would just depress me.'

'It certainly depressed me.'

'You can always make an offer on this place when they throw me inside for corrupting a minor.'

Holmes looked up, saw that Rebus was smiling, and gave a relieved grin.

'The guy's story's already coming apart at the seams.'

'Did you ever doubt it?'

'Of course not. Anyway, I thought these might cheer you up.' Holmes brandished a large manilla envelope, which had been discreetly tucked inside his cord jacket. Rebus hadn't seen this cord jacket before, and supposed it to be the Detective Constable's flat-buying uniform.

'What are they?' said Rebus, accepting the packet.

'Pics. Last night's raid. Thought you might be interested.'

Rebus opened the envelope and withdrew a set of ten-by-eight black and whites. They showed the more or less blurred shapes of men scrambling across waste ground. What light there was had about it a halogen starkness, sending up huge black shadows and capturing some faces in chalky states of shock and surprise.

'Where did you get these?'

'That DS Hendry sent them across with a note sympathising over Nell. He thought these might cheer me up.'

'I told you he was a good bloke. Any idea which one of these goons is the DJ?'

Holmes leapt from his seat and crouched beside Rebus, who was holding a photograph at the ready.

'No,' Holmes said, 'there's a better shot of him.' He thumbed through the set until he found the picture he was looking for. 'Here we are. That one there. That's McCallum.'

Rebus studied the fuzzy semblance before him. The look of fear, so distinct against the blurred face, could have been drawn by a child. Wide eyes and a mouth puckered into an 'O', arms suspended as though between rapid flight and final surrender.

Rebus smiled a smile that reached all the way up to his eyes.

'You're sure this is him?'

'One of the PCs at the station recognised him. He said he once got McCallum to sign an autograph for him.'

'I'm impressed. Shouldn't think he'll be signing too many more though. Where are they holding him?'

'Everybody they arrested has gone to Dunfermline nick'.

'That's nice for them. By the by, did they nab the ringleaders?'

'Each and every one. Including Brightman. He was the boss.'

'Davy Brightman? The scrappie?'

'That's him.'

'I played against that bugger at football a couple of times when I was at school. He played left back for his team when I was on the wing for ours. He gave me a good studding one match.'

'Revenge is sweet,' said Holmes.

'It is that, Brian.' Rebus was studying the photograph again. 'It is that.'

'Actually, a couple of the punters did scarper apparently, but they're all on film. The camera never lies, eh, sir?'

Rebus began to sift through the other pictures. 'A powerful tool, the camera,' he said. His face suddenly changed.

'Sir? Are you all right?'

Rebus's voice was reduced to a whisper. 'I've just had a revelation, Brian. A whatsit . . .? epiphany, is it?'

'No idea, sir.' Holmes was sure now that something inside his superior had snapped.

'Epiphany, yes. I *know* where this has all been leading, Brian. I'm sure of it. That bastard on Calton Hill said something about pictures, some pictures everybody was interested in. They're *Ronnie's* pictures.'

'What? The ones in his bedroom?'

'No, not those.'

'The ones at Hutton's studio then?'

'Not quite. No, I don't know exactly *where* these particular pictures are, but I've got a bloody good idea. "Hide" can be a noun, Brian. Come on.'

'Where?' Holmes watched as Rebus sprang from his chair, heading for the door. He started to collect the photographs, which Rebus had let fall from his hands.

'Never mind those,' Rebus ordered, slipping on a jacket.

'But where the hell are we going?'

'You just answered your own question,' Rebus said, turning back to grin at Holmes. 'That's exactly where we're going.'

'But *where?*'

'To hell, of course. Come on.'

It was turning cold. The sun had just about tired itself out, and was retiring from the contest. The clouds were sticking-plaster pink. Two great final sunbeams shone down like torchlight upon Pilmuir, and picked out just the one building, leaving the other houses in the street untouched. Rebus sucked in breath. He had to admit, it was quite a sight.

'Like the stable at Bethlehem,' said Holmes.

'A damned queer stable,' Rebus retorted. 'God's got a funny sense of humour if this is His idea of a joke.'

'You did say we were going to hell.'

'I wasn't expecting Cecil B. DeMille to be in on it though. What's going on there?'

Almost hidden by the day's last gasp of sunlight, a van and a hire skip were parked directly in front of Ronnie's house.

'The council?' Holmes suggested. 'Probably cleaning the place up.'

'Why, in God's name?'

'There's plenty that need housing,' Holmes replied. Rebus wasn't listening. As the car pulled to a stop, he was out and walking briskly towards the skip. It was filling up with the detritus of the squat's interior. There were sounds of hammering from within. In the back of the van, a workman supped from a plastic cup, his thermos clutched in his other hand.

'Who's in charge here?' Rebus demanded.

The workman blew on the contents of his cup, then took another swig before replying. 'Me, I suppose.' His eyes were wary. He could smell authority a mile off. 'This is a legitimate tea-break.'

'Never mind that. What's going on?'

'Who wants to know.'

'CID wants to know.'

He looked hard at Rebus's harder face, and made up his mind instantly. 'Well, we got word to come and clean this place up. Make it habitable.'

'On whose orders?'

'I don't know. Somebody's. We just take the chitty and go do the job.'

'Right.' Rebus had turned from the man and was walking up the path to the front door. Holmes, having smiled apologetically at the foreman, followed. In the living room, two workmen in overalls and thick red rubber gloves were whitewashing the walls. Charlie's pentagram had already been covered, its outline barely visible through the drying layer of paint. The men looked towards Rebus, then to the wall.

'We'll cover it up next coat,' said one. 'Don't worry yourself about that.'

Rebus stared at the man, then marched past Holmes out of the room. He started to climb the stairs, and turned into Ronnie's bedroom. Another workman, much younger than the two downstairs, was gathering Ronnie's few belongings together into a large black plastic bag. As Rebus entered the room, the boy was caught, frozen, stuffing one of the paperbacks into the pocket of his overalls.

Rebus pointed to the book.

'There's a next of kin, son. Put it in the bag with the rest.'

Something about his tone persuaded the teenager to obey.

'Come across anything else interesting?' Rebus asked now, hands in pockets, approaching the teenager.

'Nothing,' the boy said, guiltily.

'In particular,' Rebus went on, as though the teenager had not spoken, 'photographs. Maybe just a few, maybe a whole packet. Hmm?'

'No. Nothing like that.'

'You're sure?'

'Sure.'

'Right. Get down to the van and bring up a crowbar or something. I want these floorboards up.'

'Eh?'

'You heard me, son. Do it.'

Holmes just stood and watched in silent appreciation. Rebus seemed to have grown in physical stature, becoming broader, taller. Holmes couldn't quite fathom the trick: maybe it had something to do with the hands in the pockets, the way the elbows jarred outwards, lending apparent substance to the frame. Whatever it was, it worked. The young workman stumbled out of the door and down the stairs.

'You're sure they'll be here?' said Holmes quietly. He tried to keep his tone level, not wishing to sound too sceptical. But Rebus was way past that stage. In Rebus's mind, the photographs were already in his hand.

'I'm certain, Brian. I can *smell* them.'

'You're sure that's not just the bathroom?'

Rebus turned and looked at him, as though seeing him for the very first time. 'You might have a point, Brian. You just might.'

Holmes followed Rebus to the bathroom. As Rebus kicked open the door, the stench embraced both men, arching them forward in a convulsive fit of gagging. Rebus brought a handkerchief from his pocket, pushed it to his face, and leaned towards the door handle, pulling the door shut again.

'I'd forgotten about that place,' he said. Then: 'Wait here.'

He returned with the foreman, a plastic dustbin, a shovel, and three small white face-masks, one of which he handed to Holmes. An elasticated band held the cardboard snout in place, and Holmes breathed deeply, testing the apparatus. He was just about to say something about the smell still being noticeable, when Rebus toed open the

202

door again, and, as the foreman angled an industrial lamp into the bathroom, walked over the threshold.

Rebus pulled the dustbin to the rim of the bath and left it there, gesturing for the lamp to be shone into the bath itself. Holmes nearly fell backwards out of the room. A fat rat, caught in the act of feasting upon the rotten contents of the bath, squealed, red eyes burning directly into the light. Rebus swung the shovel down and cut the animal in two neat halves. Holmes spun from the room and, lifting the mask, retched against the damp wall. He tried taking gulps of air, but the smell was overpowering, the nausea returning in quickening floods.

Back inside the room, the foreman and Rebus exchanged a smile which wrinkled their eyes above the face-masks. They had seen worse than this – much worse – in their time. Then, neither man naive enough to want to linger, they set to work, the foreman holding the lamp while Rebus shovelled the contents of the bath slowly into the dustbin. The mess of raw sewage ran slickly from the shovel, spattering Rebus's shirt and trousers. He ignored it, ignored everything but the task at hand. He had done dirtier jobs in the Army, dirtier jobs by far during his failed training in the SAS. This was routine. And at least here there was some purpose to the task, some end in view.

Or so he hoped.

Holmes meantime was wiping his moist eyes with the back of his hand. Through the open door he could see the progress being made, eerie shadows cast across the wall and ceiling by the lamp, as one silhouette shovelled shit into a bin, filling it noisily. It was like a scene from some latter-day *Inferno*, lacking only the devils to goad the damned workers on. But these men looked, if not happy in their work, then at least ... well, *professional* sprang to mind. Dear God, all he wanted was a flat to call his own, and the occasional holiday, and a decent car. And Nell, of course. This would make a funny story for her one day.

But the last thing he felt like doing was smiling.

Then he heard the cackle of laughter, and, looking around him, it took several moments to realise that it was coming from the bathroom, that it was John Rebus's laugh, and that Rebus was dipping his hand into the mess, drawing it out again with something clinging to it. Holmes didn't even notice the thick rubberised gloves which protected Rebus up to his elbows. He simply turned and walked downstairs on brittle legs.

'Got you!' Rebus cried.

'There's a hose outside,' the foreman said.

'Lead on,' said Rebus, shaking the packet free of some of its clots. 'Lead on, Macduff.'

'The name's MacBeth,' the foreman called back, heading for the stairway.

In the cool, fresh air, they hosed down the package, standing it up against the front wall of the house as they did so. Rebus peered at it closely. A red plastic bag, like the carrier from a record shop, had been wrapped around some cloth, a shirt or the like. The whole had been stuck down with a roll's worth of sellotape, then tied with string, knotted resolutely in the middle.

'Clever little tyke, weren't you, Ronnie?' Rebus said to himself as he picked up the package. 'Cleverer than they could ever have thought.'

At the van, he threw down the rubber gloves, shook the foreman's hand, and exchanged the names of local watering holes with him, making promises of a drink, a nippy sweetie some night in the future. Then he headed for the car, Holmes following sheepishly. All the way back to Rebus's flat, Holmes didn't once dare to suggest that they open a window and let in some fresh air.

Rebus was like a child on a birthday morning who has just found his surprise. He clutched the parcel to him, staining his shirt even more, yet seemed loath to open it.

204

Now that he possessed it, he could forestall the revelation. It would happen; that was all that mattered.

When they arrived at the flat, however, Rebus's mood changed again, and he dashed to the kitchen for some scissors. Holmes meantime made his excuses and went to the bathroom, scrubbing his hands, bared arms, and face thoroughly. His scalp itched, and he wished he could throw himself into the shower and stand beneath it for an hour or two.

As he was coming out of the bathroom, he heard the sound from the kitchen. It was the antithesis of the laughter he had heard earlier, a kind of exasperated wail. He walked quickly to the kitchen, and saw Rebus standing there, head bowed, hands held out against the worktop as though supporting himself. The packet was open in front of him.

'John? What's wrong?'

Rebus's voice was soft, suddenly tired. 'They're just pictures of a bloody boxing match. That's all they are. Just bloody sports photos.'

Holmes came forward slowly, fearing noise and movement might crack Rebus completely.

'Maybe,' he suggested, peering over Rebus's slumped shoulder, 'maybe there's somebody in the crowd. In the audience. This Hyde could be one of the spectators.'

'The spectators are just a blur. Take a look.'

Holmes did. There were twelve or so photographs. Two featherweights, no love lost, were slugging it out. There was nothing subtle about the contest, but nothing unusual about it either.

'Maybe it's Hyde's boxing club.'

'Maybe,' said Rebus, not really caring any more. He had been so sure that he would find the pictures, and so sure that they would prove the final, clinching piece of the puzzle. Why were they hidden away so carefully, so cunningly? And so well protected. There had to be a reason.

'Maybe,' said Holmes, who was becoming irritating again, 'maybe there's something we're missing. The cloth they're wrapped in, the envelope . . .?'

'Don't be so bloody thick, Holmes!' Rebus slammed a hand against the worktop, and immediately calmed. 'Sorry. Jesus, sorry.'

'That's all right,' Holmes said coldly. 'I'll make some coffee or something. Then why don't we take a *good* look at those snaps? Eh?'

'Yes,' Rebus said, pushing himself upright. 'Good idea.' He headed towards the door. 'I'm going to take a shower.' He turned and smiled at Holmes. 'I must stink to high heaven.'

'A very agricultural smell, sir,' Holmes said, smiling also. They laughed at the shared reference to Farmer Watson. Then Rebus went to have his shower, and Holmes made the coffee, jealous of the sounds from the bathroom. He took another look at the photographs, a close look, hoping for something, something he could use to impress Rebus with, to cheer Rebus up just a little.

The boxers were young, photographed from ringside or near as dammit. But the photographer – Ronnie McGrath presumably – hadn't used a flash, depending instead upon the smoky lights above the ring. Consequently, neither boxers nor audience were recognisable as distinct individuals. Their faces were grainy, the outlines of the combatants themselves blurred with sluggish movement. Why hadn't the photographer used a flash?

In one photo, the right-hand side of the frame was dark, cut off at an angle by something getting in the way of the lens. What? A passing spectator? Somebody's jacket?

It struck Holmes with sudden clarity: the *photographer's* jacket had got in the way, and it had done so because the photos were being taken surreptitiously, from beneath a jacket. This would explain the poor quality of the photos, and the uneven angles of most of them. So there *had* to be a reason for them, and they had to be the clue Rebus was seeking. All they had to do now was discover just *what* kind of clue.

The shower became a drip, then died altogether. A few moments later, Rebus appeared clad only in a towel, holding it around his gut as he went to the bedroom to change. He was balancing with one foot poised above a trouser leg when Holmes burst in, waving the photographs.

'I think I've got it!' he exclaimed. Rebus looked up, surprised, then slipped on the trousers.

'Yes,' he said. 'I think I've worked it out, too. It came to me just now in the shower.'

'Oh.'

'So fetch us a coffee,' said Rebus, 'and let's go into the living room and see if we've worked out the same thing. Okay?'

'Right,' said Holmes, wondering again why it was that he'd joined the police when there were so many more rewarding careers out there to be had.

When he arrived in the living room, carrying the two mugs of coffee, Rebus was pacing up and down, his telephone handset wedged against his ear.

'Right,' he was saying. 'I'll wait. No, no, I won't call back. I said I'll *wait*. Thank you.'

Taking the coffee from Holmes, he rolled his eyes, exhibiting disbelief at the stupidity of the person on the other end of the telephone.

'Who is it?' Holmes mouthed silently.

'The council,' said Rebus aloud. 'I got a name and an extension number from Andrew.'

'Who's Andrew?'

'Andrew MacBeth, the foreman. I want to find out who

207

authorised the cleaning out of the house. A bit of a coincidence that, don't you think? Cleaning it out just as we were about to do a bit of poking around.' He turned his attention to the handset. 'Yes? That's right. Oh, I see.' He looked at Holmes, his eyes betraying nothing. 'How might that have happened?' He listened again. 'Yes, I see. Oh yes, I agree, it does seem a bit curious. Still, these things happen, eh? Roll on computerisation. Thanks for your help anyway.'

He pressed a button, kiling the connection. 'You probably caught the gist of that.'

'They've no record of who authorised the clear-out?'

'Quite so, Brian. The documentation is all in order, but for the little matter of a signature. They can't understand it.'

'Any handwriting to go on?'

'The chitty Andrew showed me was typed.'

'So, what are you saying?'

'That Mr Hyde seems to have friends everywhere. In the council, for starters, but probably in the police, too. Not to mention several less savoury institutions.'

'What now?'

'Those pictures. What else is there to go on?'

They studied each frame closely, taking their time, pointing out this or that blur or detail, trying ideas out on one another. It was a painstaking business. And throughout Rebus was muttering to himself about Ronnie McGrath's final words to Tracy, about how they had been the key throughout. The triple meaning: make yourself scarce, beware a man called Hyde, and I've hidden something away. So clever. So compact. Almost *too* clever for Ronnie. Maybe the meanings had been there without his realising it himself. . . .

At the end of ninety minutes, Rebus threw the final photograph down onto the floor. Holmes was half lying along the settee, rubbing his forehead with one hand as he held up one of the pictures in the other, his eyes refusing to focus any longer.

'It's no use, Brian. No use at all. I can't make sense out of any of them, can you?'

'Not a lot,' Holmes admitted. 'But I take it Hyde wanted – wants – these pictures badly.'

'Meaning?'

'Meaning he knows they exist, but he doesn't know how crude they are. He thinks they show something they don't.'

'Yes, but what? I'll tell you something, Ronnie McGrath had bruises on his body the night he died.'

'Not surprising when you remember that someone dragged his body down the stairs.'

'No, he was already dead then. This was before. His brother noticed, Tracy noticed, but nobody ever asked. Somebody said something to me about rough trade.' He pointed towards the scattering of snapshots. 'Maybe this is what they meant.'

'A boxing match?'

'An illegal bout. Two unmatched kids knocking blue hell out of one another.'

'For what?'

Rebus stared at the wall, looking for the word he lacked. Then he turned to Holmes.

'The same reason men set up dog fights. For kicks.'

'It all sounds incredible.'

'Maybe it *is* incredible. The way my mind is just now, I could believe bombers have been found on the moon.' He stretched. 'What time is it?'

'Nearly eight. Aren't you supposed to be going to Malcolm Lanyon's party?'

'Jesus!' Rebus sprang to his feet. 'I'm late. I forgot all about it.'

'Well, I'll leave you to get ready. There's not much we

can do about this.' Holmes gestured towards the photographs. 'I should visit Nell anyway.'

'Yes, yes, off you go, Brian.' Rebus paused. 'And thanks.'

Holmes smiled and shrugged his shoulders.

'One thing,' Rebus began.

'Yes?'

'I don't have a clean jacket. Can I borrow yours?'

It wasn't a great fit, the sleeves being slightly too long, the chest too small, but it wasn't bad either. Rebus tried to seem casual about it all as he stood on Malcolm Lanyon's doorstep. The door was opened by the same stunning Oriental who had been by Lanyon's side at The Eyrie. She was dressed in a low-cut black dress which barely reached down to her upper thighs. She smiled at Rebus, recognising him, or at least pretending to do so.

'Come in.'

'I hope I'm not late.'

'Not at all. Malcolm's parties aren't run by the clock. People come and go as they please.' Her voice had a cool but not unpleasant edge to it. Looking past her, Rebus was relieved to see several male guests wearing lounge suits, and some wearing sports jackets. Lanyon's personal (Rebus wondered just *how* personal) assistant led him into the dining room, where a barman stood behind a table laden with bottles and glasses.

The doorbell rang again. Fingers touched Rebus's shoulder. 'If you'll excuse me,' she said.

'Of course,' said Rebus. He turned towards the barman. 'Gin and tonic,' he said. Then he turned again to watch her pass through the large hallway towards the main door.

'Hello, John.' A much firmer hand slapped Rebus's shoulder. It belonged to Tommy McCall.

'Hello, Tommy.' Rebus accepted a drink from the

barman, and McCall handed over his own empty glass for a refill.

'Glad you could make it. Of course, it's not quite as lively as usual tonight. Everyone's a bit subdued.'

'Subdued?' It was true, the conversations around them were muted. Then Rebus noticed a few black ties.

'I only came along because I thought James would have wanted it that way.'

'Of course,' Rebus said, nodding. He'd forgotten all about James Carew's suicide. Christ, it had only happened this morning! It seemed like a lifetime ago. And all these people had been Carew's friends or acquaintances. Rebus's nostrils twitched.

'Had he seemed depressed lately?' he asked.

'Not especially. He'd just bought himself that car, remember. Hardly the act of a depressed man!'

'I suppose not. Did you know him well?'

'I don't think any of us knew him well. He kept himself pretty much to himself. And of course he spent a lot of time away from town, sometimes on business, sometimes staying on his estate.'

'He wasn't married, was he?'

Tommy McCall stared at him, then took a large mouthful of whisky. 'No,' he said. 'I don't believe he ever was. It's a blessing in a way.'

'Yes, I see what you mean,' said Rebus, feeling the gin easing itself into his system. 'But I still don't understand why he would do it.'

'It's always the quiet ones though, isn't it? Malcolm was just saying that a few minutes ago.'

Rebus looked around them. 'I haven't seen our host yet.'

'I think he's in the lounge. Shall I give you the tour?'

'Yes, why not?'

'It's quite a place.' McCall turned to Rebus. 'Shall we

211

start upstairs in the billiards room, or downstairs at the swimming pool?'

Rebus laughed and shook his empty glass. 'I think the first place to visit is the bar, don't you?'

The house was stunning, there was no other word for it. Rebus thought briefly of poor Brian Holmes, and smiled. You and me both, kid. The guests were nice, too. He recognised some of them by face, some by name, a few by reputation, and many by the titles of the companies they headed. But of the host there was no sign, though everyone claimed to have spoken with him 'earlier in the evening'.

Later, as Tommy McCall was becoming noisy and inebriated, Rebus, by no means on his steadiest legs himself, decided on another tour of the house. But alone this time. There was a library on the first floor, which had received cursory attention on the first circuit. But there was a working desk in there, and Rebus was keen to take a closer look. On the landing, he glanced around him, but everyone seemed to be downstairs. A few guests had even donned swimsuits, and were lounging by (or in) the twenty-foot-long heated pool in the basement.

He turned the heavy brass handle and slipped into the dimly lit library. In here there was a smell of old leather, a smell which took Rebus back to past decades – the 'twenties, say, or perhaps the 'thirties. There was a lamp on the desktop, illuminating some papers there. Rebus was at the desk before he realised something: the lamp had not been lit on his first visit here. He turned and saw Lanyon, standing against the far wall with his arms folded, grinning.

'Inspector,' he said, his voice as rich as his tailoring. 'What an interesting jacket that is. Saiko told me you'd arrived.'

Lanyon walked forward slowly and extended a hand, which Rebus took. He returned the firm grip.

'I hope I'm not . . .' he began. 'I mean, it was kind of you. . . .'

'Good lord, not at all. Is the Superintendent coming?'

Rebus shrugged his shoulders, feeling the jacket tight across his back.

'No, well, never mind. I see that like me you are a studious man.' Lanyon surveyed the shelves of books. 'This is my favourite room in the whole house. I don't know why I bother holding parties. It is expected, I suppose, and that's why I do it. Also of course it is interesting to note the various permutations, who's talking with whom, whose hand just happened to squeeze whose arm a touch too tenderly. That sort of thing.'

'You won't see much from here,' Rebus said.

'But Saiko tells me. She's marvellous at catching that sort of thing, no matter how subtle people think they are being. For example, she told me about your jacket. Beige, she said, cord, neither matching the rest of your wardrobe nor quite fitting your figure. Therefore borrowed, am I right?'

Rebus applauded silently. 'Bravo,' he said. 'I suppose that's what makes you such a good lawyer.'

'No, years and years of study are what have made me a good lawyer. But to be a *known* lawyer, well, that demands a few simple party tricks, such as the one I've just shown you.'

Lanyon walked past Rebus and stopped at the writing desk. He sifted through the papers.

'Was there anything special you were interested in?'

'No,' said Rebus. 'Just this room.'

Lanyon glanced towards him, smiling, not quite believing. 'There are more interesting rooms in the house, but I keep those locked.'

'Oh?'

'One doesn't want *everyone* to know just what paintings one has collected for example.'

'Yes, I see.'

Lanyon sat at the desk now, and slipped on a pair of half-moon glasses. He seemed interested in the papers before him.

'I'm James Carew's executor,' he said. 'That's what I've been trying to sort out, who will benefit from his will.'

'A terrible business.'

Lanyon seemed not to understand. Then he nodded. 'Yes, yes, tragic.'

'I take it you were close to him?'

Lanyon smiled again, as though he knew this same question had been asked of several people at the party already. 'I knew him fairly well,' he said at last.

'Did you know he was homosexual?'

Rebus had been hoping for a response. There was none, and he cursed having played his trump card so soon in the game.

'Of course,' Lanyon said in the same level voice. He turned towards Rebus. 'I don't believe it's a crime.'

'That all depends, sir, as you should know.'

'What do you mean?'

'As a lawyer, you must know that there are still certain laws. . . .'

'Yes, yes, of course. But I hope you're not suggesting that James was involved in anything sordid.'

'Why do *you* think he killed himself, Mr Lanyon? I'd appreciate your professional opinion.'

'He was a friend. Professional opinions don't count.' Lanyon stared at the heavy curtains in front of his desk. 'I don't know why he committed suicide. I'm not sure we'll ever know.'

'I wouldn't bet on that, sir,' said Rebus, going to the door. He stopped, hand on the handle. 'I'd be interested to know who *will* benefit from the estate, when you've worked it all out of course.'

Lanyon was silent. Rebus opened the door, closed it behind him, and paused on the landing, breathing deeply. Not a bad performance, he thought to himself. At the very least it was worthy of a drink. And this time he would toast – in silence – the memory of James Carew.

Nursemaid was not his favourite occupation, but he'd known all along that it would come to this.

Tommy McCall was singing a rugby song in the back of the car, while Rebus waved a hasty goodbye to Saiko, who was standing on the doorstep. She even managed a smile. Well, after all he was doing her a favour in quietly removing the loud drunkard from the premises.

'Am I under arrest, John?' McCall yelled, interrupting his song.

'No, now shut up, for Christ's sake!'

Rebus got into the car and started the engine. He glanced back one last time and saw Lanyon join Saiko on the doorstep. She seemed to be filling him in on events, and he was nodding. It was the first Rebus had seen of him since their confrontation in the library. He released the handbrake, pulled out of the parking space, and drove off.

'Left here, then next right.'

Tommy McCall had had too much to drink, but his sense of direction seemed unimpaired. Yet Rebus had a strange feeling. . . .

'Along to the end of this road, and it's the last house on the corner.'

'But this isn't where you live,' Rebus protested.

'Quite correct, Inspector. This is where my brother lives. I thought we'd drop in for a nightcap.'

'Jesus, Tommy, you can't just –'

'Rubbish. He'll be delighted to see us.'

As Rebus pulled up in front of the house, he looked out of his side window and was relieved to see that Tony McCall's living room was still illuminated. Suddenly, Tommy's hand thrust past him and pushed down on the horn, sending a loud blare into the silent night. Rebus pushed the hand away, and Tommy fell back into his seat, but he'd done enough. The curtains twitched in the McCall living room, and a moment later a door to the side of the house opened and Tony McCall came out, glancing back nervously. Rebus wound down the window.

'John?' Tony McCall seemed anxious. 'What's the matter?'

But before Rebus could explain, Tommy was out of the car and hugging his brother.

'It's my fault, Tony. All mine. I just wanted to see you, that's all. Sorry though, sorry.'

Tony McCall took the situation in, glanced towards Rebus as if to say *I don't blame you*, then turned to his brother.

'Well, this is very thoughtful of you, Tommy. Long time no see. You'd better come in.'

Tommy McCall turned to Rebus. 'See? I told you there'd be a welcome waiting for us at Tony's house. Always a welcome at Tony's.'

'You'd better come in, too, John,' said Tony.

Rebus nodded unhappily.

Tony directed them through the hall and into the living room. The carpet was thick and yielding underfoot, the furnishings looking like a showroom display. Rebus was afraid to sit, for fear of denting one of the puffed-up cushions. Tommy, however, collapsed immediately into a chair.

'Where's the wee ones?' he said.

'In bed,' Tony answered, keeping his voice low.

216

'Ach, wake them up then. Tell them their Uncle Tommy's here.'

Tony ignored this. 'I'll put the kettle on,' he said.

Tommy's eyes were already closing, his arms slumped either side of him on the arms of the chair. While Tony was in the kitchen, Rebus studied the room. There were ornaments everywhere: along the length of the mantelpiece, covering the available surfaces of the large wallunit, arranged on the surface of the coffee table. Small plaster figurines, shimmering glass creations, holiday souvenirs. The arms and backs of chairs and sofa were protected by antimacassars. The whole room was busy and ill at ease. Relaxation would be almost impossible. He began to understand now why Tony McCall had been out walking in Pilmuir on his day off.

A woman's head peered round the door. Its lips were thin and straight, eyes alert but dark. She was staring at the slumbering figure of Tommy McCall, but caught sight of Rebus and prepared a kind of smile. The door opened a little wider, showing that she was wearing a dressing gown. A hand clutched this tight around her throat as she began to speak.

'I'm Sheila, Tony's wife.'

'Yes, hello, John Rebus.' Rebus made to stand, but a nervous hand fluttered him back down.

'Oh yes,' she said, 'Tony's talked about you. You work together, don't you?'

'That's right.'

'Yes.' Her attention was wandering, and she turned her gaze back to Tommy McCall. Her voice became like damp wallpaper. 'Would you look at him. The successful brother. His own business, big house. Just look at him.' She seemed about to launch into a speech on social injustice, but was interrupted by her husband, who was now squeezing past her carrying a tray.

'No need for you to get up, love,' he said.

'I could hardly sleep through that horn blaring, could I?' Her eyes now were on the tray. 'You've forgotten the sugar,' she said critically.

'I don't take sugar,' Rebus said. Tony was pouring tea from the pot into two cups.

'Milk first, Tony, then tea,' she said, ignoring Rebus's remark.

'It doesn't make a blind bit of difference, Sheila,' said Tony. He handed a cup to Rebus.

'Thanks.'

She stood for a second or two watching the two men, then ran a hand down the front of her dressing gown.

'Right then,' she 'said. 'Good night.'

'Good night,' concurred Rebus.

'Try not to be too long, Tony.'

'Right, Sheila.'

They listened, sipping tea, as she climbed the stairs to her bedroom. Then Tony McCall exhaled.

'Sorry about that,' he said.

'What for?' said Rebus. 'If a couple of drunks had walked into *my* home at this time of night, you wouldn't *want* to hear the reception I'd give them! I thought she stayed remarkably calm.'

'Sheila's always remarkably calm. On the outside.'

Rebus nodded towards Tommy. 'What about him?'

'He'll be all right where he is. Let him sleep it off.'

'Are you sure? I can take him home if you –'

'No, no. Christ, he's my brother. I think a chair for the night is called for.' Tony looked across towards Tommy. 'Look at him. You wouldn't believe the tricks we got up to when we were kids. We had the neighbourhood terrified of what we'd do next. Chap-Door-Run, setting bonfires, putting the football through somebody's window. We were wild, I can tell you. Now I never see him unless he's like this.'

'You mean he's pulled this stunt before?'

'Once or twice. Turns up in a taxi, crashes out in the chair. When he wakes up the next morning, he can't believe where he is. Has breakfast, slips the kids a few quid, and he's off. Never phones or visits. Then one night we hear the taxi chugging outside, and there he is.'

'I didn't realise.'

'Ach, I don't know why I'm telling you, John. It's not your problem, after all.'

'I don't mind listening.'

But Tony McCall seemed reluctant to go further. 'How do you like this room?' he asked instead.

'It's nice,' Rebus lied. 'A lot of thought's gone into it.'

'Yes.' McCall sounded unconvinced. 'A lot of money, too. See those little glass bauble things? You wouldn't believe how much one of those can cost.'

'Really?'

McCall was examining the room as though he were the visitor. 'Welcome to my life,' he said at last. 'I think I'd rather have one of the cells down the station.' He got up suddenly and walked across to Tommy's chair, then crouched down in front of his brother, one of whose eyes was open but glazed with sleep. 'You bugger,' Tony McCall whispered. 'You bugger, you bugger.' And he bowed his head so as not to show the tears.

It was growing light as Rebus drove the four miles back to Marchmont. He stopped at an all night bakery and bought warm rolls and refrigerated milk. This was the time when he liked the city best, the peaceful camaraderie of early morning. He wondered why people couldn't be happy with their lot. *I've got everything I've never wanted and it isn't enough.* All he wanted now was sleep, and in his bed for a change rather than on the chair. He kept playing the scene over and over: Tommy McCall dead to the world, saliva on his chin, and Tony McCall crouched in front of him, body shaking with emotion. A brother was a terrible thing. He was a lifelong competitor, yet you couldn't hate him without hating yourself. And there were other pictures too: Malcolm Lanyon in his study, Saiko standing at the door, James Carew dead in his bed, Nell Stapleton's bruised face, Ronnie McGrath's battered torso, old Vanderhyde with his unseeing eyes, the fear in Calum McCallum's eyes, Tracy with her tiny fists. . . .

If I am the chief of sinners, I am the chief of sufferers also. Carew had stolen that line from somewhere . . . but where? Who cares, John, who cares? It would just be another bloody thread, and there were far too many of those already, knotted into an impenetrable tangle. Get home, sleep, forget.

One thing was for sure: he'd have some wild dreams.

Saturday

Or, if you shall so prefer to choose, a new province of knowledge and new avenues to fame and power shall be laid open to you, here, in this room, upon the instant.

In fact, he didn't dream at all. And when he woke up, it was the weekend, the sun was shining, and his telephone was ringing.

'Hello?'

'John? It's Gill.'

'Oh, hello, Gill. How are you?'

'I'm fine. What about you?'

'Great.' This was not a lie. He hadn't slept so well in weeks, and there was not a trace of hangover within him.

'Sorry to ring so early. Any progress on the smear?'

'Smear?'

'The things that kid was saying about you.'

'Oh, that. No, I haven't heard anything yet.' He was thinking about lunch, about a picnic, about a drive in the country. 'Are you in Edinburgh?' he asked.

'No, Fife.'

'Fife? What are you doing there?'

'Calum's here, remember.'

'Of course I remember, but I thought you were steering clear of him?'

'He wanted to see me. Actually, that's why I'm calling.'

'Oh?' Rebus wrinkled his brow, curious.

'Calum wants to talk to you.'

'To *me*? Why?'

'He'll tell you that himself, I suppose. He just asked me to tell you.'

Rebus thought for a moment. 'Do you want me to talk to him?'

'Can't say I'm much bothered either way. I told him I'd pass on the message, and I told him it was the last favour he could expect from me.' Her voice was as slick and cool as a slate roof in the rain. Rebus felt himself sliding down that roof, wanting to please her, wanting to help. 'Oh yes,' she said, 'and he said that if you sounded dubious, I was to tell you it's to do with Hyde's.'

'Hydes?' Rebus stood up sharply.

'H-y-d-e-apostrophe-s.'

'Hyde's what?'

She laughed. 'I don't know, John. But it sounds as if it means *some*thing to you.'

'It does, Gill. Are you in Dunfermline?'

'Calling from the station's front desk.'

'Okay. I'll see you there in an hour.'

'Fine, John.' She sounded unconcerned. 'Bye.'

He cut the connection, put his jacket on, and left the flat. The traffic was busy towards Tollcross, busy all the way down Lothian Road and winding across Princes Street towards Queensferry Road. Since the deregulation of public transport, the centre of the city had become a black farce of buses: double deckers, single deckers, even mini-buses, all vying for custom. Locked behind two claret-coloured LRT double deckers and two green single deckers, Rebus began to lose his tiny cache of patience. He slammed his hand down hard on the horn and pulled out, revving past the line of stalled traffic. A motorcycle messenger, squeezing through between the two directions of slower traffic, had to swerve to avoid the imminent accident, and slewed against a Saab. Rebus knew he should stop. He kept on going.

If only he'd had one of those magnetic flashing sirens, the kind CID used on the roofs of their cars whenever they were late for dinner or an engagement. But all he had were his headlights – full-beam – and the horn. Having cleared the tailback, he eased his hand off the horn, switched off the lamps, and cruised into the outside lane of the widening road.

Despite a pause at the dreaded Barnton roundabout, he made good time to the Forth Road Bridge, paid the toll, and drove across, not too fast, wanting, as ever, to take in the view. Rosyth Naval Dockyard was below him on the left. A lot of his schoolfriends ('lot' being relative: he'd never made that many friends) had slipped easily into jobs at Rosyth, and were probably still there. It seemed to be about the only place in Fife where work was still available. The mines were closing with enforced regularity. Somewhere along the coast in the other direction, men were burrowing beneath the Forth, scooping out coal in a decreasingly profitable curve. . . .

Hyde! Calum McCallum knew something about Hyde! Knew, too, that Rebus was interested, so word must have got around. His foot pressed down further on the accelerator. McCallum would want a trade, of course: charges dropped, or somehow jigged into a shape less damning. Fine, fine, he'd promise him the sun and the moon and the stars.

Just so long as he knew. Knew who Hyde was; knew where Hyde was. Just so long as he knew. . . .

The main police station in Dunfermline was easy to find, situated just off a roundabout on the outskirts of the town. Gill was easy to find, too. She was sitting in her car in the spacious car park outside the station. Rebus parked next to her, got out of his car and into the passenger side of hers.

'Morning,' he said.

'Hello, John.'

'Are you okay?' This was, on reflection, perhaps the most unnecessary question he had ever posed. Her face had lost colour and substance, and her head seemed to be shrinking into her shoulders, while her hands gripped the

225

steering wheel, fingernails rapping softly against the top of the dashboard.

'I'm fine,' she said, and they both smiled at the lie. 'I told them at the desk that you were coming.'

'Anything you want me to tell our friend?'

Her voice was resonant. 'Nothing.'

'Okay.'

Rebus pushed open the car door and closed it again, but softly, then he headed towards the station entrance.

She had wandered the hospital corridors for over an hour. It was visiting time, so no one much minded as she walked into this and that ward, passing the beds, smiling down occasionally on the sick old men and women who stared up at her with lonely eyes. She watched families decide who should and should not take turns at grandpa's bedside, there being two only at a time allowed. She was looking for one woman in particular, though she wasn't sure she would recognise her. All she had to go on was the fact that the librarian would have a broken nose.

Maybe she hadn't been kept in. Maybe she'd already gone home to her husband or boyfriend or whatever. Maybe Tracy would be better off waiting and going to the library again. Except that they'd be watching and waiting for her. The guard would know her. The librarian would know her.

But would *she* know the librarian?

A bell rang out, drilling into her the fact that visiting hours were coming to an end. She hurried to the next ward, wondering: what if the librarian's in a private room? Or in another hospital? Or. . . .

No! There she was! Tracy stopped dead, turned in a half-circle, and walked to the far end of the ward. Visitors were saying their goodbyes and take cares to the patients. Everybody looked relieved, both visitors and visited. She mingled with them as they put chairs back into stacks and donned coats, scarves, gloves. Then she paused and looked back towards the librarian's bed. There were flowers all around it, and the single visitor, a man, was leaning over the librarian to kiss her lingeringly on the forehead. The librarian squeezed the man's hand and. . . . And the man looked familiar to Tracy. She'd seen him before. . . . At the police station! He was some friend of Rebus's, and he was a policeman! She remembered him checking on her while she was being held in the cells.

Oh Jesus, she'd attacked a policeman's wife!

She wasn't sure now, wasn't sure at all. Why had she come? Could she go through with it now? She walked with one family out of the ward, then rested against the wall in the corridor outside. Could she? Yes, if her nerve held. Yes, she could.

She was pretending to examine a drinks vending machine when Holmes sauntered through the swinging ward doors and walked slowly down the corridor away from her. She waited a full two minutes, counting up to one hundred and twenty. He wasn't coming back. He hadn't forgotten anything. Tracy turned from the vending machine and made for the swing doors.

For her, visiting time was just beginning.

She hadn't even reached the bed when a young nurse stopped her.

'Visiting hour's finished now,' the nurse said.

Tracy tried to smile, tried to look normal; it wasn't easy for her, but lying was.

'I just lost my watch. I think I left it at my sister's bed.' She nodded in Nell's direction. Nell, hearing the conversation, had turned towards her. Her eyes opened wide as she recognised Tracy.

'Well, be as quick as you can, eh?' said the nurse, moving away. Tracy smiled at the nurse, and watched her push through the swing doors. Now there were only the patients in their beds, a sudden silence, and her. She approached Nell's bed.

'Hello,' she said. She looked at the chart attached to the end of the iron bedstead. 'Nell Stapleton,' she read.

'What do you want?' Nell's eyes showed no fear. Her voice was thin, coming from the back of her throat, her nose having no part in the process.

'I want to tell you something,' Tracy said. She came close to Nell, and crouched on the floor, so that she would be barely visible from the doors of the ward. She thought this made her look as though she were searching for a lost watch.

'Yes?'

Tracy smiled, finding Nell's imperfect voice amusing. She sounded like a puppet on a children's programme. The smile vanished quickly, and she blushed, remembering that the reason she was here was because *she* was responsible for this woman being here at all. The plasters across the nose, the bruising under the eyes: all her doing.

'I came to say I'm sorry. That's all, really. Just, I'm sorry.'

Nell's eyes were unblinking.

'And,' Tracy continued, 'well . . . nothing.'

'Tell me,' said Nell, but it was too much for her. She'd done most of the talking while Brian Holmes had been in, and her mouth was dry. She turned and reached for the jug of water on the small cupboard beside the bed.

'Here, I'll do that.' Tracy poured water into a plastic beaker, and handed it to Nell, who sipped, coating the inside of her mouth. 'Nice flowers,' said Tracy.

'From my boyfriend,' said Nell, between sips.

'Yes, I saw him leaving. He's a policeman, isn't he? I know he is, because I'm a friend of Inspector Rebus's.'

'Yes, I know.'

'You do?' Tracy seemed shocked. 'So you know who I am?'

'I know your name's Tracy, if that's what you mean.'

Tracy bit her bottom lip. Her face reddened again.

'It doesn't matter, does it?' Nell said.

'Oh no.' Tracy tried to sound nonchalant. 'It doesn't matter.'

'I was going to ask . . .'

'Yes?' Tracy seemed keen for a change of subject.

'What were you going to do in the library?'

This wasn't quite to Tracy's liking. She thought about it, shrugged, and said: 'I was going to find Ronnie's photographs.'

'Ronnie's photographs?' Nell perked up. What little Brian had said during visiting hour had been limited to the progress of Ronnie McGrath's case, and especially the discovery of some pictures at the dead boy's house. What was Tracy talking about?

'Yes,' she said. 'Ronnie hid them in the library.'

'What were they exactly? I mean, why did he need to hide them?'

Tracy shrugged. 'All he told me was that they were his life insurance policy. That's exactly what he said, "life insurance policy".'

'And where exactly did he hide them?'

'On the fifth floor, he said. Inside a bound volume of something called the *Edinburgh Review*. I think it's a magazine.'

'That's right,' said Nell, smiling, 'it is.'

Brian Holmes was made light-headed by Nell's telephone call. His first reaction, however, was pure shock, and he chastised her for being out of bed.

'I'm still in bed,' she said, her voice becoming indistinct in her excitement. 'They brought the payphone to my bedside. Now listen. . . .'

Thirty minutes later, he was being shown down an aisle on the fifth floor of Edinburgh University Library. The

229

member of staff checked complicated decimal numbers exhibited at each stack, until, satisfied, she led him down one darkened row of large bound titles. At the end of the aisle, seated at a study desk by a large window, a student stared disinterestedly towards Holmes, a pencil crunching in his mouth. Holmes smiled sympathetically towards the student, who stared right through him.

'Here we are,' said the librarian. '*Edinburgh Review* and *New Edinburgh Review*. It becomes "New" in 1969, as you can see. Of course, we keep the earlier editions in a closed environment. If you want those years specifically, it will take a little time –'

'No, these are fine, really. These are just what I need. Thank you.'

The librarian bowed slightly, accepting his thanks. 'You *will* remember us all to Nell, won't you?' she said.

'I'll be talking to her later today. I won't forget.'

With another bow, the librarian turned and walked back to the end of the stack. She paused there, and pressed a switch. Strip lighting flickered above Holmes, and stayed on. He smiled his thanks, but she was gone, her rubber heels squeaking briskly towards the lift.

Holmes looked at the spines of the bound volumes. The collection was not complete, which meant that someone had borrowed some of the years. A stupid place to hide something. He picked up 1971–72, held its spine by the forefingers of both his right and left hands, and rocked it. No scraps of paper, no photographs were shaken free. He put the volume back on the shelf and selected its neighbour, shook it, then replaced it.

The student at the study desk was no longer looking through him. He was looking *at* him, and doing so as if Holmes were mad. Another volume yielded nothing, then another. Holmes began to fear the worst. He'd been hoping for something with which to surprise Rebus, something to tie up all the loose ends. He'd tried contacting the Inspector, but Rebus wasn't to be found, wasn't anywhere. He had vanished.

The photos made more noise than he'd expected as they slid from the sheaves and hit the polished floor, hit it with their glossy edges, producing a sharp crack. He bent and began to gather them up, while the student looked on in fascination. From what he could see of the images strewn across the floor, Holmes already felt disappointment curdling his elation. They were copies of the boxing match pictures, nothing more. There were no new prints, no revelations, no surprises.

Damn Ronnie McGrath for giving him hope. All they were was life insurance. On a life already forfeit.

He waited for the lift, but it was busy elsewhere, so he took the stairs, winding downwards steeply, and found himself on the ground floor, but in a part of the library he didn't know, a sort of antiquarian bookshop corridor, narrow, with mouldering books stacked up against both walls. He squeezed through, feeling a sudden chill he couldn't place, and found himself opening a door onto the main concourse. The librarian who had shown him around was back behind her desk. She saw him, and waved frantically. He obeyed the command and hurried forward. She picked up a telephone and pressed a button.

'Call for you,' she said, stretching across the desktop to hand him the receiver.

'Hello?' He was quizzical: who the hell knew he was here?

'Brian, where in God's name have you been?' It was Rebus, of course. 'I've been trying to find you everywhere. I'm at the hospital.'

Holmes's heart deflated within his chest. 'Nell?' he said, so dramatically that even the librarian's head shot up.

'What?' growled Rebus. 'No, no, Nell's fine. It's just that she told me where to find you. I'm phoning from the hospital, and it's costing me a fortune.' In confirmation, the pips came, and were followed by the chankling of coins in a slot. The connection was re-established.

'Nell's okay,' Brian told the librarian. She nodded, relieved, and turned back to her work.

'Of course she is,' said Rebus, having caught the words. 'Now listen, there are a few things I want you to do. Have you got a pen and paper?'

Brian found them on the desk. He smiled, remembering the first telephone conversation he'd ever had with John Rebus, so similar to this, a few things to be done. Christ, so much had been done since. . . .

'Got that?'

Holmes started. 'Sorry, sir,' he said. 'My mind was elsewhere. Could you repeat that?'

There was an audible sound of mixed anger and excitement from the receiver. Then Rebus started again, and this time Brian Holmes heard every word.

Tracy couldn't say why it was that she'd visited Nell Stapleton, or why she'd told Nell what she had. She felt some kind of bond, not merely because of what she'd done. There was something about Nell Stapleton, something wise and kind, something Tracy had lacked in her life until now. Maybe that's why she was finding it so hard to leave the hospital. She had walked the corridors, drunk two cups of coffee in a cafe across the road from the main building, wandered in and out of Casualty, X-Ray, even some clinic for diabetics. She'd tried to leave, had walked as far as the city's art college before turning round and retreading the two hundred paces to the hospital.

And she was entering the side gates when the men grabbed her.

'Hey!'

'If you'll just come with us, miss.'

They sounded like security men, policemen even, so she didn't resist. Maybe Nell Stapleton's boyfriend wanted to see her, to give her a good kicking. She didn't care. They were taking her towards the hospital entrance, so she didn't resist. Not until it was too late.

At the last moment, they stopped short, turned her, and pushed her into the back of an ambulance.

'What's −! Hey, come on!' The doors were closing, locking, leaving her alone in the hot, dim interior. She thumped on the doors, but the vehicle was already moving off. As it pulled away, she was thrown against the doors, then back onto the floor. When she had recovered herself, she saw that the ambulance was an old one, no longer used for its original purpose. Its insides had been gutted, making it merely a van. The windows had been boarded over, and a metal panel separated her from the driver. She clawed her way to this panel and began hitting it with her fists, teeth gritted, yelling from time to time as she remembered that the two men who had grabbed her at the gates were the same two men who'd been following her that day on Princes Street, that day she'd run to John Rebus.

'Oh God,' she murmured, 'oh God, oh God.'

They'd found her at last.

The evening was sticky with heat, the streets quiet for a Saturday.

Rebus rang the doorbell and waited. While he waited, he looked to left and right. An immaculate double row of Georgian houses, stone frontages dulled black through time and car fumes. Some of the houses had been turned into offices for Writers to the Signet, chartered accountants, and small, anonymous finance businesses. But a few a precious few − were still very comfortable and well-appointed homes for the wealthy and the industrious. Rebus had been to this street before, a long time ago now in his earliest CID days, investigating the death of a young girl. He didn't remember much about the case now. He was too busy getting ready for the evening's pleasures.

He tugged at the black bow tie around his throat. The whole outfit, dinner jacket, shirt, bow tie and patent shoes, had been hired earlier in the day from a shop on George Street. He felt like an idiot, but had to admit that, examining himself in his bathroom mirror, he looked pretty sharp. He wouldn't be too out of place in an establishment like Finlay's of Duke Terrace.

The door was opened by a beaming woman, young, dressed exquisitely, and greeting him as though wondering why he didn't come more often.

'Good evening,' she said. 'Will you come in?'

He would, he did. The entrance hall was subtle. Cream paint, deep pile carpeting, a scattering of chairs which might have been designed by Charles Rennie Mackintosh, high backs and looking extraordinarily uncomfortable to sit in.

'I see you're admiring our chairs,' the woman said.

'Yes,' Rebus answered, returning her smile. 'The name's Rebus, by the way. John Rebus.'

'Ah yes. Finlay told me you were expected. Well, as this is your first visit, would you like me to show you around?'

'Thank you.'

'But first, a drink, and the first drink is always on the house.'

Rebus tried not to be nosey, but he was a policeman after all, and not being nosey would have gone against all that he held most dear. So he asked a few questions of his hostess, whose name was Paulette, and pointed to this and that part of the gaming club, being shown the direction of the cellars ('Finlay has their contents insured for quarter of a million'), kitchen ('our chef is worth his weight in Beluga'), and guest bedrooms ('the judges are the worst, there are one or two who always end up sleeping here, too drunk to go home'). The lower ground floor housed the cellars and kitchen, while the ground floor comprised a quiet bar area, and the small restaurant, with cloakrooms and an office. On the first floor, up the carpeted staircase and past the collection of eighteenth- and nineteenth-century Scottish paintings by the likes of Jacob More and David Allan, was the main gaming area: roulette, blackjack, a few other tables for card games, and one table given over to dice. The players were business-men, their bets discreet, nobody losing big or winning big. They held their chips close to them.

Paulette pointed out two closed rooms.

'Private rooms, for private games.'

'Of what?'

'Poker mainly. The serious players book them once a month or so. The games can go on all night.'

'Just like in the movies.'

'Yes,' she laughed. 'Just like the movies.'

The second floor consisted of the three guest bedrooms, again locked, and Finlay Andrews' own private suite.

'Off limits, of course,' Paulette said.

'Of course,' Rebus concurred, as they started downstairs again.

So this was it: Finlay's Club. Tonight was quiet. He had seen only two or three faces he recognised: an advocate, who did not acknowledge him, though they'd clashed before in court, a television presenter, whose dark tan looked fake, and Farmer Watson.

'Hello there, John.' Watson, stuffed into suit and dress shirt, looked like nothing more than a copper out of uniform. He was in the bar when Paulette and Rebus went back in, his hand closed around a glass of orange juice, trying to look comfortable but instead looking distinctly out of place.

'Sir.' Rebus had not for one moment imagined that Watson, despite the threat he had made earlier, would turn up here. He introduced Paulette, who apologised for not being around to greet him at the door.

Watson waved aside her apology, revolving his glass. 'I was well enough taken care of,' he said. They sat at a vacant table. The chairs here were comfortable and well padded, and Rebus felt himself relax. Watson, however, was looking around keenly.

'Finlay not here?' he asked.

'He's somewhere around,' said Paulette. 'Finlay's always around.'

Funny, thought Rebus, that they hadn't bumped into him on their tour.

'What's the place like then, John?' Watson asked.

'Impressive,' Rebus answered, accepting Paulette's smile like praise from a teacher to a doting pupil. 'Very impressive. It's much bigger than you'd think. Wait till you see upstairs.'

'And there's the extension, too,' said Watson.

'Oh yes, I'd forgotten.' Rebus turned to Paulette.

'That's right,' she said. 'We're building out from the back of the premises.'

'Building?' said Watson. 'I thought it was a fait accompli?'

'Oh no.' She smiled again. 'Finlay is very particular. The flooring wasn't quite right, so he had the workmen rip it all up and start again. Now we're waiting on some marble arriving from Italy.'

'That must be costing a few bob,' Watson said, nodding to himself.

Rebus wondered about the extension. Towards the back of the ground floor, past toilets, cloakroom, offices, walk-in cupboards, there must be another door, ostensibly the door to the back garden. But now the door to the extension, perhaps.

'Another drink, John?' Watson was already on his feet, pointing at Rebus's empty glass.

236

'Gin and fresh orange, please,' he said, handing over the glass.

'And for you, Paulette?'

'No, really.' She was rising from the chair. 'Work to do. Now that you've seen a bit of the club, I'd better get back to door duties. If you want to play upstairs, the office can supply chips. A few of the games accept cash, but not the most interesting ones.'

Another smile, and she was gone in a flurry of silk and a glimpse of black nylon. Watson saw Rebus watching her leave.

'At ease, Inspector,' he said, laughing to himself as he headed for the bar where the barman explained that if he wanted drinks, he only had to signal, and an order would be taken at the gentlemen's table and brought to them directly. Watson slumped back into his chair again.

'This is the life, eh, John?'

'Yes, sir. What's happening back at base?'

'You mean the little sodomite who made the complaint? He's buggered off. Disappeared. Gave us a false address, the works.'

'So I'm off the butcher's hook?'

'Just about.' Rebus was about to remonstrate. 'Give it a few more days, John, that's all I'm asking. Time for it to die a natural death.'

'You mean people are talking?'

'A few of the lads have had a laugh about it. I don't suppose you can blame them. In a day or so, there'll be something else for them to joke about, and it'll all be forgotten.'

'There's nothing *to* forget!'

'I know, I know. It's all some plot to keep you out of action, and this mysterious Mr Hyde's behind it all.'

Rebus stared at Watson, his lips clamped shut. He could yell, could scream and shout. He breathed hard instead, and snatched at the drink when the waiter placed the tray on the table. He'd taken two gulps before the waiter informed him that he was drinking the other gentleman's orange juice. His own gin and orange was the one still on the tray. Rebus reddened as Watson, laughing again, placed a five-pound note on the tray. The waiter coughed in embarrassment.

'Your drinks come to six pounds fifty, sir,' he told Watson.

'Ye gods!' Watson searched in his pocket for some change, found a crumpled pound note and some coins, and placed them on the tray.

'Thank you, sir.' The waiter lifted the tray and turned away before Watson had the chance to ask about any change that might be owing. He looked at Rebus, who was smiling now.

'Well,' Watson said, 'I mean, six pounds fifty! That would feed some families for a week.'

'This is the life,' Rebus said, throwing the Superintendent's words back at him.

'Yes, well said, John. I was in danger of forgetting there can be more to life than personal comfort. Tell me, which church do you attend?'

'Well, well. Come to take us all in, have you?' Both men turned at this new voice. It was Tommy McCall. Rebus checked his watch. Eight thirty. Tommy looked as though he'd been to a few pubs en route to the club. He sat down heavily in what had been Paulette's chair.

'What're you drinking?' He snapped his fingers, and the waiter, a frown on his face, came slowly towards the table.

'Sirs?'

Tommy McCall looked up at him. 'Hello, Simon. Same again for the constabulary, and I'll have the usual.'

Rebus watched the waiter as McCall's words sank in. That's right, son, Rebus thought to himself, we're the police. Now why should that fact frighten you so much?

238

The waiter turned, seeming to read Rebus's mind, and headed stiffly back to the bar.

'So what brings you two here?' McCall was lighting a cigarette, glad to have found some company and ready to make a night of it.

'It was John's idea,' Watson said. 'He wanted to come, so I fixed it with Finlay, then reckoned I might as well come along, too.'

'Quite right.' McCall looked around him. 'Nobody much in tonight though, not yet leastways. The place is usually packed to the gunnels with faces you'd recognise, names you'd know like you know your own. This is tame tonight.'

He had offered round his pack of cigarettes, and Rebus had taken one, which he now lit, inhaling gratefully, regretting it immediately as the smoke mixed with the alcohol fumes in his chest. He needed to think fast and hard. Watson and now McCall: he had planned on dealing with neither.

'By the way, John,' Tommy McCall said, 'thanks for the lift last night.' His tone made the subtext clear to Rebus. 'Sorry if it was any trouble.'

'No trouble, Tommy. Did you sleep well?'

'I never have trouble sleeping.'

'Me neither,' interrupted Farmer Watson. 'The benefits of a clear conscience, eh?'

Tommy turned to Watson. 'Shame you couldn't get to Malcolm Lanyon's party. We had a pretty good time, didn't we, John?'

Tommy smiled across at Rebus, who smiled back. A group at the next table were laughing at some joke, the men drawing on thick cigars, the women playing with their wrist jewellery. McCall leaned across towards them, hoping perhaps to share in the joke, but his shining eyes and uneven smile kept him apart from them.

'Had many tonight, Tommy?' Rebus asked. McCall, hearing his name, turned back to Rebus and Watson.

'One or two,' he said. 'A couple of my trucks didn't deliver on time, drivers on the piss or something. Lost me two big contracts. Drowning my sorrows.'

'I'm sorry to hear that,' Watson said with sincerity. Rebus nodded agreement, but McCall shook his head theatrically.

'It's nothing,' he said. 'I'm thinking of selling the business anyway, retiring while I'm still young. Barbados, Spain, who knows. Buy a little villa.' His eyes narrowed, his voice dropping to a whisper. 'And guess who's interested in buying me out? You'll never guess in a million years. Finlay.'

'Finlay Andrews?'

'The same.' McCall sat back, drew on his cigarette, blinking into the smoke. 'Finlay Andrews.' He leaned forward again confidentially. 'He's got a finger in quite a few pies, you know. It's not just this place. He's got this and that directorship, shares here there and everywhere, you name it.'

'Your drinks.' The waiter's voice had more than a note of disapproval in it. He seemed to want to linger, even after McCall had pitched a ten-pound note onto the tray and waved him away.

'Aye,' McCall continued after the waiter had retreated. 'Fingers in plenty of pies. All strictly above board, mind. You'd have a hellish job proving otherwise.'

'And he wants to buy you out?' Rebus asked.

McCall shrugged. 'He's made a good price. Not a great price, but I won't starve.'

'Your change, sir.' It was the waiter again, his voice cold as a chisel. He held the salver out towards McCall, who stared up at him.

'I didn't want any change,' he explained. 'It was a tip. Still,' he winked at Rebus and Watson, scooping the coins from the tray, 'if you don't want it, son, I suppose I might as well have it back.'

'Thank you, sir.'

Rebus loved this. The waiter was giving McCall every kind of danger signal there was, but McCall was too drunk or too naive to notice. At the same time, Rebus was aware of complications which might be about to result from the presence of Superintendent Watson and Tommy McCall at Finlay's, on the night Finlay's erupted.

There was a sudden commotion from the entrance hall, raised voices, boisterous rather than angry. And Paulette's voice, too, pleading, then remonstrative. Rebus glanced at his watch again. Eight fifty. Right on time.

'What's going on?' Everybody in the bar was interested, and a few had risen from their seats to investigate. The barman pushed a button on the wall beside the optics, then made for the hall. Rebus followed. Just inside the front door Paulette was arguing with several men, dressed in business suits but far the worse for wear. One was telling her that she couldn't refuse him, because he was wearing a tie. Another explained that they were in town for the evening and had heard about the club from someone in a bar.

'Philip, his name was. He told us to say Philip had said it was okay and we could come in.'

'I'm sorry, gentlemen, but this is a *private* club.' The barman was joining in now, but his presence was unwanted.

'Talking to the lady here, pal, okay? All we want is a drink and maybe a wee flutter, isn't that right?'

Rebus watched as two more 'waiters', hard young men with angular faces, came quickly down the stairs from the first floor.

'Now look –'

'Just a wee flutter '

'In town for the night –'

'I'm sorry –'

'Watch the jacket, pal –'

'Hey! –'

Neil McGrath struck the first blow, catching one of the heavies with a solid right to the gut, doubling the man over. People were gathering in the hallway now, leaving the bar and the restaurant untended. Rebus, still watching the fight, began to move backwards through the crowd, past the door to the bar, past the restaurant, towards the cloakroom, the toilets, the office door, and the door behind that.

'Tony! Is that you?' It had to happen. Tommy McCall had noticed his brother Tony as one of the apparent out-of-town drunks. Tony, his attention diverted, received a blow to the face which sent him flying back against the wall. 'That's my brother you're punching!' Tommy was in there now too, mixing it with the best of them. Constables Neil McGrath and Harry Todd were fit and healthy young men, and they were holding their own. But when they saw Superintendent Watson, they automatically froze, even though he could have no idea who they were. Each was caught with a sickening blow, which woke them to the fact that this was for real. They forgot about Watson and struck out for all they were worth.

Rebus noticed that one of the fighters was hanging back just a little, not really throwing himself into it. He stayed near the door, too, ready to flee when necessary, and he kept glancing towards the back of the hallway, where Rebus stood. Rebus waved an acknowledgment. Detective Constable Brian Holmes did not wave back. Then Rebus turned and faced the door at the end of the hallway, the door to the club's extension. He closed his eyes, screwed up his courage, made a fist of his right hand, and brought it flying up into his own face. Not full strength, some self-protection circuit wouldn't let him do that, but hard. He wondered how people managed to slit their wrists, then

242

opened his watering eyes and checked his nose. There was blood smeared over his top lip, dripping from both nostrils. He let it drip, and hammered on the door.

Nothing. He hammered again. The noise of the fight was at its height now. *Come on, come on.* He pulled a handkerchief from his pocket and held it below his nostrils, catching droplets of brightest crimson. The door was unlocked from within. It opened a couple of inches and eyes peered out at Rebus.

'Yeah?'

Rebus pulled back a little so the man could see the commotion at the front door. The eyes opened wide with surprise, and the man glanced back at Rebus's bloody face before opening the door wider. The man was hefty, not old, but with hair unnaturally thin for his age. As if to compensate for this, he had a copious moustache. Rebus remembered Tracy's description of the man who had followed her the night she'd come to his flat. This man would fit that description.

'We need you out here,' Rebus said. 'Come on.'

The man paused, thinking it over. Rebus thought he was about to close the door again, and was getting ready to kick out with all his might, but the man pulled open the door and stepped out, passing Rebus. Rebus slapped the man's muscular back as he went.

The door was open. Rebus stepped through, sought the key, and locked it behind him. There were bolts top and bottom. He slid the top one across. Let nobody in, he was thinking, and nobody out. Then, and only then, did he look around him. He was at the top of a narrow flight of stairs, concrete, uncarpeted. Maybe Paulette had been right. Maybe the extension wasn't finished after all. It didn't look like it was meant to be part of Finlay's Club though, this staircase. It was too narrow, almost furtive. Slowly, Rebus moved downwards, the heels of his hired shoes making all-too-audible sounds against the steps.

Rebus counted twenty steps, and figured that he was now below the level of the building's lower ground floor, somewhere around cellar level or a bit below that even. Maybe planning restrictions *had* got Finlay Andrews after all. Unable to build up, he had built *down*. The door at the bottom of the stairs looked fairly solid. Again, a utilitarian-looking construction, rather than decorative. It would take a good twenty-pound hammer to break through this door. Rebus tried the handle instead. It turned, and the door opened.

Utter darkness. Rebus shuffled through the door, using what light there was from the top of the stairs to make out what he could. Which was to say, nothing. It looked like he was in some kind of storage area. Some big empty space. Then the lights came on, four rows of strip lights on the ceiling high above him. Their wattage low, they still gave enough illumination to the scene. A small boxing ring stood in the centre of the floor, surrounded by a few dozen stiff-backed chairs. This *was* the place then. The disc jockey had been right.

Calum McCallum had needed all the friends he could get. He had told Rebus all about the rumours he'd heard, rumours of a little club within a club, where the city's increasingly jaded begetters of wealth could place some 'interesting bets'. A bit out of the ordinary, McCallum had said. Yes, like betting on two rent boys, junkies paid handsomely to knock the daylights out of one another and keep quiet about it afterwards. Paid with money and drugs. There was no shortage of either now that the high rollers had spun north.

Hyde's Club. Named after Robert Louis Stevenson's villain, Edward Hyde, the dark side of the human soul. Hyde himself was based on the city's Deacon Brodie, businessman by day, robber by night. Rebus could smell guilt and fear and rank expectation in this large room. Stale cigars and spilt whisky, splashes of sweat. And amongst it all moved Ronnie, and the question which still needed to be answered. Had Ronnie been paid to photograph the influential and the rich – without their knowing they were being snapped, of course? Or had he been freelancing, summoned here only as a punchbag, but stealthy enough to bring a hidden camera with him? The answer was perhaps unimportant. What mattered was that the owner of this place, the puppet-master of all these base desires, had killed Ronnie, had starved him of his fix and then given him some rat poison. Had sent one of his minions along to the squat to make sure it looked like a simple case of an overdose. So they had left the quality powder beside Ronnie. And to muddy the water, they had moved the body downstairs, leaving it in candlelight. Thinking the tableau shockingly effective. But by candlelight they hadn't seen the pentagram on the wall, and they hadn't meant anything by placing the body the way they had.

Rebus had made the mistake of reading too much into the situation, all along. He had blurred the picture himself, seeing connections where there were none, seeing plot and conspiracy where none existed. The real plot was so much bigger, the size of a haystack to his needle.

'Finlay Andrews!' The shout echoed around the room, hanging emptily in air. Rebus hauled himself up into the boxing ring and looked around at the chairs. He could almost see the gleaming, gloating faces of the spectators. The canvas floor of the ring was pockmarked with brown stains, dried blood. It didn't end here, of course. There were also the 'guest bedrooms', the locked doors behind which 'private games' were played. Yes, he could visualise the whole Sodom, held on the third Friday of the month, judging by James Carew's diary. Boys brought back from Calton Hill to service the clients. On a table, in bed, wherever. And Ronnie had perhaps photographed it all. But Andrews had found out that Ronnie had some insurance, some photos stashed away. He couldn't know, of course, that they were next to useless as weapons of blackmail or evidence. All he knew was that they existed.

So Ronnie had died.

Rebus climbed out of the ring and walked past one row of chairs. At the back of the hall, lurking in shadow, were two doors. He listened outside one, then outside the other. No sounds, yet he was sure. . . . He was about to open the door on the left, but something, some instinct, made him choose the right-hand door instead. He paused, turned the handle, pushed.

There was a light switch just inside the door. Rebus found it, and two delicate lamps either side of the bed came on. The bed was against the side wall. There wasn't much else in the room, apart from two large mirrors, one against the wall opposite the bed, and one above the bed. The door clicked shut behind Rebus as he walked over to the bed. Sometimes he had been accused by his superiors of having a vivid imagination. Right now, he shut his imagination out altogether. Stick to the facts, John. The fact of the bed, the fact of the mirrors. The door clicked again. He leapt forwards and yanked at the handle, but it was fast, the door locked tight.

'Shit!' He stood back and kicked out, hitting the belly of the door with the heel of his shoe. The door trembled, but held. His shoe did not, the heel flapping off. Great, bang went his deposit on the dress hire. Hold on though, think it through. Someone had locked the door, therefore someone was down here with him, and the only other place they could have been hiding was the other room, the room next to this. He turned again and studied the mirror opposite the bed.

'Andrews!' he yelled to the mirror. 'Andrews!'

The voice was muffled by the wall, sounding distant, but still lucid.

'Hello, Inspector Rebus. Nice to see you.'

Rebus almost smiled, but managed to hide it.

'I wish I could say the same.' He stared into the mirror, visualising Andrews standing directly behind it, watching him. 'A nice idea,' he said, making conversation, needing time to gather his strength and his thoughts. 'People screwing in one room, while everyone else is free to watch through a two-way mirror.'

'Free to watch?' The voice seemed closer. 'No, not free, Inspector. Everything costs.'

'I suppose you set the camera up in there too, did you?'

'Photographed and framed. Framed being quite apt under the circumstances, don't you think?'

'Blackmail.' It was an observation, nothing more.

'Favours merely. Often given without question. But a photograph can be a useful tool when favours are being withheld.'

'That's why James Carew committed suicide?'

'Oh no. That was your doing really, Inspector. James told me you'd recognised him. He thought you might be able to follow your nose from him back to Hyde's.'

'You killed him?'

'*We* killed him, John. Which is a pity. I liked James. He was a good friend.'

'Well, you have lots of friends, don't you?'

There was laughter now, but the voice was level, elegiac almost. 'Yes, I suppose they'd have a job finding a judge to try me, an advocate to prosecute me, fifteen good men and true to stand as jury. They've all been to Hyde's. All of them. Looking for a game with just a little more edge than those played upstairs. I got the idea from a friend in London. He runs a similar establishment, though perhaps with a less sharp edge than Hyde's. There's a lot of new money in Edinburgh, John. Money for all. Would you like money? Would you like a sharper edge to your life? Don't tell me you're happy in your little flat, with your music and your books and your bottles of wine.'

247

Rebus's face showed surprise. 'Yes, I know quite a bit about you, John. Information is *my* edge.' Andrews' voice fell. 'There's a membership available here if you want it, John. I think maybe you *do* want it. After all, membership has its privileges.'

Rebus leaned his head against the mirror. His voice was a near whisper.

'Your fees are too high.'

'What's that?' Andrews' voice seemed closer than ever, his breathing almost audible. Rebus's voice was still a whisper.

'I said your fees are too high.'

Suddenly, he pulled back an arm, made a fist, and pushed straight through the mirror, shattering it. Another trick from his SAS training. Don't punch *at* something; always punch *through*, even if it's a brick wall you're attacking. Glass splintered around him, digging into the sleeve of his jacket, seeking flesh. His fist uncurled, became a claw. Just through the mirror, he found Andrews' throat, clamped it, and hauled the man forward. Andrews was shrieking. Glass was in his face, flakes of it in his hair, his mouth, prickling his eyes. Rebus held him close, teeth gritted.

'I said,' he hissed, 'your fees are too high.' Then he brought his other hand into a fresh new fist and placed a blow on Andrews' chin, releasing him so that the unconscious figure fell back into the room.

Rebus pulled off the useless shoe and tapped away the shards of glass which still clung around the edges of the frame. Then, carefully, he hauled himself through into the room, went to the door, and opened it.

He saw Tracy immediately. She was standing hesitantly in the middle of the boxing ring, arms hanging by her sides.

'Tracy?' he said.

'She may not hear you, Inspector Rebus. Heroin can do that, you know.'

Rebus watched as Malcolm Lanyon stepped out from the shadows. Behind him were two men. One was tall, well built for a man of his mature years. He had thick black eyebrows and a thick moustache tinged with silver. His eyes were deep-set, his whole face louring. He was the most Calvinist-looking thing Rebus had ever seen. The other man was stouter, less justified in his sinning. His hair was curly but thinning, his face scarred like a knuckle, a labourer's face. He was leering.

Rebus stared at Tracy again. Her eyes were like pinpoints. He went to the ring and climbed in, hugging her to him. Her body was totally compliant, her hair damp with sweat. She might have been a life-sized rag doll for all the impetus in her limbs. But when Rebus held her face so that she had to look back at him, her eyes glimmered, and he felt her body twitch.

'*My* edge,' Lanyon was saying. 'It seems I needed it.' He glanced towards the room where Andrews was lying unconscious. 'Finlay said he could handle you himself. Having seen you last night, I doubted that.' He beckoned to one of the men. 'See if Finlay's going to be all right.' The man headed off. Rebus liked the way the odds were going.

'Would you care to step into my office and talk?' he said.

Lanyon considered this, saw that Rebus was a strong man, but that he had his hands full with the girl. Also, of course, Lanyon had his men, while Rebus was alone. He walked to the ring, grabbed onto a rope, and hauled himself up and in. Now, face to face with Rebus, he saw the cuts on Rebus's arm and hand.

'Nasty,' he said. 'If you don't get those seen to. . . .'

'I might bleed to death?'

'Exactly.'

Rebus looked down at the canvas, where his own blood was making fresh stains beside those of nameless others. 'How many of them died in the ring?' he asked.

'I really don't know. Not many. We're not animals, Inspector Rebus. There may have been the occasional . . . accident. I seldom came to Hyde's. I merely introduced new members into it.'

'So when do they make you a judge?'

Lanyon smiled. 'Not for a considerable time yet. But it *will* happen. I once attended a club similar to Hyde's in London. Actually, that's where I met Saiko.' Rebus's eyes widened. 'Oh yes,' Lanyon said, 'she's a very versatile young woman.'

'I suppose Hyde's has given you and Andrews carte blanche throughout Edinburgh?'

'It has helped with the odd planning application, the odd court case just happening to go the right way, that sort of thing.'

'So what happens now that I know all about it?'

'Ah, well, you needn't worry there. Finlay and I see a long-term future for you in the development of Edinburgh as a great city of commerce and industry.' The guard below chuckled.

'What do you mean?' asked Rebus. He could feel Tracy's body tensing, growing strong again. How long it would last he couldn't know.

'I mean,' Lanyon was saying, 'that you could be preserved in concrete, supporting one of the new orbital roads.'

'You've done that before, have you?' The question was rhetorical; the goon's chuckle had already answered it.

'Once or twice, yes. When there was something that needed clearing away.'

Rebus saw that Tracy's hands were slowly closing into fists. Then the goon who had gone to see Andrews came back.

'Mr Lanyon!' he called. 'I think Mr Andrews is pretty bad!'

Just then, as Lanyon turned from them, Tracy flew from Rebus with a terrifying shriek and swung her fists in a low arc, catching Lanyon with a sickening thump between his legs. He didn't so much fall as deflate, gagging as he went, while Tracy stumbled, the effort having been too great, and fell to the canvas.

Rebus was quick, too. He grabbed Lanyon and pulled him upright, locking his arm behind his back with one hand while the other hand went to his throat. The two heavies made a move towards the ring, but Rebus dug his fingers into Lanyon's flesh just a little deeper, and they hesitated. There was a moment's stalemate before one of them made a dash for the stairs, closely followed by his partner. Rebus was breathing heavily. He released his grip on Lanyon and watched him crumple to the floor. Then, standing in the centre of the ring, he counted softly to ten – referee style – before raising one arm high into the air.

Upstairs, things had quietened down. The staff were tidying themselves up, but held their heads high, having acquitted themselves well. The drunks – Holmes, McCall, McGrath and Todd – had been seen off, and Paulette was smoothing the rumpled atmosphere with offers of free drinks all round. She saw Rebus coming through the door of Hyde's, and froze momentarily, then turned back into the perfect hostess, but with her voice slightly less warm than before, and her smile counterfeit.

'Ah, John.' It was Superintendent Watson, glass still in hand. 'Wasn't that a tussle? Where did you disappear to?'

'Is Tommy McCall around, sir?'

'Somewhere around, yes. Heard the offer of a free drink and headed in the direction of the bar. What have you done to your hand?'

Rebus looked down and saw that his hand was still bleeding in several places.

'Seven years bad luck,' he said. 'Do you have a minute, sir? There's something I'd like to show you. But first I need to phone for an ambulance.'

'But why, for God's sake? The rumpus is over, surely?'

Rebus looked at his superior. 'I wouldn't bet on that, sir,' he said. 'Not even if the chips were on the house.'

Rebus made his way home wearily, not from any real physical tiredness, but because his mind felt abused. The stairwell almost defeated him. He paused on the first floor, outside Mrs Cochrane's door, for what seemed minutes. He tried not to think about Hyde's, about what it meant, what it had been, what emotions it had serviced. But, not consciously thinking of it, bits of it flew around inside his head anyway, little jagged pieces of horror.

Mrs Cochrane's cats wanted out. He could hear them on the other side of the door. A cat-flap would have been the answer, but Mrs Cochrane didn't believe in them. Like leaving your door open to strangers, she had said. Any old moggie could just waltz in.

How true. Somehow, Rebus found that little unwrapped parcel of strength which was necessary to climb the extra flight. He unlocked his door and closed it again behind him. Sanctuary. In the kitchen, he munched on a dry roll while he waited for the kettle to boil.

Watson had listened to his story with mounting unease and disbelief. He had wondered aloud just how many important people were implicated. But then only Andrews and Lanyon could answer that. They'd found some video film as well as an impressive selection of still photographs. Watson's lips had been bloodless, though many of the faces meant nothing to Rebus. Still, a few of them did. Andrews had been right about the judges and the lawyers.

Thankfully, there were no policemen on display. Except one.

Rebus had wanted to clear up a murder, and instead had stumbled into a nest of vipers. He wasn't sure any of it would come to light. Too many reputations would fall. The public's faith in the beliefs and institutions of the city, of the country itself would be shattered. How long would it take to pick up the pieces of *that* broken mirror? Rebus examined his bandaged wrist. How long for the wounds to heal?

He went into the living room, carrying his tea. Tony McCall was seated in a chair, waiting.

'Hello, Tony,' Rebus said.

'Hello, John.'

'Thanks for your help back there.'

'What are friends for?'

Earlier in the day, when Rebus had asked for Tony McCall's help, McCall had broken down.

'I know all about it, John,' he had confessed. 'Tommy took me along there once. It was hideous, and I didn't stick around. But maybe there are pictures of me ... I don't know ... Maybe there are.'

Rebus hadn't needed to ask any more. It had come spilling out like beer from a tap: things bad at home, bit of fun, couldn't tell anyone about it because he didn't know who already knew. Even now he thought it best to keep quiet about it. Rebus had accepted the warning.

'I'm still going ahead,' he had said. 'With you or without. Your choice.'

Tony McCall had agreed to help.

Rebus sat down, placed the tea on the floor, and reached into his pocket for the photograph he had lifted from the files at Hyde's. He threw it in McCall's direction. McCall lifted it, stared at it with fearful eyes.

'You know,' Rebus said, 'Andrews was after Tommy's

haulage company. He'd have had it, too, and at a bargain-basement price.'

'Rotten bastard,' McCall said, tearing the photograph methodically into smaller and smaller pieces.

'Why did you do it, Tony?'

'I told you, John. Tommy took me along. Just a bit of fun –'

'No, I mean why did you break into the squat and plant that powder on Ronnie?'

'Me?' McCall's eyes were wider than ever now, but the look in them was still fear rather than surprise. It was all guesswork, but Rebus knew he was guessing right.

'Come on, Tony. Do you think Finlay Andrews is going to let any names stay secret? He's going down, and he's got no reason to let anyone's head stay above water.'

McCall thought about this. He let the bits of the photograph flutter into the ashtray, then set light to them with a match. They dissolved to blackened ash, and he seemed satisfied.

'Andrews needed a favour. It was always "favours" with him. I think he'd seen *The Godfather* too many times. Pilmuir was my beat, my territory. We'd met through Tommy, so he thought to ask me.'

'And you were happy to oblige.'

'Well, he had the picture, didn't he?'

'There must've been more.'

'Well . . .' McCall paused again, crushed the ash in the ashtray with his forefinger. A fine dust was all that was left. 'Yes, hell, I was happy enough to do it. The guy was a junkie after all, a piece of rubbish. And he was already dead. All I had to do was place a little packet beside him, that's all.'

'You never questioned why?'

'Ask no questions and all that.' He smiled. 'Finlay was offering me membership, you see. Membership of Hyde's. Well, I knew what that meant. I'd be on nodding terms with the big boys, wouldn't I? I even started to dream about career advancement, something I hadn't done in quite some time. Let's face it, John, we're tiny fish in a small pool.'

'And Hyde was offering you the chance to play with the sharks?'

McCall smiled sadly. 'I suppose that was it, yes.'

Rebus sighed. 'Tony, Tony, Tony. Where would it have ended, eh?'

'Probably with you having to call me "sir",' McCall answered, his voice firming up. 'Instead of which, I suppose the trial will see me on the front of the scum sheets. Not quite the kind of fame I was looking for.'

He rose from the chair.

'See you in court,' he said, leaving John Rebus to his flavourless tea and his thoughts.

Rebus slept fitfully, and was awake early. He showered, but without any of his usual vocal accompaniment. He telephoned the hospital, and ascertained that Tracy was fine, and that Finlay Andrews had been patched up with the loss of very little blood. Then he drove to Great London Road, where Malcolm Lanyon was being held for questioning.

Rebus was still officially a non-person, and DS Dick and DC Cooper had been assigned to the interrogation. But Rebus wanted to be close by. He knew the answers to all their questions, knew the sorts of trick Lanyon was capable of pulling. He didn't want the bastard getting away with it because of some technicality.

He went to the canteen first, bought a bacon roll, and, seeing Dick and Cooper seated at a table, went to join them.

'Hello, John,' Dick said, staring into the bottom of a stained coffee mug.

'You lot are early birds,' Rebus noted. 'You must be keen.'

'Farmer Watson wants it out of the way as soon as poss, sooner even.'

'I'll bet he does. Look, I'm going to be around today, if you need me to back up anything.'

'We appreciate that, John,' said Dick, in a voice which told Rebus his offer was as welcome as a dunce's cap.

'Well . . .' Rebus began, but bit off the sentence, and ate his breakfast instead. Dick and Cooper seemed dulled by the enforced early rise. Certainly, they were not the most vivacious of table companions. Rebus finished quickly and rose to his feet.

'Mind if I take a quick look at him?'

'Not at all,' said Dick. 'We'll be there in five minutes.'

Passing through the ground-floor reception area, Rebus almost bumped into Brian Holmes.

'Everyone's after the worm today,' Rebus said. Holmes gave him a puzzled, sleepy look. 'Never mind. I'm off to take a peek at Lanyon-alias-Hyde. Fancy a bit of voyeurism?'

Holmes didn't answer, but fell in stride with Rebus.

'Actually,' Rebus said, 'Lanyon might appreciate that image.' Holmes gave him a more puzzled look yet. Rebus sighed. 'Never mind.'

'Sorry, sir, bit of a late night yesterday.'

'Oh, yes. Thanks for that, by the way.'

'I nearly died when I saw the bloody Farmer staring at the lot of us, him in his undertaker's suit and us pretending to be pissed Dundonians.'

They shared a smile. Okay, the plan had been lame, conceived by Rebus during the course of his fifty-minute drive back from Calum McCallum's cell in Fife. But it had worked. They'd got a result.

'Yes,' Rebus said. 'I thought you looked a bit nervy last night.'

'What do you mean?'

'Well, you were doing your Italian army impression, weren't you? Advancing backwards, and all that.'

Holmes stopped dead, his jaw dropping. 'Is that the thanks I get? We put our careers on the line for you last night, all four of us. You've used me as your gofer – go find this, go check that – as a bit of bloody shoeleather, half the time for jobs that weren't even official, you've had my girlfriend half killed –'

'Now wait just one second –'

'– and all to satisfy your own curiosity. Okay, so there are bad guys behind bars, that's good, but look at the scales. You've got them, the rest of us have got sod all except a few bruises and no bloody soles on our shoes!'

Rebus stared at the floor, almost contrite. The air flew from his nostrils as from a Spanish bull's.

'I forgot,' he said at last. 'I meant to take that bloody suit back this morning. The shoes are ruined. It was you talking about shoeleather that reminded me.'

Then he set off again, along the corridor, towards the cells, leaving Holmes speechless in his wake.

Outside the cell, Lanyon's name had been printed in chalk on a board. Rebus went up to the steel door and pulled aside the shutter, thinking how it reminded him of the shutter on the door of some prohibition club. Give the secret knock and the shutter opened. He peered into the cell, started, and groped for the alarm bell situated beside the door. Holmes, hearing the siren, forgot to be angry and hurt and hurried forward. Rebus was pulling at the edge of the locked door with his fingernails.

'We've got to get in!'

'It's locked, sir.' Holmes was afraid: his superior looked absolutely manic. 'Here they come.'

A uniformed sergeant came at an undignified trot, keys jangling from his chain.

'Quick!'

The lock gave, and Rebus yanked open the door. Inside, Malcolm Lanyon lay slumped on the floor, head resting against the bed. His feet were splayed like a doll's. One hand lay on the floor, some thin nylon wire, like a fishing-line, wrapped around the knuckles, which were blackened. The line was attached to Lanyon's neck in a loop which had embedded itself so far into the flesh that it could hardly be seen. Lanyon's eyes bulged horribly, his swollen tongue obscene against the blood-darkened face. It was like a last macabre gesture, and Rebus watched the tongue protruding towards him, seeming to take it as a personal insult.

He knew it was way too late, but the sergeant loosened the wire anyway and laid the corpse flat on the floor. Holmes was resting his head against the cold metal door, screwing shut his eyes against the parody inside the cell.

'He must've had it hidden on him,' the sergeant said, seeking excuses for the monumental blunder, referring to the wire which he now held in his hands. 'Jesus, what a way to go.'

Rebus was thinking: he's cheated me, he's cheated me. I wouldn't have had the guts to do that, not slowly choke myself. . . . I could never do it, something inside would have stopped me. . . .

'Who's been in here since he was brought in?'

The sergeant stared at Rebus, uncomprehending.

'The usual lot, I suppose. He had a few questions to answer last night when you brought him in.'

'Yes, but *after* that?'

'Well, he had a meal when you lot went. That's about it.'

'Sonofabitch,' growled Rebus, stalking out of the cell and back along the corridor. Holmes, his face white and slick, was a few steps behind, and gaining.

'They're going to bury it, Brian,' Rebus said, his voice an angry vibrato. 'They're going to bury it, I know they are, and there'll be no cross marking the spot, nothing. A junkie died of his own volition. An estate agent committed suicide. Now a lawyer tops himself in a police cell. No connection, no crime committed.'

'But what about Andrews?'

'Where do you think we're headed?'

They arrived at the hospital ward in time to witness the efficiency of the staff in a case of emergency. Rebus hurried forward, pushing his way through. Finlay Andrews, lying on his bed, chest exposed, was being given oxygen while the cardiac apparatus was installed. A doctor held the pads in front of them, then pushed them slowly against Andrews' chest. A moment later, a jolt went through the body. There was no reading from the machine. More oxygen, more electricity. . . . Rebus turned away. He'd seen the script; he knew how the film would end.

'Well?' said Holmes.

'Heart attack.' Rebus's voice was bland. He began to walk away. 'Let's call it that anyway, because that's what the record will say.'

'So what next?' Holmes kept pace with him. He, too, was feeling cheated. Rebus considered the question.

'Probably the photos will disappear. The ones that matter at any rate. And who's left to testify? Testify to what?'

'They've thought of everything.'

'Except one thing, Brian. *I* know who they are.'

Holmes stopped. 'Will that matter?' he called to his superior's retreating figure. But Rebus just kept walking.

There was a scandal, but it was a small one, soon forgotten. Shuttered rooms in elegant Georgian terraces soon became light again, in a great resurrection of spirit. The deaths of Finlay Andrews and Malcolm Lanyon were reported, and journalists sought what muck and brass they could. Yes, Finlay Andrews had been running a club which was not strictly legitimate in all of its dealings, and yes, Malcolm Lanyon had committed suicide when the authorities had begun to close in on this little empire. No, there were no details of what these 'activities' might have been.

The suicide of local estate agent James Carew was in no way connected to Mr Lanyon's suicide, though it was true the two men were friends. As for Mr Lanyon's connection with Finlay Andrews and his club, well, perhaps we would never know. It was no more than a sad coincidence that Mr Lanyon had been appointed Mr Carew's executor. Still, there were other lawyers, weren't there?

And so it ended, the story petering out, the rumours dying a little less slowly. Rebus was pleased when Tracy announced that Nell Stapleton had found her a job in a cafe/deli near the University Library. One evening, however, having spent some time in the Rutherford Bar, Rebus decided to opt for a takeaway Indian meal before home. In the restaurant, he saw Tracy, Holmes and Nell Stapleton at a corner table, sharing a joke with their meal. He turned and left without ordering.

Back in his flat, he sat at the kitchen table for the umpteenth time, writing a rough draft of his letter of resignation. Somehow, the words failed to put across any of his emotions adequately. He crumpled the paper and tossed it towards the bin. He had been reminded in the restaurant of just how much Hyde's had cost in human terms, and of how little justice there had been. There was a knock at the door. He had hope in his heart as he opened it. Gill Templer stood there, smiling.

In the night, he crept through to the living room, and switched on the desk lamp. It threw light guiltily, like a constable's torch, onto the small filing cabinet beside the stereo. The key was hidden under a corner of the carpet, as secure a hiding place as a granny's mattress. He opened the cabinet and lifted out a slim file, which he carried to his chair, the chair which had for so many months been his bed. There he sat, composed, remembering the day at James Carew's flat. Back then he had been tempted to lift Carew's private diary and keep it for himself. But he had resisted temptation. Not the night at Hyde's though. There, alone in Andrews' office for a moment, he had filched the photograph of Tony McCall. Tony McCall, a friend and colleague with whom, these days, he had nothing in common. Except perhaps a sense of guilt.

He opened the file and took out the photographs. He had taken them along with the one of McCall. Four photographs, lifted at random. He studied the faces again, as he did most nights when he found sleep hard to come by. Faces he recognised. Faces attached to names, and names to handshakes and voices. Important people. Influential people. He'd thought about this a lot. Indeed, he had thought about little else since that night in Hyde's club. He brought out a metal wastepaper bin from beneath the desk, dropped the photographs into it, and lit a match, holding it over the bin, as he had done so many times before.

READING
GROUP
NOTES

HIDE &
SEEK

© Rankin

ABOUT IAN RANKIN

Ian Rankin, OBE, writes a huge proportion of all the crime novels sold in the UK and has won numerous prizes, including in 2005 the Crime Writers' Association Diamond Dagger. His work is available in over 30 languages, home sales of his books exceed one million copies a year, and several of the novels based around the character of Detective Inspector Rebus – his name meaning 'enigmatic puzzle' – have been successfully transferred to television.

Introduction to DI John Rebus

The first novels to feature Rebus, a flawed
but resolutely humane detective, were not an
overnight sensation, and success took time
to arrive. But the wait became a period that
allowed Ian Rankin to come of age as a writer,
and to develop Rebus into a thoroughly
believable, flesh-and-blood character straddling
both industrial and post-industrial Scotland;
a gritty yet perceptive man coping with his
own demons. As Rebus struggled to keep
his relationship with daughter Sammy alive
following his divorce, and to cope with the
imprisonment of brother Michael, while all the
time trying to strike a blow for morality against
a fearsome array of sinners (some justified and
some not), readers began to respond in their
droves. Fans admired Ian Rankin's re-creation
of a picture-postcard Edinburgh with a vicious
tooth-and-claw underbelly just a heartbeat away,
his believable but at the same time complex
plots and, best of all, Rebus as a conflicted man
trying always to solve the unsolvable, and to do
the right thing.

As the series progressed, Ian Rankin refused
to shy away from contentious issues such as
corruption in high places, paedophilia and illegal

immigration, combining his unique seal of tight
plotting with a bleak realism, leavened with
brooding humour.

In Rebus the reader is presented with a rich and
constantly evolving portrait of a complex and
troubled man, irrevocably tinged with the sense
of being an outsider and, potentially, unable to
escape being a 'justified sinner' himself. Rebus's
life is intricately related to his Scottish environs
too, enriched by Ian Rankin's attentive depiction
of locations, and careful regard to Rebus's
favourite music, watering holes and books, as
well as his often fraught relationships with
colleagues and family. And so, alongside Rebus,
the reader is taken on an often painful,
sometimes hellish journey to the depths of
human nature, always rooted in the minutiae
of a very recognisable Scottish life.

The Oxford Bar – Rebus and many of the characters who appear in the novels are regulars of the Ox – as is Ian Rankin himself. The pub is now synonymous with the Rebus novels to the extent that one of the regular medical examiners called in to assist with investigations is named after the pub's owner, John Gates.

Edinburgh plays an important role throughout the Rebus novels; a character itself, as brooding and as volatile as Rebus. The Edinburgh depicted in the novels is far short of

the beautiful city that tourists in their thousands flood to
visit. Hidden behind the historic buildings and elegant
façades is the world that Rebus inhabits.

For general discussion regarding the Rebus series

How does Ian Rankin reveal himself as an author interested in using fiction to 'tell the truths the real world can't'?

There are similarities between the lives of the author and his protagonist – for instance, both Ian Rankin and Rebus were born in Fife, lost their mothers at an early age, have children with physical problems – so is it useful therefore to think of John Rebus and Ian Rankin as each other's alter egos?

Could it be said that Rebus is trying to make sense in a general way of the world around him, or is he seeking answers to the 'big questions'? And is it relevant therefore that he is a believer in God and comes from a Scottish Presbyterian background? Would Rebus see confession in both the religious and the criminal sense as similar in any way?

How does Ian Rankin explore notions of Edinburgh as a character in its own right? In what way does he contrast the glossy public and seedy private faces of the city with the public and private faces of those Rebus meets?

How does Ian Rankin use musical sources – the Elvis references in *The Black Book*, for instance, or the Rolling Stones allusions in *Let It Bleed* – as a means of character development through the series? What does Rebus's own taste in music and books say about him as a person?

What do you think about Rebus as a character? If you have read several or more novels from the series, discuss how his character is developed.

If Rebus has a problem with notions of 'pecking order' and the idea of authority generally, what does it say about him that he chose careers in hierarchical institutions such as the Army and then the police?

How does Rebus relate to women: as lovers, flirtations, family members and colleagues?

Do the flashes of gallows humour as often shown by the pathologists but sometimes also in Rebus's own comments increase or dissipate narrative tension? Does Rebus use black comedy for the same reasons the pathologists do?

Do Rebus's personal vulnerabilities make him under-standing of the frailties of others?

How does the characterisation of Rebus compare to other long-standing popular detectives from British authors such as Holmes, Poirot, Morse or Dalgleish? And are there more similarities or differences between them?

HIDE & SEEK

Life is moving forward for Rebus. Newly promoted to
Detective Inspector and with a new partner, the likeable
DS Brian Holmes, and with the *Knots & Crosses* success
behind him, Rebus should be feeling settled and confident.
But when he is called to a bizarrely staged death, almost
immediately he feels out of his depth: the clues don't
seem to make much sense and it's not even clear what
this case is really about or, indeed, whether a murder
has in fact even taken place.

As Rebus and Holmes are led a merry dance through
the backstreets of the dingier side of the city, gradually the
trail leads them back to the glossy façade of 'respectable'
Edinburgh, where upright stalwarts of society unleash
their depravations behind a sleekly foreboding exterior,
and Rebus sees that they will fight to the death to keep
their secrets hidden. Only this time it's neither he nor
his loved-ones who are under threat . . .

As Rebus confronts the different aspects of the
Edinburgh he inhabits, he tries (and almost fails) to
connect a strange series of deaths; and at the same time
the reader is treated to a vivid warts-and-all tour of the
city so visceral one can almost smell and hear it, and an
ending that refuses to answer questions of natural justice.

Discussion points for *Hide & Seek*

Ian Rankin saw *Hide & Seek* as a companion piece
to *Knots & Crosses*, especially in his allusions to
The Strange Case of Dr Jekyll and Mr Hyde. How does
he reveal the relationship between the two books?

Two other non-Rebus novels were written between *Knots
& Crosses* and *Hide & Seek* (neither was very successful,
selling only 500 hardback copies apiece). Does Ian
Rankin's extra writing experience show in *Hide & Seek*?

To open *Hide & Seek,* a quotation is used from
The Strange Case of Dr Jekyll and Mr Hyde: 'My devil
had long been caged, he came out roaring.' Would you
say that this refers more to the murderer or to Rebus?

Has Rebus's promotion to DI changed him? Has the
confidence shown in him by his superiors at work
translated into new confidence in social situations in
his private life? Why hasn't he told Rhona about the
end of his relationship with colleague Gill Templer?

Does Rebus treat Brian Holmes fairly? Does Rebus feel
close to him? And how good is Holmes at looking after
himself?

How does Rebus respond to the suggestion made by
a colleague that there may be an occult aspect to the
case? Is Ian Rankin being playful when he says that
Rebus is on a 'witch hunt'?

Is Rebus sympathetic when questioning young people? Does he deal similarly with his daughter Sammy?

Discussing the 'real' Edinburgh, it is claimed that the justified sinners, men like Burke and Hare, or Deacon Brodie, have been 'cleaned up for the tourists'. *'And sure enough* [says the interviewee], *it's all still here, the past replaying itself in the present.'* Would Rebus agree with this comment? And when he visits the rundown estates of Edinburgh, does Rebus feel slightly like a tourist himself?

'Rebus believed in good and evil, and believed stupid people could be attracted toward the latter.' Is the reader supposed to infer that Rebus might give credence to the idea that intelligent people are not attracted to evil?

Carew's suicide note says, *'If I am the chief of sinners, I am the chief of sufferers too.'* How does Rebus respond to this?

Rebus wonders why he didn't tell Gill Templer immediately about the complaint against him. Why didn't he?

When Ronnie McGrath shrieks *'Hide!'*, in what ways might this be understood, and why does it take Rebus such a long time to consider the various implications?

What is the reader's response to the novel's ending? Is Rebus pleased or disappointed with the way things turned out?